MEELIS FRIEDENTHAL

THE WILLOW KING

The Birds of the Muses

TRANSLATED BY MATTHEW HYDE

PUSHKIN PRESS

LONDON

Pushkin Press
71-75 Shelton Street,
London WC2H 9JQ

Original text © Meelis Friedenthal 2012
Translation © Matthew Hyde 2017

First published in Estonian as *Mesilased* in 2012
This translation first published by Pushkin Press in 2017

This book has been supported by the Estonian
Cultural Endowment, Traducta programme

EESTI KULTUURKAPITAL

1 3 5 7 9 8 6 4 2

ISBN 978 1 782271 74 1

Set in Monotype Baskerville by Tetragon, London
Printed in Great Britain by the CPI Group, UK

www.pushkinpress.com

I T HAD BEEN RAINING WITHOUT END. The rain had rotted the crops in the fields; it had caused mildew on the wooden walls of the houses, and made the ships' decks as wet as seaweed. Laurentius had been eating rotten bread for several months now, and living in mildewed houses; during the last week he had been slipping on the wet decks too. Black bile had accumulated in him like the sludge which collects on a stick thrust into the river. Finally, he stepped from the rocking boat onto the harbour quay, onto the slippery boards knocked onto poles rammed deep into the silt, and he looked unsurely at his surroundings. As gusts of wind from the low sky blew drops of water into his face, he tried to comprehend what kind of country this could be, where he had come of his own free will. The bare strip of shore, with its white sand and lone bulrushes, and the uniform grey clouds closely resembled the harbour which he had set out from. Set against the backdrop of grey sky the postal ship's masts looked just as before, and the sailcloth stretched across them was as grey and impassive as when he had started his journey. Alongside the wharf, which stretched far out into the sea, a breakwater could be seen, half-submerged under the muddy water, and at the end of it an old watch house was stooping low into the water. Clearly no one had used it for some time.

Ruined buildings of this kind could be found at any harbour, and despite the wretchedness of the scene it had a reassuring effect on him. Here too the harbours had been rebuilt; here too they had been extended to accommodate new ships, and the old watch houses had been left neglected.

He sighed and fiddled uneasily with the cover of his cage, which was dripping wet.

He had managed to bring all his trappings with him without too much trouble. One chest knocked together from oak boards had fully accommodated all the things which he had thought necessary to take on his studies. Now it was at the tollhouse together with the other goods transported in the ship's hold, and he probably wouldn't be able to get hold of it until evening. The ship's cargo and the passengers' personal baggage had been carefully checked and anything which could be liable for tax had been noted down. He had not had any bother on that front, since he had nothing of any value with him. His few personal books were all officially authorized, and he had only brought the bare minimum of medicaments. The difficulties were caused by his rose-ringed parakeet in its cage. He had already been warned back home that transporting the bird wasn't likely to be the easiest of undertakings, and that the conditions on his journey could prove too much for it. But he had no wish to leave his companion behind, and so he had decided to take the risk. Now that he had arrived, his main concern was to get the bird out of the cold rain and into the warmth as soon as possible.

Despite his wide-brimmed hat the rainwater was trickling down Laurentius' face, and he had to wipe it out of his eyes. He glanced under his coat flap at his pocket watch and began to look for someone who could direct him to a tavern, and perhaps later bring his chest from the tollhouse. He didn't dare entrust his cage to anyone. He had to act quickly now since the roads were already in a poor state, and he could not delay the onward journey any longer. The autumn rainfalls were becoming more violent and had already started to erode the soft roads, so it was getting more difficult to traverse them with every day. The air was also starting to turn icy cold, and he feared his parakeet might fall ill. He had to find a carriage or cart and start travelling towards Dorpat as soon as possible.

"Hey!" Laurentius called out.

The harbour quay was glistening-wet from rain, and only a few curious onlookers had braved the vile weather to come and wait for the boats to arrive. They had probably already decided that there was little chance of finding work, so they didn't at first think to react to Laurentius' call. The seamen had unloaded the ship's cargo near the tollhouse, and the haulers who worked for the merchants were thronging over there. Some of them had started heaving the slippery boxes and damp bags onto the carts with looks of bored indifference on their faces, while the harbour officials marked up the goods.

Laurentius called out again.

"Hey, you there!"

A bystander in a flimsy, worn-out coat looked up blankly and Laurentius gestured to beckon him over, just in case he had not understood. The man looked like a character from one of the paintings by the gloomy artists of the Middle Ages which he had seen back in Holland. Tangles of hair of an indeterminate colour protruded from under a lopsided felt hat; his nose was red and swollen, and a pockmarked chin could be made out underneath his sparse stubble. It occurred to Laurentius that a sign hanging under the man's neck reading

"Villainy" would have suited him very well. Those sorts could be found loitering about every harbour, and one's gut feeling about them based on their appearance was usually right. But they were always the most in the know about the town's inns and hostels, so some use could be had from them. They would be sure to swindle you, of course; the only question was by how much.

"Please direct me to a decent inn," Laurentius instructed curtly, and then watched as the man turned round and set off without uttering a word. Hopefully he had understood what Laurentius said, although it was possible that he had just guessed at the meaning.

Laurentius lifted up his parakeet cage, and, cradling it in his arms, followed the man in the direction of town. The bird started squawking agitatedly.

"Shh, Clodia, be quiet."

They walked on into the thickening dusk, and Laurentius tried to rock the cage as little as possible. Against the backdrop of the evening sky he could see the threatening silhouettes of the sheer city walls, formed from stacks of sturdy boulders, rotund medieval fortress towers and four tall church spires. The lower town buildings were swallowed up in the sodden mist which was seeping from the heavy clouds. The man walking ahead of him was unexpectedly fleet of foot, and looked like he knew very well where he wanted to end up. But by now Laurentius could feel his old illness flaring up with increasing severity. The constant damp permeated everywhere, making everything waterlogged, and he now felt more vulnerable to it than in earlier years. The surfeit of black bile which was seething inside him would not normally have caused such listlessness until late autumn, but this year the rains had started on Midsummer Day, and the endless spatter had swathed his internal organs, his heart and his brain in a sticky mist. Even when he had stepped off the ship onto dry land, and walked on the flat paving stones, rubbed to a smooth shine, the memory of the swaying sea made him feel as if he were forcing his way through a bog. Every step was a strain.

"Uh," he muttered under his breath. "Just a bit further."

He looked at the hunched back of the ragamuffin walking ahead of him, and decided that he should definitely send someone else to go and fetch his chest. There was often trouble to be had from this kind of chance character picked up at the harbour. The innkeeper should be able to help him. He tried to remember the currency which was used in Reval; several passengers on the ship had offered their views, from which he concluded that he couldn't hope for full clarity on the matter. *Ars apodemica*, the books about the art of travelling, made almost no reference to the situation in Estonia and Livonia—there was just some general guidance on what was worth seeing, and the best way of taking in the surroundings. These lands and their cities were completely uncharted from an apodemic perspective—after all, anyone who travelled for personal pleasure would go elsewhere, to the south. To the places of culture and history. Laurentius' head had started throbbing, and he could remember nothing relevant at all.

"Very well," he eventually decided. "One sixth of an öre should be sufficient."

It was nearly pitch black by the time they came to a stop under a yellow lantern which illuminated an unexpectedly decent-looking inn, situated just a short way from the city gates. The ragamuffin turned towards Laurentius with his hand outstretched. Laurentius had already fished out a small coin from his pocket in advance, and now he dropped it into the man's palm, making sure to look towards the ground as he did so. The man quickly checked the money and then smiled broadly.

"Damn," thought Laurentius. "I gave him too much after all."

He turned and started to enter the inn, pushing his cage through the door ahead of him.

"Would he desire anything else?" enquired the ragamuffin in unexpectedly good German.

Laurentius faltered. He knew that the ones who latch on to you were usually the worst kind of scoundrel, and he would normally have been happy to see the man make a swift departure.

"I need to start moving in the direction of Dorpat," he found himself saying. "And as quickly as possible."

He could send someone else for his chest, but there was probably no harm in asking the way. The stagecoaches were supposed to pass through at some point; on the ship they had told him that a group of travellers departed for Dorpat almost every week. He had been shown two possible routes on the map—both of them took several days, longer depending on the road conditions.

The man cast another glance at the parakeet cage, bowed somehow insincerely and left.

Laurentius shrugged his shoulders and entered the inn. He placed his cage on the table closest to the fireplace, lifted the damp, dark cloth from it, and stood watching his parakeet preen itself on the perch.

"So, Clodia, ready for another journey?" Laurentius asked.

The heat radiating from the hearth had a restorative effect, warming the parakeet's freezing body and lifting Laurentius' mood. He took a folded piece of paper from his pocket and scattered some seeds from it onto the bottom of the cage. He had not been sure if he would find sunflower seeds anywhere in these parts, so he had brought some with him. As usual, the other guests who had been idly standing around quickly thronged round the cage, hoping to get a closer look at the strange, coloured bird.

"So where does one of them kind hail from?"

"What does it eat?"

"Can it sing?"

Laurentius started explaining. On the one hand, dragging his parakeet around with him was troublesome and inconvenient—and not just for Laurentius: clearly the bird suffered even more—but it was also a wonderful way of getting to know people. Clodia had already been a great help to him in this respect on the ship.

"So you're a university student, are you?" someone asked, getting up from behind one of the tables.

"Yes," Laurentius replied. It seemed that the man had already had an eye on him for some time—he could always sense that acutely, and he had learnt to keep his own gaze fixed on the ground, so as not to look straight into some curious bystander's eyes accidentally. He had realized as a young man that this always led to trouble. At first people grew suspicious of him; then they would hold their fingers crossed behind their backs as they talked to him, or even turn street corners to avoid him. The safest thing was to keep his gaze fixed on the ground.

"I wouldn't advise you to go to Dorpat at this time," said the man.

Notwithstanding his outward politeness, there was a sarcastic ring to the man's words, and his use of the polite form of address seemed somehow mocking.

"Why is that?" Laurentius remonstrated. He knew, of course, what kind of arguments might be made against going to Dorpat.

"They're going through bad times down there. Even the professors have become most slack in performing their duties. And summer was wet, so famine is inevitable, and all the prices will go up," the man said.

"But it's like that everywhere now," Laurentius responded.

Laurentius let his gaze slide momentarily across the man's proud, scornful countenance, and concluded from the short sword hanging from his belt that he must be a nobleman. Laurentius had already heard that they had a particular antipathy towards Dorpat.

"But my stipend is for Dorpat," Laurentius explained.

"Ha!" said the man with a dismissive shake of his hand.

Laurentius carefully opened the door of his cage, and lifted his parakeet out on one finger. The bird knew him well and could sense his moods, and Laurentius found its familiar presence reassuring, just like a good friend whom he could rely on for support and advice.

The bird rocked comically as it tried to steady itself on the parchment-like skin of his hand, which was covered in stains from the tinctures and medicaments which he took. It gave him an affectionate peck on the fingernail. The curious onlookers stepped back to a safe distance, as if they were afraid the bird could attack them at any moment, as if Laurentius had produced a little demon from his cage. He gave the bird a tender pat, and he felt the warmth of its body, the blood concealed under the feathers and skin, the life flowing within. His parakeet had been with him for as long as he could remember. He had suffered from a surfeit of black bile ever since he was born, and that was why his godfather Pastor Theodus had originally given him Clodia as a present. Theodus had got the idea from Plutarch, who had referred to birds in his *Table Talks* as an effective treatment for the kind of ailments which afflicted Laurentius. His parakeet's sanguine tweeting and jolly behaviour had indeed kept Laurentius' temperament balanced and helped him cope better with his illness. It was thanks to his parakeet that he had managed to deal with the summer rains so well.

"That bird of yours won't survive the journey to Dorpat, you can be sure of that," said the nobleman, clearly not wanting to let Laurentius off the hook.

"It certainly looks as if I will need to find a closed carriage, and then depart for Dorpat as soon as possible. I wasn't anyway planning to go by foot," Laurentius explained.

He knew very well that the majority of university students walked the journey, and that only a small number of them could allow themselves the luxury of paying for a carriage, but in his current situation it seemed like the only option.

The nobleman looked straight at him and grinned.

Laurentius turned his head quickly aside, smiled, and gave Clodia a tender pat. "I have had her for nearly ten years now, I know what she can cope with. She stands the cold very well."

"Don't you go with just anyone. These are troubled times; you might well be robbed," the nobleman said.

"I know. But there is not a great deal one could take from me," Laurentius replied.

He thought it best not to mention the ornate pocket watch hidden under his clothes. This exquisite and valuable timepiece was the work of an English master craftsman, and was another gift from his godfather Theodus.

"I would take your coat for starters. And that hat of yours looks pretty decent. Your life could always be taken from you too," said the nobleman.

Laurentius could not detect any threat in the man's voice; it sounded more like he was making a matter-of-fact statement. Maybe he had once had his own hat stolen, and been left slumped by the roadside, half-dead. Human life is fragile, after all. It endures within the body's confines like a thing of wonder, like birds held aloft in the sky, like the stars suspended in the superlunary ethereal sphere.

Laurentius tried to impart a learned tone to his voice. "If it was never mine from the beginning, then no one can take it from me."

"Have you previously studied anywhere?"

Laurentius nodded.

"You're getting yourself tangled up with dodgy company down there in Dorpat—they are the worst bunch of boozers and carousers in the whole of the Swedish state. And the Swedes are known for their drunkenness," said the man disdainfully.

Laurentius frowned and looked around the room uneasily. The conversation had already started to irk him. He needed to find the tavern keeper, so that he could rent a room and enquire about getting to Dorpat. He had no wish to begin discussing the finer details of his life with complete strangers.

But he couldn't resist responding to the man's critical comments with a dig of his own. "Do you speak from personal experience?" he asked.

The man smiled broadly and sat down next to Laurentius. "In one sense you're right, of course. What business is it of mine what your plans are? But it is plain to see that you are not a Swede yourself. What parts do you hail from anyway?"

Laurentius was a bit taken aback at the question, and he pulled away instinctively. Of course he had been right. Now he felt embarrassed for having mocked the man like that. This was exactly the kind of situation that the travel guides advised one to avoid. "I beg your pardon. I didn't for one moment intend to be rude," he said.

"Your apology is accepted," said the nobleman.

"In any case, I do want to get to Dorpat as soon as possible. The road conditions are getting worse with every day, and I'm aware that it takes almost a week to get there." Laurentius reached into the small cage and the bird amenably hopped off his hand back onto its perch.

"Where is the host?" Laurentius enquired.

"I own this inn," the nobleman informed him. "The innkeeper is in town dealing with some matters."

"This is your inn?" Laurentius asked.

"Listen, why are you in such a desperate hurry to get to Dorpat anyway?" the nobleman asked, ignoring his question. It looked like he was already handsomely drunk, and there was a revelrous haughtiness in his voice which didn't bode well. "Have you been in some sort of bother? People normally go to Dorpat if they have not been accepted anywhere else, or if they are short of means. You don't look like you belong to either category."

"Dorpat is the city most devoted to the Muses," Laurentius explained.

"So you're going there to enlighten yourself, are you? Very well, I won't poke around in your secrets any more," the nobleman said.

"What is that supposed to mean?" Laurentius asked.

"I predict you won't catch much of a glimpse of intellectual life this autumn and winter. But there will definitely be plenty of other sights for you to witness," the nobleman said.

Laurentius got up and started pacing anxiously around the room. He took his watch from his pocket and glanced at it. He immediately regretted taking it out in public, but it was too late now. Flustered, he dropped the watch back into his breast pocket.

"Very well," he mumbled to himself.

He still had some time for a walk around town before the city gates were shut. He wondered if the nobleman really did not realize that if he had already reached Estonia then he wasn't likely to change his plans on the basis of some idle inn talk. That kind of wet, chicken-hearted behaviour was only fit for those who had no respect for intellectual discipline. But he did have respect; he had to.

"I'm sorry, but I have to leave now," Laurentius told the nobleman.

"Well, go then. But I warn you, you will live to regret your decision," the nobleman replied.

"Can I leave my cage here?" Laurentius asked.

MONDAY

"MMM, AAHH."

He breathed the air in and out. In the cool of the autumn evening the warm, damp breath condensed into a mist which was momentarily suspended in front of his face. This was his expiration, from within his body, and it showed that his spirit was present, that he was alive. Instead of taking someone's pulse it was possible to put a mirror in front of his mouth and establish from the mist which formed there whether that person was alive. Whether he was still able to produce moisture, to demonstrate that his soul was present.

"Alive," he whispered with a nod, before stepping into the carriage together with the other passengers.

He chose a seat under a window which consisted of little more than holes hacked into the lead plating, and he watched as the other passengers got into that soulless box constructed from metal and wood, and sat down in their places, breathing heavily. They were all alive, all of them moving; they all knew their purpose, and where they were headed. They had already been sitting and waiting to depart for two days and all the subjects of conversation had been exhausted. The excitement which Laurentius had initially felt about embarking on the journey had turned into a bored torpor, tinged with distress about Clodia.

The carriage driver flicked the reins, and the casket began moving forward on its wooden wheels. It had been sitting there like a hollow monument, like a shell, but once the people had entered it had taken on life, and now it departed as if to some plan, swaying and shaking as it got under way. An object which had no will of its own had gained a soul, and from that soul a life. But did the people inside the casket give their souls away to an external body, or did they somehow keep them as their own, for their own use?

"When I climb into the carriage," Laurentius pondered, "am I still myself, or have I taken on a new body, a body which no longer takes steps but rolls along on wheels, a body which can only move on roads covered with dirt and rough gravel?"

"What?" Laurentius' neighbour asked.

"Nothing…" Laurentius replied.

"Didn't you just say something?" the neighbour asked again.

"I was just mumbling to myself, it's not important. Forgive me," Laurentius explained.

Laurentius rested his head against the side of the carriage, pretending that he was trying to get to sleep. But the passengers' new, collective body was seeking its way; the large spoked wheels were engaging with the sharp-edged ruts, which in places had already collapsed into large potholes, and his head knocked painfully against the lead plating to the jarring rhythm.

"Ouch!" Laurentius exclaimed.

He was thinking about his parakeet. It looked like the characters in the inn had fed her something as soon as he had left for town—although they had all denied it vehemently. By the time he got back, Clodia had already begun to shake. The trembling and listlessness had lasted all night; his bird had not eaten or drunk anything at all, and by the following evening she had already given up the ghost. Laurentius had watched the onset of death in distress. First the feeble shivering, then the loss of balance, then her gaze became dull and hazy. Clodia had not survived two days on Estonian soil. It was not his fault that she died, but that was no consolation. Whether he was to blame or not, his pet bird was dead. Now the little spadger lay stiff and lifeless in her cage, on the baggage deck at the back of the carriage.

Laurentius had not wanted to leave her behind, so he decided to take her to Dorpat with him. He had managed to arrange a place in a carriage, and so had decided against going on foot. Maybe it really was as dangerous on the roads as people said.

"A new body," began the woman sitting next to him again. "A new body, you said, or something like that… but how does that new body get here?"

"We take it on ourselves."

"How's that? I thought that you were talking about your parakeet again. Now I don't understand anything at all."

Laurentius clenched his hands into fists and opened them again. These were his hands, his body. Were they part of him in the same way that he was now part of the carriage? This was his carriage, his journey. Was it also his cage?

The woman made a deliberate gesture of placing her hands on top of her travel bag.

"Forgive me," said Laurentius.

There was really nothing much to explain anyway; it was quite a mundane story, but for some reason he didn't want to repeat it all again. When the passengers had first introduced themselves in Reval he had told them about his parakeet, but none of them had understood why he was so upset. For them a parakeet was just an expensive, exotic bird. They sympathized with him just as they would sympathize with a merchant whose cargo had sunk in a storm. These things happen, can't be helped, life goes on… Laurentius sighed and fell silent, resting his head against the lead panelling and letting the cool metal soothe the sore spot, like a spoon soothes a bump. Life goes on.

"What does it mean then, this new body?" the woman asked, refusing to let go of the subject.

The woman's husband had been cautiously holding his peace, but now he grimaced and shook his head, clearly irritated. "Now, don't start all that again," he told his wife.

Laurentius tensely looked down at the floor, wondering how he could change the subject—the woman's voice had already started to sound shrill and agitated. Those carriage conversations could often become strange and awkward. Laurentius didn't have a gift for getting on with other people, much as he would have liked to.

"I was just thinking that to start with, the soul is inside the body. But souls are of course immortal," he said eventually. "So, in short, my question is: when the body dies, where do the souls go to before their resurrection?"

"What do you mean? Surely they're with God?" the woman said.

"But where is God?" asked Laurentius.

"In the sky, everywhere," the woman answered.

"Exactly, but then there must be souls everywhere. Here as well," Laurentius suggested.

"You mean to say that there are spirits here in this carriage?" the woman surmised snappily.

"No, not like that… more like memories," Laurentius said.

"So then," concluded the woman victoriously. "If there are memories in this carriage, and the memories are souls, then this carriage should be alive. But it's not, is it? It can't have children!"

Laurentius thought of Aristotle and the beds. "Not all living people have children," he said.

The woman turned away from Laurentius and sat glowering angrily in the direction of the central gangway.

"It's not about having children, of course," Laurentius added.

But the woman was silent, almost obstinately, resolutely so. It occurred to Laurentius that he could tell his story once again, to explain the reason for his glum mood. But he had done so several times already, and it seemed pointless to do so again. It probably wasn't worth bothering his fellow passengers with it. Clodia had always helped him to get on with people, livening things up with her cheerful tweeting. Her company was exactly what he needed at that moment. But now his childhood companion was lying wrapped in a sheet in her cage, wedged between sodden cases. Dead.

"Awful," he mumbled quietly to himself.

"What did you say?" the woman asked.

"Nothing," Laurentius replied.

"I'm sure I heard something," said the woman gruffly, but then she fell silent again. The other four passengers were looking at them incredulously—Laurentius and the woman had been trying the whole journey to start a polite conversation, but their attempts had come to nothing.

Laurentius sighed in exasperation, closed his eyes, and started making a serious effort to get to sleep. The carriage shook monotonously, the wheels engaging the furrows in the weathered road surface with a regular measured rhythm, like the swinging of a clock's pendulum. He imagined that the carriage was a large golem made by Rabbi Eliyah, with people stuffed into its stomach like strips of paper, each one with the name of the Lord written on it. But how does that strip of paper feel inside the machine's stomach? Does it have its own place there, or is it just passing through, whiling away the time in boredom? What is it like inside a human? Where does the soul come from, and where does it go? What about inside his parakeet?

Laurentius shook his head and looked around uneasily. He didn't want to get bogged down in those kinds of thoughts—he had to make sure he stayed rational. But he couldn't help himself. Fragments of thoughts, individual sentences and memories permeated the edge of his consciousness like blood soaking into a bandage. This was the wound of his consciousness, which he dressed and treated, but to no avail. Laurentius had tried to immerse himself in learning, literature, theatre, other people's company, anything to soothe the wound and help it heal. But it festered; the same thoughts kept returning, and the bad blood kept rising to the surface.

He heard a clattering sound. The carriage had driven straight into one of the larger potholes, jolting the passengers, whose faces contorted in alarm. A travel bag fell off the knees of the man sitting opposite onto the floor.

"Ouch!" someone exclaimed.

The bag had fallen sideways onto the neighbouring passenger's feet.

"Sorry, I nodded off for a moment and hit my head," explained the man, rubbing his ear with a vexed expression.

"The state of the roads here is worse than anywhere I have travelled… Now, over in Sweden they've got proper roads. The ground is firmer there, of course—there aren't so many marshes. But here…"

The woman just mumbled something angrily to herself.

The man prattled on, as if he had been holding himself back for some time and the jolt had caused him to start unburdening himself of everything which had been on his mind.

"The local landowners are supposed to keep the roads here in good order, but do they hell. They'll do anything to avoid it. And the state of the roadside inns does not even bear mentioning. In some of them you're lucky if you get anything besides beer and spirit. You have to sleep on mouldy straw on the mud floor. And yet everything is so damned expensive. The inns in Sweden are decent: you get warm food in every one, and there are beds with fresh straw everywhere. I tell you, it's a different thing altogether."

Laurentius sat up in his chair and smiled ruefully. From his experience the situation in Sweden was not in fact much better. He folded his coat flap so that he had a thick bit of material to put between his forehead and the side of the carriage. It cushioned him from the jolting a bit, but it did nothing at all to shield him from the man's persistent chatter. The patter of raindrops against the outside of the carriage got stronger and stronger, drumming against his temple. The woven yarn of his coat turned fuzzy from the damp, and a barely noticeable mustiness started wafting out from between the fibres. He had in fact been lucky to get a place in a closed carriage. The majority of carriages travelling between Reval and Dorpat were little more than open hay carts, and the passengers got drenched in the cold rain just as the coachman and the footman were now.

"Hmm, vile," puffed the man sitting opposite him as he concluded his angry tirade against the roads and inns of Estonia and Livonia. He stretched out his legs, which were clad in muddy boots, far in front of him.

Meanwhile, Laurentius was still thinking about his parakeet lying there limply in her cage, wondering whether he should put her into a smaller box. It seemed odd to carry a dead bird around in a cage like that. But he had got so used to dragging around that wire box, so used to hearing the cheeping coming from inside it, to talking with Clodia and taking care of her. She had always been quite happy sitting on his hand and pecking at his fingers. Her small feathered body had felt unexpectedly warm, almost as if she had a fever, and so full of life. But it seemed wrong to bring a cage with a dead bird into the carriage. The other passengers might think even worse of him than they already did.

"Indeed," said Laurentius without addressing anyone in particular. Silence ensued, and he coughed hesitantly. He closed his eyes and tried to think about what he would do once he arrived in Dorpat. First, he should get himself settled into lodgings; then he could go to pay his first visit to the university. In place of any clear thoughts, however, he heard the monotonous rumble of the carriage's wooden wheels, the surging murmur of the wind, the rattling of the passengers' cases tied together under the cloth cover, and the ceaseless spatter of rain. His head shook to the carriage's jarring rhythm, and his temple knocked painfully against the pillow he had made from his folded coat. Not a single clear and comprehensible thought, just complete disarray.

"Mm," Laurentius mumbled.

He opened his eyes, sat upright, and looked at the other people in the carriage. They all had downcast gazes; they were all sitting there quietly minding their own business. Now he could observe them properly. The woman next to him was sitting in a cramped position, as if she had been pushed up sideways against the carriage's wooden seat. Her head was turned in the other direction, looking away. Her body was right there next to him, to be sure, but it looked like its owner was somewhere else. A body without eyes, unseeing, lifeless. Just an empty bag. Laurentius felt the need to speak, to talk to someone, but he couldn't think what to say. He was afraid he might start an argument out of nothing again.

He took his watch from his pocket and inspected the dial with its single hand. Soon it would be completely dark outside. He bent forwards towards the window, so that he could see out through the small holes. A view of the outside world opened up before his eyes. A mottled river, flowing unwittingly towards its goal. Leaves of many hues, sprinkled with glittering beads of rainwater. Lone forest clearings, sliding slowly past. But nothing that could hold his eye for long, nothing that could help his thoughts cohere. He was in need of Clodia's supportive twittering right now, but all he had for company were the other passengers, half-asleep, half-conscious. He tried to banish the thoughts which were racing backwards and forwards in his head, scattering here and there, but the battle with the demons of his memory only made the images more distinct, gave them a form. Monsters born of reason.

Laurentius coughed, and he felt a grating in his throat. He was finding it hard to breathe.

He slowly became aware of an acrid stench which was seeping into the carriage. At first it had been barely perceptible, but now it was gradually becoming all-engulfing, dominating his senses completely, overpowering him like sleep overpowers a weary body.

He spun around in panic. Where was the smell coming from? The other passengers were calmly sitting in their seats, not so much as wrinkling their noses. He reached forwards towards the window and looked out again. That stench must be coming from somewhere! In the distance he could see the dark silhouette of a building, a colossus of massive beams standing in the ominous, nightmarish half-light which came with the onset of dusk. Straining to see past the rainwater which was dripping in through the window holes, he wiped the wet inner surface clean, leaving a greyish, muddy streak in the palm of his hand. There, through the mist, next to a forest glade gleaming wet with rain, he could make out collapsed walls, misshapen rafters knocked together from planks of wood, flapping shingle roofing and bristling poles. Was that a barn? There was not a single light to be seen, not a single sign of life coming from the building's carcass.

The stench must be coming from somewhere over there, from those splayed, mildewed rafters, decided Laurentius. Definitely from over there.

He looked to see whether anyone might have made a bonfire near the barn, although it was clear that in this weather no one could keep a fire burning for long. There was no flickering yellow glow of flame to be seen, just a dull, lifeless scene set against a backdrop of darkening blue sky. But somewhere there must be something, some substance, some liquid, some decay from which the poisonous smell was seeping. Maybe it was rotten hay smouldering inside the barn?

He pressed his head against the cold metal plating and peered through the window to try to get a better view of the surroundings, but all he could see through the narrow metal slits was the jolting landscape, getting darker and darker, just individual details which didn't add up to any whole.

Laurentius tried to align his eye with one of the larger holes, but at that very moment the carriage jolted violently, causing him to knock his brow painfully against the cold iron, and everything started swimming in front of his eyes. He let out a muffled groan. The other passengers anxiously sat up in their seats and pressed their hands against the sides of the carriage for support. He heard a rattling sound, at first barely audible, but slowly getting louder and louder, until suddenly the seats tilted sideways, and there was a loud crash, followed by the sound of the coachman swearing and whoaing the horses. The carriage came to an abrupt halt. For a moment silence reigned, to be broken by the thwack of cases falling from the baggage deck onto the muddy road behind.

"Aah!" Laurentius cried out.

He rubbed the sore spot on his head and started trying to lift himself out of the lopsided carriage, although it proved no easy task. When he finally managed to get the door open, he saw that the coachman and the woman's footman were already bustling about at the back of the carriage. Fortunately, the spoked wheel had not been too seriously damaged: it had just come off its axle and was lying to one side, half-lodged in the mud.

"I'm going to need help with that," declared the coachman. "I'm hardly likely to get it back on by myself. Everyone out."

"But it's raining, isn't it?" the woman sitting next to Laurentius said in an irked tone.

"Let the lady stay where she is," said the coachman in response. "How much can she weigh in any case?"

Laurentius straightened his back and surveyed the scene. By the roadside there were a few lone trees which the wind had not yet stripped of their autumn leaves, and through their grey trunks he could see a brown forest glade. On higher ground in the middle of it stood a blackened barn, the same one which Laurentius had been trying to make out through the carriage window. Something about the scene sent a cold shiver running down his spine. That acrid stench was in his nostrils again, like some horrific memory which he had been struggling to subdue. The essence of black bile, mixed with acid, maybe sulphur, was pouring down on the passengers and the carriage with the raindrops. The vile breath crept through their damp clothing, under their hats and through their hair, past their skin and into their nostrils, and then onwards to their lungs, flesh and hearts. First on the tongue, then in the nose—acrid, sharp, hostile and unexpected. He could vaguely remember that some time ago, a very long time ago, he had experienced a similar smell, a similar horror. The particles of this stench, the essence of which carried the memories, hooked their barbs into the inner cavities of his nose, into the roof of his mouth, and moved onwards through the long passages to his brain, and then to his soul. The smell overpowered him, bringing with it memories of a horrific scene, with murder, rape and people wailing in distress, a scene which he would never forget. It wore away at the old experiences which had been dulled by the passage of years, leaving them freshly exposed. Blood flowed from the wound. He could still remember—how could he not?

"Excuse me," Laurentius said, trying to get the coachman's attention.

He anxiously rubbed his nose, and even tried to hold his nostrils shut, but in vain. The smell had permeated every-where and he feared that there was no hope of being free of it. A feeling of dread started to overcome him. Meanwhile, the other passengers were bustling about at the end of the carriage pole, looking almost cheerful.

"It's as if some Satan put a curse on that there wheel," fumed the coachman. "I looked over everything meself before we set out, and there weren't nothing wrong. Some devil must've put the evil eye on it."

"Excuse me!" Laurentius said despairingly. But the coach-man didn't even look in his direction; he just carried on swearing to himself, as if he were chanting a prayer or spell.

"Hey, what's the matter with you?! Come and take hold of this end and we'll lift it together," instructed the man who had been cursing the state of the local roads.

"Have you noticed that smell as well?" asked Laurentius.

"I beg your pardon?" the man asked.

"That smell," Laurentius repeated.

"I can't smell a thing. I've had a heavy cold the last few days. Maybe the wind is carrying it from somewhere nearby. The locals burn all sorts of rubbish," the man said.

Laurentius shook his head, looked around again, and rubbed his nose anxiously. His head was spinning.

"Now, all together, heave!" the coachmen yelled.

Laurentius grabbed hold of the carriage with the others. Straining their muscles, pushing their boots deep into the mud, they eventually managed to lift the carriage to the right height, and the driver began to beat the wheel back on, continuing to mutter something to himself in time with the hammer blows. But inside Laurentius, inside his thoughts and in his brain, the barbed stench was spreading with ever-greater strength; the black bile was diffusing ever wider, reaching into all of his limbs: horror, odium, hell. But where were they?

"Where are we now, anyway?" Laurentius asked.

The coachman mumbled something incomprehensible, nodded towards the road, and carried on beating the wheel with his hammer. Flustered, Laurentius didn't dare ask more questions; he just stood there looking uneasily at the surroundings. Where indeed could they be?

"We're almost there now, just a little further to go. I reckon Dorpat would have been in sight before nightfall," explained one of the men when they finally put the carriage back down. "It was bad luck about that wheel, to be sure; now it will be properly dark by the time we arrive. Best gather up the baggage quickly."

Laurentius smiled and tried to summon up a friendly expression. "It's a real bother, to be sure."

Thankfully his case was still there on the baggage deck. But the cage containing his dead parakeet was not to be seen, and nor did it appear to be among the things scattered across the muddy road. Laurentius strained to look in the direction of the dark clearing. The other passengers huffed and puffed irately as they lifted their cases up onto the back of the carriage, and the footman tied them fast, while the carriage driver continued to potter about near the wheel. Laurentius looked around as if he were searching for something. But it was barely possible to make out any clear details through the twilight and spattering rain. Taking care to avoid the long puddles he stepped a couple of paces away from the carriage wheel.

He winced as he felt a hot sensation moving slowly upwards from his stomach to his head. This was the hot, moist humour, the one which caused anger and fear.

A couple of yards away, stooping in the shadow of a tall thick fir tree, stood a raggedy hunchbacked figure with sunken features. He was holding Laurentius' parakeet cage. The cage door had been torn open, and Laurentius could see something brightly coloured in the ragamuffin's spindly, bone-white hand. The strange stench was getting stronger and stronger. The ragged figure croaked a couple of words in an incomprehensible language and seemed to try to smile. From inside the grey tuft of beard a mouth appeared, full of crooked, dark stumps of differing sizes.

"Give that back to me," said Laurentius, trying to make his voice sound assured and assertive.

Still smiling, the figure stood upright and grabbed Laurentius by the shoulders. Light-blue eyes, almost the same colour as the summer sky, goggled at him from sunken sockets. Laurentius wanted to avert his gaze. He never looked other people in the eye if he could avoid it. But this time he couldn't look away or close his eyes. He stared into the old man's eyes, and there, amid the bluish-grey, he saw pain and death. A starving old man, driven away from wherever he went, too old and skinny to work, too scruffy and sick for anyone to care for.

"I can't…" Laurentius began to explain. He still couldn't turn his gaze away. But by now it was probably too late.

"I must not," Laurentius said.

The old man turned round and galloped off at a surprisingly sprightly pace in the direction of the rotting barn.

Laurentius stood and watched him go, unable to do anything. He should have gone after him, grabbed the cage, maybe offered some money, but a torpor caused by the stench and his fear held him fast like a wall. The black bile had engulfed him, pushed him into a dead end; he couldn't react quickly enough. He was afraid of the little old man.

"We're leaving now. Before it gets really dark," someone hollered from over by the carriage.

At first Laurentius didn't answer; he just stood staring blankly at the black barn and rubbing his nose. The stench was washing over him in waves; it seemed to be radiating from the surrounding trees and the rotten rafters of the barn, like light from a candle. Or did it come from Laurentius himself? Was he the candle?

"Hey!" someone called again.

Laurentius shook his head and started walking slowly back towards the carriage. "Didn't you see?"

"What? Hurry up now," said one of the other passengers.

"There was someone there," Laurentius said.

"My good man, it was probably just a patch of mist," said the passenger.

"My cage…" he began, but he knew there was no sense in trying to explain. By now the stench was almost suffocating him; he couldn't stand being there any longer.

Monday Evening

THE OUTSKIRTS OF TOWN were always the same. Clearings would suddenly start to appear between the forest trees, swiftly followed by lone, unlit hovels. Architectural complexity and yellow lantern light were reserved for the centre of town; here in the hazy interim zone there were just shabby buildings, workshops of various descriptions, tanners and their stinking vats, all those people who due to their trades or social standing were not allowed into town, or who chose not to pass through its walls. Here the town was yet to start, but the countryside had already started fading away. Nevertheless, people still talked about the edge of town, as if it were possible to draw a dividing line, beyond which the countryside abruptly ceases to exist. Where was that sharp boundary which separates the town from the countryside, the end from the beginning? Was it the town wall? Of course not—the cloisters, inns, graveyards and allotments indicated that the town had started well before then. Where are the outer limits of my being? Are they my skin, my hair, my clothes, my cage? The stagecoach?

Laurentius closed his eyes, but the stench had not gone anywhere. At first he had been afraid that it was too vile ever to get used to, then he thought that he might be able to forget it at least for a while. But as soon as he started to take cheer in that thought it came back, filling his nostrils with all its former strength, and he could think of nothing else. He knew that it was because of the crime he had committed and the oppressive guilt which would not leave him alone for a moment. But where was it coming from? He felt so overcome with disgust that he decided to pray quietly to himself. But even prayer could not help. Where was his dear Clodia when he needed her?

Laurentius shifted restlessly in his seat. "Aren't we there yet?" he asked, addressing no one in particular.

"We should be arriving at the inn any moment now. You can't make out anything in this darkness. There should be a lantern hanging outside it," the man sitting opposite said.

Laurentius nodded, rummaged about in his pocket for a handkerchief, and wiped his face. He bent forwards to look out of the window, but he could make out very little through the little holes. Just a uniform, indeterminate dimness, together with the hazy outlines of the occasional hut and the odd bystander watching them as they went past. In the distance he could see the contours of the city walls and the bastion mounds.

"I can't see a single light," Laurentius said.

"Aha," the other passenger responded.

Laurentius closed his eyes and tried to focus his thoughts. The stench was continuing to waft into his nostrils, as if an iron demon had breathed a soul forged on an anvil into him. The new soul had entered him and started to displace the vapour which had previously been suspended there, which he had brought with him from another place, from another country.

Without knowing fully why, he stared to panic.

"Now you can see it," the man sitting opposite announced jubilantly.

The coachman geed the horses, and the carriage turned. It rumbled across the sunken kerbstones leading onto a small square which was edged with a row of wooden stakes. The light of the high-hanging lanterns illuminated innumerable rippling puddles, covering the uneven muddy surface of the yard. As the large carriage wheels pressed down into the puddles they created momentary furrows of dryness, before the water lapped back into position. Tiny water droplets fell onto the puddles' surface, causing concentric ripples, and the wind whistled between the dripping spokes of the carriage wheels.

"We're here!" the man sitting opposite called out in a triumphant voice, as if he had been driving the carriage himself and had managed to steer it to safe harbour through many ordeals and hardships. The other passengers began to stir and gather up their bundles.

The leather-clad door opened with a creak; the coachman warned the passengers to be careful descending the steps, and one by one they stepped out onto the grey flagstones which had been placed at the edge of the square for that very purpose. Laurentius sat and waited for the rest of the passengers to get off, watching how the woman sitting next to him hoisted up her voluminous dress so that she could stand up and make her way out of the carriage.

"Is that everyone?" the coachman asked.

"Forgive me," Laurentius mumbled, and he got up. His legs were trembling. He stood on the footboard for a moment, taking deep breaths of the air outside. Some kind of vapour wafted past his face, and he could detect the smells of sulphur, iron and tin.

"Easy there," the coachman said to Laurentius.

He stood on the square and watched as the small horses were led to stable, tossing their manes, while the coachman swore to himself. The wind had picked up and was tearing bits of straw from the thatched roofs. The debris spun through the air before landing in the puddles where it lay, floating on the surface. Laurentius was the last to clatter his way in through the inn door. Once inside, he hoped to get himself and his case out of sight of the other guests as quickly as possible. For some reason he had the feeling that everyone was watching him suspiciously, and this wasn't helped by the agoraphobia which he always felt in such places. Would this be the moment when someone pointed the finger at him? Several other guests had gathered around the chipped stone hearth to warm their hands, and they turned towards the door as he entered. Some of the others were sitting at the wobbly little tables by the wall, and they also peered over at him curiously.

"Good evening to you all," he mumbled in the brief silence which ensued as he entered, and made a line straight for the host.

"One night please," he announced, glancing at the innkeeper.

The clerkish-looking innkeeper appraised Laurentius for a moment before directing him to a small chamber at the back of the inn, where there were two beds positioned almost side by side.

"There is one free space here," said the host, pointing at a wooden case which was already standing by the wall. "The window hardly lets in any draught at all. But you will have to share the bed. The other gentleman is still in town taking care of some business, but he is sure to be back by evening."

Laurentius sighed. Sharing a bed was a familiar necessity which could often prove rather tedious, especially if one's bedmate happened to be a drunkard.

"Understood. I will bear that in mind," Laurentius said.

He dragged his case to the head of the bed. The small window above had a thick pane of glass in it, but it hadn't yet been filled with straw for winter, so it was safe to assume that the damp and chill of the night would come seeping into the room. But this was still better than the roadside guest houses, where he had been forced to sleep on nothing more than his coat, spread out on the bare floor. He had good reason to fear that if his bedmate were restless, then not much would come of his efforts to sleep here either. But nor did he have much choice in the matter—they put several people together to sleep in all of the guest houses. It saved on space—and it was warmer like that.

"Thank you," he said politely.

The host gave him an encouraging nod, and pulled the door shut behind him, leaving a reassuring ray of light shining into the room through the chink at the bottom.

Laurentius sat down on the mattress filled with birch leaves, and leant back against the wall. None of the other guests had gone to bed yet, and he could hear a racket coming from the neighbouring room. Someone had even started singing in an inebriated voice.

"Drunkards again," he mumbled to himself.

Laurentius shook his head apprehensively, and started reading an evening prayer in a half-whisper. Through the thin bedroom door he could hear almost every word being said in the public room, and he couldn't focus on any of the lines of his prayer apart from "preserve us from evil".

"Amen," he said in a slightly louder voice, and he looked out of the window.

It occurred to him that it might be appropriate to say an intercessory prayer for his parakeet, but he couldn't make up his mind. It was true that Clodia had been a bird, and that she therefore had no rational soul, but creatures who spent so much time in the company of humans eventually became one with their beings and desires, and with their soul's phantasms, and they began to change. Plutarch had tried to comfort his wife after their daughter's death by comparing the soul to a bird which has flown its cage. If the bird had been in the cage for a short time, then it would fly out quickly, but if it had been there longer, then the bird would have grown accustomed to the cage; it would have become its home, and it would not be able to leave so easily. When little children play with dolls made from cloth and wood, the dolls respond to them. For the children they are beings with souls, and causing them distress is the same as causing distress to a living person. Those wooden dolls and scraps of cloth are given a life and a purpose by the children, just as the carriage gained a life and purpose when the passengers travelled in it; just as the cage has a life and purpose when a bird is inside it. In a similar way Clodia had long been one with his soul; she had balanced his soul's humours with her warmth, acting as a counterweight to his melancholy. Together, they had formed a single whole, like an artist and the brush he holds in his hand. They were immiscible and yet undissolvable. If Ovid had dedicated an elegy to his beloved parakeet, then why should Laurentius not pray for his? After all, he had spent every single day over nearly ten years tending to Clodia's well-being, and she in turn had helped to keep him balanced. But now his spadger was gone, seized by some raggedy old man.

> Our soul is like a bird
> escaped from the fowler's snare:
> The snare was broken
> and so we escaped.

Noting that the Psalm also compared the soul to a bird, Laurentius nodded and read it through to the end, trying not to let any other thoughts distract him. But the stench in his nostrils was constantly reminding him of its presence, like a throbbing pain, which interfered with his concentration and distracted his attention. He stopped reading and rested his head in his hands.

"Very well," Laurentius said resignedly.

With a sigh he opened his case and took out a small bottle containing a dark tincture which was intended only for extreme eventualities. He swigged down half a mouthful and wrinkled his nose. The tincture tasted horribly bitter, but he hoped it would counteract the disgusting smell. He cast a final glance out of the window, and then wrapped himself determinedly in his coat. He had been up for too long; now only sleep could cure him.

"Bedtime," Laurentius told himself.

The birch leaves rustled in his mattress, giving off a barely detectable scent of fresh forest; evidently they had just been replaced. He hadn't had the chance to sleep on such a decent bed the whole journey; normally all there was for a mattress was a piece of sheeting thrown on top of some trampled, mouldy straw. The last time he slept on a feather mattress had been before setting out on his journey, when he had been awaiting his departure at his godfather's house. Laurentius curled up in bed, and the events of the past day started to come back to him. The images flashed before his eyes and the fragments of conversation echoed in his ears, mixing with the voices from the public room. As the prattling voices whirled round his head the old man who had grabbed his cage came back to him again and again, and with him came the stench. Even after taking the tincture, it was still wafting into his nostrils. Laurentius closed his eyes tight shut and pressed his face closer to the birch leaves, hoping that their pure scent would drive away the vileness. He tried to imagine a warm summer meadow, a forest glade illuminated by radiant sunshine, with bright, lush greenery all around. He could hear birds twittering and chirping, and bees buzzing. The sky was bright blue, and far above, in the uppermost layers of the humid sphere which was wreathed around the planet, a couple of long flaxen clouds were visible, making the boundless blueness of the heavenly vaults appear even higher. He let himself sink into the rustling grass and lie in wait under the imaginary axis of the azure sphere. He could smell the sweet scent of roses and the powerful woody aroma of thyme. He could almost see the dodecahedral cosmos, ethereal, clear and pure.

"To sleep, perchance to dream," Laurentius whispered to himself. But then the ragged old man's light-blue eyes came back to him.

The spatter of rain outside started to get louder. Drops of water splashed against the windowpane; the wind roared like a fire in the hearth; there was a clattering and creaking sound coming from somewhere. The lantern hanging above the door outside started swaying violently, its jerky dance casting a trembling opaque light onto the walls of the room.

Laurentius raised his head in alarm.

There was a rotten stench flooding in through the wide gap between the window frame and the wall and even the smell of the rustling summer birch leaves couldn't deflect it from his nose. Laurentius jerked upright and looked angrily outside.

There was a caped figure standing there. Through the green glass of the windowpane it had a strange, deathly hue, and its hair was stuck to its face and shoulders in dark matted strands.

Laurentius gazed in horror. The hunched creature was standing at the edge of the circle of lantern light, out in the heavy spattering rain, and it didn't seem to care that the hem of its cape was floating in a puddle: the water had already soaked into the coarse fibres of the fabric and was moving greedily upwards. Through the rainwater which was flowing down the windowpane the figure's face was wavy and distorted, preventing Laurentius from catching sight of any expression.

Without thinking what he was doing, Laurentius jumped up from his bed and rushed through the hubbub of the public room and out through the front door of the inn. But by the time he had got outside into the rain the apparition had gone, and even after splashing about for a while at the perimeter of the lantern light and the darkness, trying to locate the spot where the figure had been standing, he couldn't see the slightest trace. Nevertheless, he was certain that there had been someone out there, standing and looking longingly in the direction of the guest house, towards the lights.

"Hey!" someone called out, and the inn door was flung wide open, sending a glaring square of light and warmth flooding out into the muddy yard.

"Yes?" Laurentius said in response.

"Have you lost something out there?" the innkeeper's voice rang out.

"No, I was just looking out of the window and thought I saw someone standing out here," Laurentius replied, and started walking back towards the inn door.

"Ahh… that will be those locals. It rained all through the summer, and now they're loitering hungrily outside everyone's house. The situation is bound to get even worse for them soon."

"But what will become of them?" Laurentius asked.

"What do you mean?" the innkeeper said, seeming not to understand the question.

But Laurentius just nodded and went back inside. After all, he knew that people starving to death was nothing surprising. It happened everywhere now.

NIGHT

I'M STARVING HUNGRY; I've got pains all over; my head is throbbing. I lean back against a spruce tree to rest. The thin lower branches prod into me, but at least the thick boughs above catch most of the rain. My clothes are soaking wet; I should make a fire, but where in this weather? Thankfully it's not far to go now. They say that everyone gets given something to eat in Dorpat. A lot of people have already gone that way—just yesterday I met two girls on the road, rushing there almost merrily. Just as if they had set off a-wooing. They didn't want to take an old granddad like me with them, of course. And right they were too: I wouldn't take me as company. My legs are completely worn out. I'm old enough not to believe those stories about free food any more. But there might just be a grain of truth in them this time. Maybe I will get given something to eat there? And anyway, there is more hope of surviving in town than out here in the forest. They haven't got the better of me yet, ha! I'm a Ugandi man—you don't get the better of us Ugandi men as easy as that! That's right, I'll have a little rest, then onwards.

In the summer and early autumn, when the berries were ripe, I could just about get by, but since the weather's turned colder, it's become completely impossible. The forests are empty; I get sent packing wherever I go; I hardly ever get so much as a drop of spirit to drink.

I can hear the branches rustling in the gusts of wind; the rainwater is trickling down my collar; there's no shelter to be had here. There's a barn over there on that hill, but I don't dare go up there. During the war the soldiers filled it up with people and set it alight; the onlookers said that evil spirits started flitting about in the flames, taking people's souls to hell. The soldiers fired at the spirits, but they couldn't harm them. Hah, everyone knows that only a silver bullet can get them. But ever since, folk have heard cackling and chortling coming from that barn; they say that witches go up there to dance their dances and take people's souls to the Devil. I'm not afraid of those old hags and codgers; there aren't really any devils up there. Although best to keep a safe distance just in case. I know they're just stories, probably just lies, but there might be a grain of truth there somewhere. Even if you never know exactly where, you just can't put your finger on it.

My lips are dry; I spit; the mucus catches on my beard and hangs there.

I hear the trample of hooves, someone whoaing horses, and then a crashing sound. I stand there in the twilight, watching as the carriage slowly tips onto its side, and the bags fall onto the ground…

I wipe my chin with the back of my hand. When you've been hungry for a long time you start to see all sorts of odd things—I've heard about that. They say you mustn't believe any of it, that it's sent by the Devil. But who knows? I've seen all sorts. People walking around with dogs' heads, and whatever you fancy. You see them when you're hungry. But that carriage over there looks grand: bright colours, big wheels. Who knows for sure if it's real, or if it just seems to be there?

My head is hurting; there's bags lying about all over the place. Right there in front of me there's some sort of wire cage. There's an odd-looking coloured bird inside it, small and skinny. I haven't eaten anything for days, and that bird would be enough for a mouthful. What's to lose? Let's give it a try. I force the cage door open.

Some frightened-looking chap in a hat approaches and whispers something. But I can hardly hear what he says.

"What do you want?" I snap back in response.

He whispers something in his soft voice, and it sounds like some kind of witchery. He grabs me by the shoulders; his eyes are dark as dirt, glimmering like coals, and he looks straight at me. I want to look away, but I can't: there are clouds of fog and shadows in his gaze, and I'm trapped there, helpless like a glow-worm. I can feel him drawing my soul from me, as if he were sucking it out through a straw. Just like I drank birch sap as a child. My head is hurting; I struggle. But then he lets me go.

"Ai!" I shout out, and I start to run.

I don't notice that the cage, the prison woven from wire, is still in my hand. I run, but my legs are heavy; my feet sink into the wet ground and slip about on the grass. I run, but then I trip on some logs, twist my leg, and fall onto the ground, straight on top of something. I'm too frightened to make a move; the wind is roaring, rainwater is dripping onto me, and the ground is cold and damp. I'm lying under the eaves of the barn; there's a rotten wall right behind me, blackened joists and beams are bristling either side, smearing their blackness onto me. I don't dare go inside, I'll be fine here where I am.

It's damp, but at least I have some shelter from the wind. I wait and listen out for footsteps. I can hear grass scrunching and rustling, and some voices whispering faintly. It sounds as if someone is breathing very close by, just the other side of the wall. I wait. I can hear some mumbling and sobbing from inside the barn. Is that witches?

Some time passes, and nothing happens. I don't dare to show myself or move about too much, so I start plucking the feathers off the bird right there and then. It's a small bird, no bigger than a sparrow, but it will be enough for a mouthful, that's for sure. Its flesh is soft; its bones are fragile—they crunch under my teeth.

I carefully poke my head round the corner, and it looks like the carriage has disappeared. Was it really there? I feel a churning in my stomach, followed by a sharp pain. Damn, maybe that bird was rotten. Maybe it had already been dead too long. The meat tasted good, sweet; there was no sickly taste of decay. But now I can taste some sort of sourness and bitterness, rising up from my stomach. Like wormwood.

I feel a pinching pain down there, like cramp. I jump up and grip hold of my stomach. Have I been without food so long that my guts can no longer cope? A couple of days ago I got a crust of bread and a swig of spirit from some inn, so things shouldn't be so bad. But the cramps don't seem to be stopping: I'm bent double from pain. I try to hold it back, but something bitter like bile starts seething up my throat. I vomit onto the ground near my feet, and then the bright-coloured bird pops out of my mouth, flaps its wings, and flies off.

Damn, I've been bewitched.

That man back there bewitched me and my soul just flew out through my mouth. What sort of cage is this? Maybe it's meant for collecting souls—the souls are locked up inside it. I should probably take it straight back to where it came from. But if that man was the Devil himself, how will I find him now? The carriage is nowhere to be seen, and it's going to be dark soon. I have to get moving.

I hear the door creak open, and the voices get shriller.

I shake my head but everything is still muddled. I shake my fist at the barn, run back down the hill, and start walking along the road. The ruts are deep and full of cold water. No problem if they headed for Dorpat—I can go there too. I was planning to go there anyway—all the more reason if I can get my soul back. That bird is sure to follow him. Although maybe it was someone else's soul that I just let out of the cage, maybe someone else's soul just flew off?

I look round. There are no crows to be seen, no magpies either, not a single bird keeping watch for my soul. What happened just now? My head is aching and throbbing; I've got cramp in my stomach. I stumble onwards; the road leads downhill and then turns, passes through some forest and comes to a meadow. A river is visible through the rain, twisting and turning past clumps of bushes; there are sinewy willows with drooping branches on either bank. The dusk is growing thicker; it's hard to make out the shapes of things; everything has started melting into one. Over yonder, between the trees, I can see a dark shape. It looks like a house, long and low like a coffin. Is that where they went? There's not a single sign of human life around it, no dogs or horses. Not a single light flickering through the windows. But Dorpat must be close by. I have to push on.

Is that their carriage in front of the house? It looks like it might be; maybe they stopped there after all. It could just be that I can't see the light in the windows from where I'm standing. It's true that if they were delayed they would have set down at the first guest house they came to—what else could they do? Let's have a closer look what's down there.

I carry on down the muddy road; the wind is whistling and whispering through the bars of the cage. Or maybe that sound is coming from somewhere else? I look round, there are trees, willows dripping with rainwater dotted here and there. But it feels as if someone is watching me from behind. I look round again, and think I can make out a crown and a cape over there. Pallid faces, deathly pale, starving lips slightly parted as if trying to utter some kind of warning.

But no, I can't let myself believe everything I see. It's just the hunger, visions—you mustn't pay attention, they say. Otherwise you end up going mad, hearing voices, running about in rings and biting people. I've seen people like that before—people who couldn't bear the hunger any longer and just gave in.

No, we're Ugandi men: you won't get the better of us that easily. I have to keep going.

TUESDAY

LAURENTIUS OPENED HIS EYES and lay there, staring blankly at the ceiling. The beams had been stained dark brown, almost black, by the peat smoke from the fireplace. A carriage drove past outside, and the windowpanes rattled. He could hear the rainwater dripping from the eaves, and the occasional voice hollering something in unfamiliar Estonian. It was morning.

He pushed himself into a sitting position and groped in his breast pocket for his watch—its single hand was between five and six. Stretched out next to him was a man with long, greasy hair, wrapped tightly in his coat, and smelling of stale beer. Maybe that was what had woken him?

"Hmm…" Laurentius mumbled to himself.

The sun had not yet risen and the hazy pre-dawn light was glimmering through the green windowpane. Laurentius never normally got up so early: someone usually had to come and wake him, and even then he would try his best to carry on sleeping. He could never manage to go to bed at the right time, and he was often plagued by insomnia, but once he had finally dropped off he never had any problem sleeping right through to midday. So far in his life he had not developed the discipline needed to get up at the same time every day—it would always depend on circumstances. And those circumstances tended to change quite frequently.

Annoyed that he had lost at least an hour of sleep, Laurentius closed his eyes and sank back into the rustling mattress. The man next to him carried on snoring luxuriantly.

"Hopeless." He already felt completely alert, fully rested. He took out his pocket watch and purposefully started to wind it up.

"Why did I wake up so early?" he asked himself.

He started to feel more and more anxious. Scraps of dreams started seeping back into his lucid morning consciousness. He had the vague feeling that he had woken up because of something which he had dreamt about, but he couldn't remember what it had been. It had not been a slow, gradual awakening; it had felt more like someone roughly shaking him awake, like being robbed in the middle of the street. Unidentified and unexpected.

"Now then," he mumbled, still deep in thought.

In that brief period when he was no longer sleeping but was still not properly awake, a silhouette of what he had seen must have impinged itself on his memory. Just a blurred recollection, but still recognizable. Through the confused fog he could see one clear image: a river and trees.

"Trees, pointed leaves, sinewy trunks," he said to himself.

He started to recall that he had also seen a house through the branches and leaves. A dark, low building. He had been standing on a muddy road in the dim light, and he had started walking, holding his birdcage in his hand. Over yonder stood a king, with a high crown and a broad dark cape. And there were alders or willows growing in thick straight rows either side of the road.

"There was something else there as well," Laurentius said to himself.

Then he remembered what had been bothering him. While he was still asleep he had desperately tried to commit everything to memory, but he had realized that it was a dream—and then he woke up.

He grabbed a quill and ink from his chest and scribbled on a blank sheet of paper. A king, willow trees, a coffin-shaped building. He knew from past experience that without any reference points his dreams were quickly lost; even the memory of them would cease to be. A couple of words were enough at first—then one could leave associative memory to do its work, as Aristotle had written. It was quite possible that some seemingly unconnected event would later enable him to recover the whole dream, or at least some part of it.

He folded the sheet of paper in two, stuffed it back into his case, and stood there irresolutely.

Images were whirling round his mind, sensory impressions of the building, the trees and... that smell. Only now did he realize that the smell from yesterday had not gone anywhere, that it had even been part of his dream. It was as if it had seeped so deep into him that it had become a part of him, so that he sometimes even forgot about it. But then inevitably it would remind him of its presence, just like a feeling of guilt over things left undone, like despairing remorse for crimes committed unwittingly.

He shook his head, knelt down beside his chest and read the first Psalm to himself:

> "And he shall be like a tree,
> planted by the rivers of water,
> that bringeth forth his fruit in his season;
> his leaf also shall not whither;
> and whatsoever he does shall prosper."

He tried to imagine the flowing waters and fruit trees, but it didn't help to calm him one bit. Instead, wiry willow trees and dark, dirty waters reared up in his mind's eye.

"Now then," he said, eventually managing to get to the end of the Psalm.

He decided not to make too much of the trees. To start with he had to go to speak to the rector and put his name on the list for matriculation with the other students. It was important to make sure he received his stipend in its entirety: even with his godfather's generosity he wouldn't be able to get by without state support.

He took a couple of brisk paces backwards and forwards and practised a few fencing moves, trying to shake off the memories of yesterday's journey, the stinking barn, the ragged old man's eyes and his dream. He bent down over his chest and inspected his neatly packed clothes. They were almost completely new, with not a single patch to be seen on them.

To be on the safe side he put on his long boots; then he straightened his shirtsleeves and adjusted his lace neckerchief so that it would be visible above his jacket collar. It had turned a bit yellow on the journey, but that couldn't be helped. Laurentius did not want the rector to think that he came from a poor family, but he certainly didn't want to make a foppish impression either.

Having finished with his garments, he checked that his sword was hanging at an appropriately gallant angle from his hip, and went through to the public room of the inn. His bedmate hadn't moved once since Laurentius had woken, and he left him lying there.

"I have some matters to take care of at the university," Laurentius announced to the innkeeper.

The innkeeper smiled and explained in a slightly patronizing tone that the university was actually not at all hard to find. It was not far from the inn, next to the church of St John, which one could spot from a distance by its metal-plated spire. So if Laurentius headed straight in the direction of the church tower he would be sure to end up at the academy.

Laurentius followed the instructions precisely, and arriving at his destination he discovered that the academy building had been completed just recently and was indeed "in the latest fashion and rather fancy", as the innkeeper had told him. Although there were other newly built houses in town, stone constructions were still in the minority, and in several places the overgrown plots bore witness to the fact that these parts had been ravaged by war just twenty years previously. But even if it had still not been fully rebuilt, the general impression which the town made was not a bad one. The streets had been paved, and judging by the way the houses had flower pots and glass windows, people lived fairly comfortably. The academy building was clean and light inside, and the wide, spacious vestibule was surprisingly cheery and welcoming. Laurentius had already started to feel much better.

The university rector, Professor Below, received him almost immediately, and was friendly and obliging throughout their conversation. He even made a point of praising his fellow professors at Dorpat, stressing that they were in no way inferior to those in Uppsala.

"Where do you plan to live?" Professor Below eventually enquired.

"I haven't managed to rent a room yet. I was hoping I could get some advice from the university. One can't normally trust the landlords in these matters."

Below sighed. "I am sure that you are aware that the lectures started a few weeks ago, and that we are therefore entitled to withhold a proportionate sum from your stipend. As far as advice is concerned, I fear that you will have to share a room with someone. The lodgings situation is truly dire currently, although no doubt you will find something eventually."

"I'm sorry, but the journey proved harder than expected. The sea was so stormy that not a single boat dared to set sail any earlier. I'm sure you know what the weather can be like in September," Laurentius replied.

But he was not convinced that that would be a good enough excuse. It was indeed well known that the sea could be stormy by September, which meant that it would have been wise for him to set out in August, not October.

Professor Below raised his eyebrows absent-mindedly and then immersed himself in the papers which Laurentius had submitted.

"Well now, I see that you gained your first degree in Leiden! I studied in Holland myself, a splendid place. Very well, let's leave your late arrival aside for now. Go to see Professor Dimberg; he is professor of mathematics and can assess your level of knowledge. Such are the formalities here. You probably don't need to go through the initiation ceremony again. It's a most unpleasant custom in any case."

Laurentius nodded a little distractedly. The university examination system had been established some time ago, when students who were little older than boys and others who experienced difficulties with their studies started coming to university. But it was probably not so much his knowledge as the possibility that he had been forced to leave Holland due to religious convictions which was the issue now. The situation in the Netherlands was known to be conducive to free think-ing, and students who arrived from there sometimes had the strangest of beliefs, from atheism or pantheism to Anabaptism and Pietism. According to official Swedish policy, however, all religious sentiments other than orthodox Lutheranism were strictly proscribed. The king himself led by example in this respect, quoting the Bible in court, and holding a very firm position regarding other denominations.

"I have indeed already been through the initiation cere-mony," Laurentius said politely, avoiding the question of his late arrival. "In that respect I would like to request that I not be assigned to any particular national group. I don't suppose that I have any compatriots studying here anyway."

The rector looked straight at him in evident surprise. "How do you know? Anyway, it's our custom to assign all students to national groups. I see no reason to make an exception in your case. That way you would get yourself lodgings as well."

"By the grace of God," Laurentius bowed low. "I am a loyal subject of Our Esteemed Majesty, but my ultimate loyalty belongs to the ruler of the heavenly hosts."

"Hmm," the rector mumbled sceptically, and Laurentius thought he saw a faint grin appear on his face. "First go and see Professor Dimberg all the same; he will definitely be interested in hearing about your religious convictions. And let's see what can be done about those lodgings."

"I'm a committed adherent of orthodox Lutheranism: the Spenerists' attitude to the Holy Scriptures and outward piety are theologically inadmissible to me. That whole approach is directly contrary to the presumption of salvation through faith alone," Laurentius said, trying to dispel any doubts regarding his theological convictions.

"Ah, is that so?" the rector said, this time with a clearly visible smile, which even seemed to convey a hint of *Schadenfreude*. "So that is your position on the matter. Most interesting."

Laurentius smiled and nodded. He didn't know what people really thought about Swedish religious policy here in Dorpat, but he could be sure that they observed it at least formally. It was anyway safest for him to try to avoid any disagreements and conflicts, even if it were among the Pietists that one would be most likely to encounter the most modern and liberal views. Pietism was gaining more and more widespread popularity among the students, and was constantly giving rise to the kinds of disagreements which he had been dragged into in Holland. Such disputes tended to get increasingly heated, and before you knew it other, more serious problems reared their head. His careless talk had been the reason he had to cut short his studies in Leiden, and he hoped that no rumours about him had arrived in Dorpat yet, especially given that the current rector had also studied in Holland; although that could also be a good reason for him not to take all the gossip as truth. Back home his godfather Theodus' friends had advised him to come to Dorpat to continue his studies. Even if nothing good was said of the general situation at the university, the Swedish state offered stipends to come and study there.

Dorpat was known for the constant altercations between the students and the military, the tense relations with the local Germans and its expensive lodgings. But notwithstanding all the downsides, many Swedish poets believed that it was one of the best settings in which to write poetry, perhaps because of those very tensions. In any case, it was definitely a pretty peripheral part of the world.

"If you would be so kind," Laurentius said, prompting the professor with a nod.

"Oh yes. If you manage to complete the examination tomorrow, then be sure to come to Thursday's banquet as well. It is our custom to organize a large reception for the students at this time of the year, so all things considered you have arrived quite opportunely."

Laurentius thanked the rector for the invitation. The gently mocking tone he had adopted when talking about Laurentius' late arrival had not bothered him, and considering the circumstances he had got off lightly. He smiled, put his hat back on, adjusted the sword hanging from his hip and left the university building. Outside, a light drizzle was falling, and Laurentius glanced up at the sky, hoping to see what the weather promised. The days were still quite long, but for some reason it already felt like it was the end of December, when one barely has time to notice the sunlight before it starts to fade. In any case, it was still raining, and gusts of wind were sending droplets of water trickling off the leaves of the trees which grew on the sloped road outside the academy building.

In the morning it had looked like the downpour might soon abate, but now there seemed to be no hope of that at all. Laurentius shook his head worriedly.

He didn't have to report for the examination until tomorrow; now the most important thing was to find himself lodgings. Laurentius wasn't inherently opposed to the idea of sharing a room with someone, and such an arrangement would make most sense financially. But people tended to share with their fellow countrymen, and it didn't seem likely he would find anyone from his parts here. He could have joined some folk from Småland or Skåne, but he didn't really want to tie himself to anyone on a purely geographical basis. Not that he had anything as such against the hyperborean notion of Gothic national unity; it just seemed rather trite to flatter oneself with a noble past like that. Scandinavia was a young region, and was still quite uncultured compared with the rest of Europe. No number of imaginary genealogies or proud histories inspired by mythology could change that.

"The land of the seven north stars," Laurentius mumbled to himself.

The legend of the stars known as Ursa Major, and the fables about the conquests of Theoderic, leader of the Goths, in the Roman Empire had been dreamt up to tickle Nordic statesmen's overweening sense of self-importance. They allowed self-promoting philosophers in the vein of Rudbeckius to come up with risible ideas, such as that Sweden was Atlantis and that Latin and Hebrew were derived from the Swedish language, for example. Even if there was the slightest chance that such things could be true, Laurentius didn't feel at all tempted to go along with this kind of chauvinism. And sharing a room might lead to other unwelcome complications.

The most sensible thing to do would be to rent a room on his own.

Laurentius adjusted his hat and looked down the muddy street. He noticed a young man walking past who was wrapped tightly in his cape, and had the appearance of a student, and he decided to call out to him. Having heard that the majority of students and professors were Swedish-speaking, he chanced using Swedish. As Robert Burton had said in his writings on religious melancholy: when in Rome, do as the Romans do.

"Greetings my good fellow. I'm newly arrived in town and would like to rent a room. I have just matriculated at the university. I don't suppose you could advise me?"

The passer-by looked straight at him and replied, in a heavy accent but with otherwise faultless Swedish: "Haven't you heard that there are plans to move the university to Pärnu? There's no point trying to get settled in here. Anyway, the rents are sky high, and after the lousy summer the price of foodstuffs has gone through the roof as well."

"Yes, I know. But it's the same everywhere now. It's not as if the situation is any easier elsewhere," said Laurentius, switching smoothly to German and trying all the time to avoid his interlocutor's gaze.

"Ah, so you're German. From which region?" the young man exclaimed, his tone growing more friendly.

"I'm actually not German. I am but a loyal subject of His Majesty. Are they really going to start moving the university in the middle of the semester?" Laurentius asked.

"Of course not. But a delegation has just arrived back from Pärnu, where the matter was discussed. It's said that they agreed with Pro-Chancellor Fischer that the university will move as soon as the buildings are made ready. Maybe as early as the end of the summer break," the young man explained eagerly. It seemed as if he had recently picked up some gossip on the subject, and was now trying to make the happy and exciting possibility more real by communicating it onwards to others.

"In that case there is sense in me renting a room at least until then," Laurentius said.

The student shook his head, seeming somewhat disappointed. "Well, yes, I suppose that there is."

TUESDAY NOON

B Y THE TIME LAURENTIUS arrived back at the inn there
was a crowd of people bustling about outside it, and
he could hear someone cursing loudly in Estonian. He had
already learnt to distinguish when the locals were swearing—the otherwise smooth-flowing speech became harsh and
disjointed, and the syllables rattled and rasped.

"*Kurat!*" someone yelled out.

A couple of men appeared and hoisted what looked like a
corpse wrapped in a sheet onto a cart. They started rolling the
cart through the puddles towards the centre of town, jostling
and shoving their way through the crowd. The limp body was
swaying about on the base of the cart and Laurentius could
see skinny, bare legs and spindly, veiny forearms poking out
from under the damp, tattered sheet. He instinctively made
the sign of the cross, turned away, and pushed his way past the
curious onlookers towards the door of the inn. The wind was
carrying a vile smell from somewhere, straight into his nostrils.

Once Laurentius had got inside, the innkeeper greeted him
with a cursory nod of the head before turning back to the
window to carry on gawping at what was happening outside.

"That won't be the end of it," he declared, squinting
through the narrow window.

"What happened?" Laurentius asked.

"I don't know exactly. There's some sort of trouble every day now." The innkeeper started recounting what he knew, obviously relishing the opportunity. "It looked like some ragamuffin was rushing about like a mad man, biting people. Some people reckoned that it must have been from hunger, others thought he had just gone funny in the head. In the end there was nothing for it but to have the tanner's lad give him a whack with his pole. Not too hard, mind you, but it still must have been a right good wallop. He's a pretty strong one, that lad, although he's not too bright. But in any case, looks like he knocked him stone dead—the old man's head is all covered in blood, and he's not moving a muscle."

Laurentius stood and listened to what the innkeeper was telling him, becoming more and more worried by the moment. "So what do they plan to do now?"

"They will probably take the lad to the guardhouse, and he may have to go before court. People saw what happened: it was clear that he didn't do it on purpose. But killing someone is no laughing matter; they'll probably give him a right going over."

Laurentius shook his head. "It looks like I will be moving out from here—would you be able to send my chest on?"

"Where to?" the innkeeper asked obligingly.

"There was a room free at Fendrius' place; a student suggested I try there. It seems quite decent."

Johannes, the student Laurentius met, had directed him to the last stone house on Cloister Street, where there was a spare room on the second floor. It turned out to be pretty expensive but it seemed he had no other option. Johannes had told him that the previous lodger moved out just a couple of days ago after some scandal, and had also advised him that decent places were not easy to come by. Some soldier or another student might snap it up straight away. In general, the locals preferred to take students in as lodgers, and would sometimes even offer them cheaper rent. The soldiers were always causing trouble, although the students were of course no angels either. In any case, Laurentius needed to act quickly.

"Aha," was all that Laurentius could manage by way of response to Johannes' story, which seemed to have a whiff of gossip about it.

He had smiled when he set eyes on the pokey little room. The furnishings consisted solely of a writing table, a fragile-looking shelf leaning against one of the walls and a bed. But it seemed to be a pleasant and comfortable enough place— there was even a small fireplace at the foot of the chimney.

"What a nice view you have here," he had said to the landlady.

With its whitewashed walls, wooden floorboards, which had been scrubbed clean with soap, and little window with a view over the city wall and out onto the wide expanse of low-lying green meadowland, the room had a homely feeling about it.

Laurentius had agreed right away to take the lodgings until the end of the semester, and he told the landlady he would move in that very same day, once he had fetched his things from the inn. She had nodded and promised to explain the house rules to him when he got back.

Laurentius had left with a good feeling; even the weather seemed to have got brighter. But his mood was quickly spoilt when he saw the crowd of people gathered in front of the inn. He already had a sense of foreboding as soon as he spotted all the curious onlookers, wrapped in their traditional grey jerkins. But when he saw the old man in his ripped clothes, his spindly legs sprawled across the wet base of the cart, his misgivings had turned into a firm conviction that something was amiss.

The innkeeper just stayed stooped down, looking out of the window, as Laurentius hurriedly gathered his things. He didn't want to stay in that vicinity for any longer than was absolutely necessary.

"How much do I owe you?" Laurentius asked the innkeeper.

"How are you paying?" the innkeeper replied.

Laurentius fished out a selection of coins from his purse and tossed them in the palm of his hand, while the innkeeper peered at them, trying to assess their value.

"Now then, let's have a look," he said, and with a deft movement of his fingers he plucked a couple of coins from Laurentius' hand. "Let's say that much? All right?"

Laurentius was still not sure of the value of the local currency or the correct prices of things, so he decided not to argue with the innkeeper's reckoning. It seemed more or less right.

"All right. Thank you," he said to the innkeeper.

As soon as he stepped outside, two stern-looking soldiers appeared in front of the tavern. They walked straight up to the tanner's lad and slapped a hand on either shoulder. Laurentius waited in the doorway, instinctively reaching down to the sword hanging from his hip, while the crowd of people grew agitated and started backing away.

"What the hell?!" someone objected raucously.

Judging by the wide, foul-smelling leather apron he was wearing, he was probably the tanner. He took two paces towards the soldiers, but then came to an abrupt standstill, as if lost in thought. "Let them take him, then! There's not much I can do about it anyway," he eventually said.

Then he turned to the lad. "You idiot! Why did you have to give it to him so hard?" he yelled.

The lad looked straight at him, wide-eyed. "I don't know what happened. I didn't mean to kill him. But as soon as I took the pole in my hands it felt like I was under a spell. The others here reckon that the old man was some kind of witch, in league with the demons. There was definitely something not right about him."

A murmur of agreement passed through the crowd, and then someone ran up holding a wire cage. It seemed very familiar to Laurentius, but he couldn't get a closer look at it because of all the rowdy people.

"He was carrying this thing with him. It looks like some fishy kind of witch's contraption," the man who found it announced triumphantly.

"What are you talking about? It's a birdcage," the tanner said gruffly.

"But where did that ragamuffin get his hands on it? You don't just find them lying about on the ground—he was definitely planning to use it for some sort of witchery," the man responded.

The din of the crowd grew louder and louder, and the soldiers started looking uneasy.

"There's nothing to see here. We're taking him with us. Everyone stay calm," one of the soldiers ordered the crowd firmly as he started leading the tanner's lad away. Spurred on by his colleague's display of initiative, the other soldier grabbed the lad by the collar, and gave him a whack in the stomach with his scabbard for good measure. The lad produced a doleful belching sound, but he seemed more upset than physically hurt. He looked about him with a forlorn, guileless expression for a while, although he clearly realized that he had no choice other than to trudge off with the soldiers.

The tanner carried on his tirade as they left. "Let them take him, then. What am I supposed to do about it? There's not much work at the moment anyway—at least the lad will get to eat the king's loaf for a while. It's not as if they'll let him starve there, after all. Plenty of this lot here would be very happy to be thrown into a cell for a while."

Having clearly decided to finish on an optimistic note he stood there looking about bellicosely, and at that point he noticed Laurentius, who was discreetly trying to check whether the cage was actually his or not. He was already pretty sure that the ragamuffin in the cart had been the same one who grabbed the cage from him up there by the barn.

"That cage is definitely some sort of witch's contraption," the tanner said to Laurentius, shoving himself up closer to him. "I don't know what kind of witchery it's used for, but there's certainly no good to be had from it. Have a look for yourself."

He pushed the cage forcefully into Laurentius' hands, just in case there were any doubt about what he wanted him to do.

"Well, have a look, then!" the tanner demanded.

There was a stifling sweet stench exuding from the man which was nearly strong enough to make Laurentius sick. It came from the pots of urine in which the tanners soaked their leather day in, day out—they stank so badly that the workshops had to be situated outside the city walls. But for Laurentius even the tanner's stench was more bearable than the smell from up by the barn, which was still swirling in his nostrils.

"But earlier you said that it was just a birdcage," objected Laurentius, trying to create the impression that he had just seen it for the first time, although of course he had made it himself and brought it with him across the sea, so was very familiar with it. He noticed that the door had been carelessly twisted to one side and needed fixing.

The tanner eyed him up and down. "You must be new in town."

"Yes," Laurentius confirmed. "I'm a student. I've just arrived."

"Be warned that they're up to all sorts of witchery here. Just recently the printer Brendeken's son had such a bad spell put on him that hair started growing on his neck and face, and he eventually ended up dead," the tanner recounted in a lecturing tone. "You probably know very well that witchery is a major concern everywhere now. God knows who's already fallen victim here, animals even."

"Yes, but what has this cage got to do with it?" Laurentius asked, refusing to drop the question.

"Well those witches have all manner of strange creatures in tow. Ravens and crows, even those foreign types of bird. They carry them round in cages. I've seen the pictures in books—the witches always have some sort of animal with them. Bugs, spiders, frogs and the like. Brendeken's lad splashed some water on Madlen's cow, and the cow started cursing him in Estonian. The hairs started growing right there and then; they were pulling them out in tufts but it was too late to help him."

"But that was a cow," Laurentius said, hoping that the tanner would recognize that a cow was unlikely to be a suitable animal for a witch.

"Every witch has some sort of animal with them," said the tanner, getting angry. "Whether a cow or crow, there's not much difference."

"Actually, there is. Witches are generally thought to be accompanied by nocturnal animals," Laurentius argued.

"But I know what a cow is. They've got horns—look at their skulls. They're horned!" the tanner insisted.

Laurentius decided it might seem suspicious if he were to start trying too hard to win the argument. It was generally better not to attract too much attention. If it were to come out that the cage in fact belonged to him then all sorts of trouble could ensue.

"Usually, yes," he said, agreeing with the tanner.

"So there you are, then," the tanner said in a victorious tone. "What did I tell you? And the fact that this old man was biting people demonstrates all the better that the demons had got to him. They force the possessed to eat human flesh, and all sorts of other abominations. I tell you, the lad did the right thing by knocking him dead. He saved the court a whole lot of time and trouble."

Laurentius couldn't think how to respond to that. He was sure that if he explained how the ragamuffin had run off with his cage it wouldn't help the tanner's lad one little bit. It might even make the situation worse—if they could claim that the old man was mad and troubled by evil spirits then the lad would have a better chance of escaping the gallows.

"Theologians are generally of the view that the majority of cases of witchcraft are just a result of a misunderstanding. One needs to conduct very thorough investigations before starting to accuse anyone of associating with demons," explained Laurentius, trying to acquaint the tanner with the religious interpretation of witchcraft. "Often people just mistakenly believe that they are witches—such delusions can occur quite often. People claim they see devils and demons, but it's actually just a goat or some other domestic animal hidden in a bush. Usually it can all be explained by superstition."

"Are you trying to say that that old man wasn't under a spell? Try thinking with your own head for a while, then you might make the obvious conclusions. Those theologians know nothing at all. I can see for myself what's what. My sight is sovereign, as they say. No special schooling needed for that," said the tanner, demonstrating his full confidence in his own native wit. "All those straw-heads in the university have just studied themselves stupid, everyone knows that."

Laurentius smiled wanly, and turned to leave. There was no sense in arguing with the tanner. Those sorts were always unshakably sure of their own wisdom, and neither theologians nor philosophers could persuade them otherwise. They knew what it meant to see something with their own eyes, and that therefore gave them absolute certainty. They believed that all the information which reached them through their sensory organs was nothing less than the absolute truth. Laurentius wasn't otherwise much of an adherent of Cartesian philosophy, but he had to agree with the freethinking Frenchman that it is the senses more than anything else which mislead us and cause us to mislead others. This was of course an acknowledged truth, which the sceptics of Antiquity had debated back in their day. Laurentius knew that one should bear in mind at all times that the senses can be deceptive, that phantasms are born there. Maybe that was why Descartes had tried so hard to adhere to the scientific method, to rule out any fanciful notions, to strive towards the clear and distinct classification of concepts. The senses were where phantasms lurked.

Laurentius walked on, not noticing that out of force of habit he had picked up his cage and was carrying it with him.

TUESDAY EVENING

L AURENTIUS HAD ALREADY NOTICED the faint ringing
in his ears when he left the inn. It was such a low-pitched
sound that his ear's auditory membrane could barely pick it
up; it was more like a vague feeling somewhere at the back
of his head, as if someone were breathing onto the nape of
his neck—a hollow throbbing in time with the pulsing of the
blood through his veins. His ears buzzed, quietly at first, but
then more persistently, until the droning and the alien breath
passed through his eyeballs and onwards into his brain. That
was how Laurentius' fever always started.

At the end of his second year at Leiden he had written a
disputation on the subject of illnesses which entered people's
bodies by penetrating their sensory organs. Some of them
entered through the eyes, others through the ears, mouth, nose
or sensitive parts of the skin. When the body was exposed to
excessive cold or damp, the tonsils would be the first to show
it, by swelling up. It was the bloating of the tonsils and the
spread of the illness in the region around them that caused the
ears to hurt. The types of illness which entered through the
open mouth or nostrils tended to irritate those organs. From
there, the infection could reach into peoples' souls. Laurentius
was pretty certain when he had put his body's humours out
of balance. In all likelihood it had been when he helped to

lift the carriage out of the mud and had lost Clodia's wire cage. That was when the vile dampness had entered his soul. It had come from the sopping, rotten surroundings, from the blackened barn, the puddles, the ragamuffin's blues eyes and the vapour he had expired, and now his body was trying to be rid of it. At least, he hoped that it was the cold and damp which had made him ill, and not something else.

He smiled ruefully.

The stench he had first become aware of up at the barn was still swirling in his nostrils—a dire, bitter smell. But now it had established itself in his internal organs too, like a kind of dry rot. The white fungus on the surface was just the outward sign of its presence; the true destructive force was in the writhing roots below, which had worked their way in so deep that even the most skilled of carpenters couldn't be completely rid of them. Only fire could destroy the fungus, just as only fever could destroy the sickness. Often the whole house had to be burned down to be rid of it, and Laurentius feared that that would be the way with him too. The dry rot of his illness, which he had carried within him since childhood, would not leave him until his body was burned. Either by the fever or at the stake. He had been searching for a cure for his sickness for as long as he could remember, but to no avail.

He had experienced the first dizzy turn, which sent hot and cold waves coursing through his body, just as he passed the German Gate and arrived inside the city walls. Pulling his coat tighter around himself, he had hurried to his lodgings. The landlady had greeted him cheerfully when they met on the ground floor, but when she noticed the dirty, twisted cage hanging from his hand she had given him a strange suspicious look.

"So you came back, then. What would you prefer? Shall I have your food brought to your room?" the landlady asked.

Laurentius gave a quick bow. "Thank you, but not now. I'm still tired from the journey. I would like to rest a while."

The landlady nodded and started to explain at length her understanding of the rental arrangements, and how she expected things to be done in her house. But all the rules and regulations just washed over Laurentius as he listlessly stood there, hugging his empty cage close to his chest. The only detail he managed to catch was that he would have to procure the straw and bedding for himself. And he was vaguely aware of the landlady stressing the rule that the tenants could only use the back stairs. He was feeling more and more wretched with every moment.

"Thank you," he said to the landlady as he turned to walk away. "I have asked for my chest to be sent here from the inn. The men should arrive soon, but right now I would like to go to my room."

The landlady seemed to look uneasily and disapprovingly at him, but she said goodbye politely enough and closed the door.

Laurentius struggled upstairs and collapsed onto the edge of his bed—his whole body felt strangely heavy, and inside his boots his legs were contorted with cramp. This wasn't the first time he had fallen ill while abroad. As the medical handbooks warned, sickness was one of the most common dangers of travelling. If the human body was used to a certain environment and had adapted its balance of humours to it, then rapid change could be physically destabilizing, and would be sure to manifest itself in the form of sickness and fever. It was therefore advisable to make frequent stops and avoid crossing excessive distances in a single day. Laurentius was not sure if he had traversed excessive distances, but it was clear that people were more susceptible while travelling, and that if they lacked the necessary spiritual fortitude, then sickness could easily set in. His parakeet had been his spiritual fortitude.

"Mmm…" Laurentius mumbled to himself.

He closed his eyes and tried to focus on something clear and comprehensible. But he still couldn't get to sleep. He knew that if a sick person let his thoughts wander, the result could be gruesome and unpleasant. He had to wait a little longer. Once his case was delivered, then he could sleep. And dream, perchance.

He shook his head and tried to make out what was outside the window.

Fragments of thoughts from his journey and his arrival in Dorpat floated through his mind, disjointed and in disarray. Some of them drifted past slowly, like heavy, phantasmagorical clouds swirling through the sky. Others moved more quickly, like birds flitting past the window. He tried to think about his parakeet, but instead of his tweeting, sanguine Clodia, the image of the old man with his dark, dripping-wet hair loomed before him. He was lying there, sprawled across the cart, his head split open.

There was a knock at the door, and he woke with a start. A while passed before he remembered where he was. He pushed himself upright with some difficulty, and hurriedly tried to make himself look a bit more presentable.

"Come in," Laurentius said, trying to make his voice sound as normal as possible.

Two men came in and, without saying a word, placed his chest by the door. One of them stretched out a hand towards Laurentius. Just as in Reval, Laurentius groped about in his purse for a while before finding a small coin. The porters nodded and left as silently as they had arrived. Probably Estonians, Laurentius thought to himself. He listened to their footsteps clumping down the wooden stairs, and then he turned and stretched out on the wooden bed boards again. Now he could sleep.

He smiled to himself, anticipating the onset of oblivion.

But the blissful sensation of lying down quickly passed as the hard base of the bed started digging into his shoulder and hip. The landlady had told him that he had to get hold of the straw for his bed himself, but he simply wasn't capable of undertaking that task in the state he was in. The cold shivers were getting stronger and stronger.

"Damn it…" Laurentius muttered.

Straining to push himself upright, Laurentius stumbled over to his case. He had no bedclothes with him other than an empty mattress and a small feather pillow. During his journey he had normally slept under his travelling cape, and now he pulled it tighter around himself. The felted wool of the cape smelt of inn rooms and dampness, somehow reinforcing the feeling that he was in unfamiliar surroundings. His feather pillow was also damp, and smelt slightly musty.

"I will try to get hold of some logs for the fire tomorrow," Laurentius told himself. There were just a couple of dark lumps of coal in the hearth, and no logs to be seen at all.

With some effort he lowered himself back onto the bed, and as he lay there various scraps of conversation from his journey started creeping back into his mind. Disconnected phrases, faces, scenes. But then these were replaced by an overwhelming fear that his sickness might take his life. Maybe when he had let the dampness seep into his body up near the barn he had tipped his health off balance for good. Now, shivering under his cape, he would gradually ebb away, and the vapour which he had breathed in and out would disappear into formless chaos.

What had they been talking about in the carriage? Life?

He stared at the cage sitting there on the table with its door twisted off. It had been Clodia's cage. The stark, reproachful emptiness of the wire box made him feel awful. Nature abhors a vacuum, emptiness, lifelessness. Something new, something different would always appear in its place.

"*Natura abhorret vacuum,*" he said to the cage. And to the rhythm of those words a fragment of verse he had once heard started coming back to him:

> If a snuffbox has been empty
> for one hundred years,
> then doubtless Old Nick
> will make his way there.

The verse throbbed in his ears like the pulsing of blood through his veins, and despite its light-hearted tone it now seemed unambiguously sinister. But maybe it was not just Old Nick who would come? Emptiness meant not existing, the absence of reality. Only God was pure being, pure actuality, as Thomas Aquinas had said. The unmoved mover. He started praying in a barely audible whisper, hoping that the familiar rhythm and lucid sense of the prayer would drive away the phantasms which the sickness had stirred in his soul. Laurentius knew that the fever was necessary to restore his body's inner balance. But when the body was already out of balance then the soul's phantasms and other external influences could easily overpower it. That was why people saw visions when they were feverous, and that was why it was essential to protect the body and the soul from any kind of malign influences while ill. He remembered how the peasant folk in Holland had spoken about a willow or alder king, who came to steal the souls of sick people. People with weak souls, especially children, would often see him, dressed in a crown and dark cape. The tall shadowy form would stand there in a dark void under bare-branched trees and beckon the sick to come with him. Laurentius knew very well that this was real witchery, and not just the peasants' imagination. His own soul had always been weak; the black bile had always ebbed and flowed inside him. But would nothingness remain in his cage, or would some other kind of reality take shape there?

"Amen," Laurentius whispered.

Finishing his prayer, he curled up in bed and listened to the landlady bustling about and talking to someone on the ground floor. Laurentius could only catch mundane, insignificant fragments of sentences from the murmuring which reached him through the floorboards, and it seemed that the landlady was just exchanging some everyday news with someone. He listened more closely, trying to work out exactly what they were talking about, but to no avail. He knew he should ask for something hot to eat and for the fire to be lit, but he felt reluctant to—he didn't want to bother anyone.

"Tincture…" he whispered to himself. "Of course, tincture."

He pushed himself upright and took a small bottle from his chest. It contained well under half of the amount of mixture he needed to treat his fever, and he already regretted not having prepared more of it earlier. Some time ago he had written out a number of essential recipes from Dioscorides' *De materia medica* and other manuals, and he had already tried most of them out on himself. He had hoped to find a cure for his ailments using Arabic inorganic chemistry and the findings of contemporary researchers. But up until now the tincture had proven the only truly effective means of relieving the pain and bringing down his fever. Although even the effect of that had grown weaker and weaker over time.

He shook his head apprehensively.

Every time Laurentius fell ill he experienced an overpowering sensation that he was inhabiting some sort of parallel reality, and that other people had only the most tenuous connection with it. They seemed distant and indistinct, as if he were sinking deeper and deeper into a well with a vertical ray of sunlight shining downwards, and the light had taken on a different quality. He would always worry that if he opened his mouth to ask something then people would look at him as if he were a foreigner who couldn't speak their language and had started trying to explain something with strange sounds and gestures. Their expressions would convey sympathy and contempt at the same time. But no, he had to stop thinking like that.

"Tincture," he whispered. "That will help."

He measured out some of the brown liquid and took a swig. There was very little left now, and he couldn't start preparing a new batch until tomorrow. He would just have to wait for the first bout of fever to do its work. In theory, a night of fever and sweating was supposed to show that the illness would soon pass, but if there was no sweating then it could last longer. Praying that he would make it through the night, Laurentius rolled up into a tight ball like a cat and tried hard to think of something other than his illness. It would have been better to worry about real problems, like the exam tomorrow and his studies. Not about some imagined spirits, the sticky dampness, his headache, the fever, a willow king and the nature of reality…

"Ah!" Laurentius cried out.

He jerked upright. He could feel a throbbing cramp in his right leg, and his side was hurting from lying on the hard wooden boards. He had an odd feeling in his stomach.

He could hear snoring coming from somewhere very close by.

Laurentius spun around in agitation, trying to see where the sound was coming from, but he could make out nothing in the darkness. Only then did he realize that night had fallen and that he had in fact been asleep for a few hours. The snoring probably belonged to one of the family members sleeping on the lower floor.

Feeling slightly more at ease, Laurentius lowered himself back into bed and started massaging his leg. His muscles had distended from the heat of the fever, and the tension was causing his calves to cramp up, making it impossible to lie comfortably. Although the stiffness may just as well have come from his journey or the hard bed.

He felt a shiver run through him as he became aware of the cold, damp air pouring in through the gaps in the window. He could just about make out the contours of low clouds through the small windowpanes. Raindrops were trickling down the uneven surface of the glass, and a small pool of water had collected on the windowsill. As he lay there, listening to the house creaking and the water dripping from the eaves, he realized that he needed to go to the toilet. But then he recalled, to his dismay, that he hadn't asked where it was, and he hadn't yet managed to get hold of a chamber pot.

"Satan and his wily ways," Laurentius swore quietly to himself.

Sometimes the latrine would be situated outside in the yard, sometimes it was inside the house.

Laurentius groped about on top of the cupboard for the fire steel and tinder, but then he remembered that he didn't even have a lamp. He hadn't paid attention to what the landlady had said about that either.

"Bother..." Laurentius muttered.

Standing upright in the pitch blackness of the room, he decided that the best thing would be to try his luck outside. He was bound to wake up the family if he started looking for a latrine inside. He left his boots under the bed and set off barefoot, treading carefully. Coming downstairs and opening the back door, he found himself in a walled yard, the size of which he couldn't determine in the darkness and rain. It was possible to make out the wavering outlines of a few objects through the wet haze, but they didn't at first add up to any kind of whole. Just some dark curves and the rippling surface of the ground, which was covered in puddles. He shuddered and pulled his travelling cape tighter around himself.

In the light shining from the doorway he gradually started to make out the roughly hewn wooden steps. A few paces away, against the backdrop of darkness, he could see the outline of a small shed, and then he picked up the bitter stench of ammonia emanating from it, familiar to him from every tanner's workshop, guest house and outhouse he had ever been to. He remembered the conversation he had had with the tanner by the inn, and couldn't help wondering, with a shudder, what had eventually happened to the old man and the tanner's lad.

Laurentius walked across the muddy ground to the shed, stepping on the cold, slippery stones which had evidently been put there for that purpose. Having got there, however, he decided it might be better not to go in after all. Who knew what his bare feet might encounter inside. Now that his eyes were used to the darkness he noticed the pretty, concentric circles which the drizzling rain was making in the puddles. His head was spinning from the fever.

"Good evening," he heard someone say.

Laurentius felt a hot flush of surprise, and hurriedly pulled up his trousers. Glancing over his shoulder he saw a figure in a long, bright shirt, standing on the steps under the awning.

"Good evening," he said hesitantly in response, trying to put himself in order as inconspicuously as possible.

"Are you the new lodger?" the figure asked.

"That's me," Laurentius confirmed.

"Have you come from afar?"

Laurentius straightened his shirt and sheepishly tiptoed across the stones back to the shelter of the awning. When he stood facing the young woman he noticed that the pale skin of her face was glowing like an encaustic painting. Leaning against the wall, Laurentius tried to smile, but he realized straight away that it hadn't turned out as he intended. It still felt as if his body were incandescent from fever, and that was making everything around him seem somehow unreal, as if it were shimmering like the hot air above an iron or brazier.

"Yes, from afar," Laurentius answered.

"Have you got anything to eat?" the girl asked him.

"To eat?" asked Laurentius, failing to understand the question.

"Yes," the girl confirmed.

"No," he said, realizing that he hadn't eaten anything all day. "I've got nothing at all to eat."

"Would you like something?" she asked.

The mud and cold water in the yard felt stinging cold against Laurentius' bare feet, and the sensation was putting him vaguely on edge. As he tried hard to think about whether he should eat, he felt his right leg start to tighten with cramp again. He couldn't bear standing there much longer. He stared at the girl's bare toes on the wet planks.

"Tomorrow. I will eat tomorrow," Laurentius finally answered.

He made a vague gesture with his hand and placed one foot on the steps. It was rude to slope off in the middle of a conversation like that, but he couldn't be on his feet any longer. And he still had the feeling that he was dreaming. Maybe he really was still asleep?

"Wait a moment—are you sure you're all right?" the girl asked.

"I have a fever," Laurentius attempted to explain.

The girl touched his forehead. "Look at me," she instructed.

"I can't. Really, I can't," Laurentius said.

"Look here," she said insistently, and she forced him to move his head round to face her. Laurentius could see that her eyes were light yellow like Attica honey, as if there were a candle burning behind them. Like gold, which would restore his strength and drive off the melancholy. He breathed a sigh of relief.

"You are sick; you must recuperate. Go and sleep," the maiden said, and it sounded like a blessing, like a benediction.

"Yes… I know. I have to sleep. Sleep," Laurentius mumbled to himself as he started walking up the steps.

The maiden smiled and waved to him as he left.

NIGHT

I FREEZE STILL FOR A MOMENT; my eyes are brimming with tears as I blink in the light of the burning brand, and the crowd is exultant.

"Freak!"

"Look now!"

The court attendant shoves the flaming stake into my face. I can sense its scorching incandescence almost touching my brown skin, and the crackling dry heat singes my eyelashes and eyebrows.

"Ah!" I cry out, and my whole body is gripped by panic. My head jerks to one side; one leg buckles backwards; my hands are trembling; my heart is pounding like a grain flail. I turn to try to flee into the darkness which beckons beyond the bright circles of torchlight, behind the crowd, somewhere far away from here.

But the court attendant blocks me, grabs me by my hair, and forces me to look at the crowd through the yellow-red blaze of the flame. The gloved hand tugs and pulls at me until my spirit is subdued, limp and yielding. The surging, droning din of the crowd also begins to subside, like rain after a storm, still spattering for a while; some voices are still murmuring somewhere; the occasional cackle of laughter rings out. There are rows of people there, men and women, young and old, some of them still children just like me. They watch me, standing in the dim night light beside the scaffold. A ragged boy, a face like mud trampled under hoof. So this is the freak, the little whelp, the one who can see the witch's mark.

"Hideous!" one of the women cries out.

"It's little wonder…"

"Shame on him!"

Hands are raised, fingers pointing at me, at my grimy face and cracked lips. People are making rings in the air with their index fingers, warding off evil and driving away shame, so that no part of this witchery will befall them, so that nothing of me or what is happening on the scaffold will follow them home. All of these people are strangers to me, but all of them fear and despise me. I have pointed the finger, and that is why this woman has been convicted of being a witch.

"Toad!" someone yells.

I press my hands against my chest, fists clenched. There is nothing I can do; it is as if time has slowed down. The air is shimmering in the heat of the torches, and the scene looks like a reflection in a worn-out silver mirror. It radiates the heat of hell; people's voices and faces become elongated; they lose all meaning; they become wretched shadows of their real selves. I cast my gaze downwards, away.

The court attendant starts to read out the verdict in a booming voice: "When the executioner has mercifully concluded his work, so that the head is separated from the body, then the body shall be burned in fire. The court has reached this verdict on the basis of the divine law of Exodus 22: 18, Leviticus 20: 6 and Deuteronomy 18: 11, and the laws of the Swedish state. Insofar as this witch has been identified by the seer boy; she bears the witch's mark in her eyes and following incarceration has confessed her guilt."

The executioner strikes.

I feel my head spinning, as if I were standing on a bridge, looking down at the fast-flowing river water below. A constant iridescence, sunlight reflecting off the rippling waters deep into the retina, blinding me. Now the shimmering heat takes the form of a sword held in the executioner's hand, a glimmer of red blood trickling down its central groove. The tip of the sword is pointing at me, away from the woman, who has collapsed forward, hunched over the wooden block. The executioner's fingers are tightly gripping the hilt of the sword, but the woman's head has lolled backwards, the hacked-through veins of her neck still pulsing with blood. Her eyes are partly shielded by thick strands of dark hair stuck to her face, and blood is trickling through her lips, bubbling between her teeth as she breaths her final breaths. But she is not yet dead.

"Ah…" I whisper.

"That is the law. Be sure that you know it!" the court attendant cries out.

I stand there; my eyes absorb the images, but my reason cannot comprehend them. They just slide under my hair and into my head, one by one, disconnected like dreams, shadows suspended in fog. Separate fragments, inexplicable parts, nothing which is clear or whole. But they scrape against me, working their way in, like death-watch beetles boring their meandering, senseless tunnels into a tree.

Her eyes seek me out…

The crowd has now overcome its initial shock and is growing ill-tempered and raucous. Some of the people in the back rows look like they are getting ready to leave, and they are discussing something among themselves in a half-whisper; a couple of the men are glowering in my direction.

But I am staring wide-eyed at the execution platform; the light is scorching my face, shrivelling my corneas.

For some reason I know that if I close my eyes everything will be hopelessly lost. They wanted me to show them the witch, so I showed them. Why did I do it? Maybe it was because I was hungry, so hungry...

The woman's eyes are bulging, goggling, as if someone were strangling her. She is struggling to breathe.

I can see it is the gaze of a dying person, full of horror and pain. She fixes that gaze on me as her last living act, and I know that if I let it go, there will be no turning back. I can see her memories, her whole life there. But the backdrop is pain and fear; there is no longer any trace of the proud madness which so scared everyone, which they were so afraid of.

The court attendant shuffles his feet uneasily, clearly unhappy that the executioner is unable to perform his duties properly. What kind of executioner is he if he cannot take her head off with one blow?

"Come on, strike her again, man!" he yells.

The executioner awkwardly lifts his sword, holds it hesitantly above the woman's head for a moment, and then strikes again as ordered.

I can no longer see the woman's eyes, but the memory of her life suddenly comes to me. Her childhood, her confirmation and her wedding. She is standing in a long white robe in front of the altar, and her groom is tall and handsome. She bears many children, and four of the boys grow up to be adults. They live well at first; they go to church on horseback, wearing their own boots, and there they listen to the rousing word of God. But then her husband falls ill with fever. He is sick for a while, and then dies. After her husband's death the woman starts paying visits to the forest, and before long she is boasting that she is in cahoots with the Devil, that she is now the Devil's bride. Her boys start to fear her; they try to restrain her, but she keeps going to the forest, because the Devil shows her people's souls, and he knows how to read them. The souls are memories, and they are everywhere.

The executioner smiles in satisfaction as the bones in the woman's neck crunch. The last tendon in her neck holds fast for a moment, but then her body and head are indeed as separate as required under law. The court attendant grabs hold of the head by the hair and lifts it triumphantly above the crowd, which has already started to thin out.

There is no exultant baying, just a couple of people shouting taunts at the executioner. The court attendant nods in satisfaction.

I collapse onto my knees, press my hands against my chest, and cry. I don't even know why. But I cry out loud, at the top of my voice; I bawl.

All the people, all their faces, seem somehow distant and distorted. Through my tears they seem as small as children, fuzzy and one-dimensional like stick men drawn with coal on white birch bark.

A figure dressed in black appears from somewhere. He comes a couple of steps closer and bows.

I watch him in silence for a while; his eyes are shiny black like coals. He has a crown on his head.

WEDNESDAY

LAURENTIUS WAS WOKEN by a clanging coming from somewhere nearby. He soon realized that it must be the bell of the church of John the Baptist right next door, which had a somehow tinny sound to it. The church itself had been built at great expense and with considerable architectural prowess, and was famous for its ornate, red-clay decorative work; it was even mentioned in some of the travel guides. The tinny sound was reportedly the result of the bell being buried underground during the last war, which had caused it some kind of damage. After all the dragging about, burial and unearthing, hairline cracks had appeared in the bronze. They were invisible to the naked eye but they somehow made its chime sound strange and hollow. It may also have been that something went wrong during the bell's casting, or that repeated ringing during the plague had caused the damage. Church bells tended to crack during traumatic events, and were often impossible to repair. Decades later the cracks would remain as testament to those times. Sometimes they would serve to warn of coming woes as well...

Laurentius pushed himself up onto his elbows and looked out of the window, but the church tower was not visible from there. All he could see was the blue-grey sky, and rain clouds. It seemed that this day would be just like all the previous ones.

"Ah," Laurentius sighed.

Due to the onset of sickness yesterday he hadn't yet managed to visit a single church. Normally he would begin his acquaintance with a town by looking at the churches; their state of repair and general appearance usually gave one a pretty accurate idea of how people lived in the city, and what their priorities were. The apodemic guides also advised starting with the town's main buildings. In some towns, one could find pigs, hens and other animals living right inside the church building, and manure-soiled straw strewn across the earth floors. Often all the pictures had been pulled down during the Reformation, creating a general impression of slovenliness and neglect. But in others there might be a guard who was paid to keep animals out of the house of worship. There would be stone-tiled floors; the rubbish would be cleaned away regularly, and the walls would be painted a puritanical white, creating an impression of order. That said something about the town itself.

Laurentius counted the peals of the bell, pondering whether he should go to the church straight away. His fever had eased a little and he almost felt well again; just the rotten smell which had fixed itself in his nostrils when he arrived in Dorpat remained, reminding him of the events of the last few days. Yesterday's events, including the ragamuffin's death and the strange meeting with the girl on the steps seemed like hazy, distant memories, even stories which someone had once told him. Had that meeting actually happened? He looked down and inspected his muddy legs, and had to conclude that he had indeed gone outside. At least that part had not been a dream. But hadn't he dreamt something as well?

Laurentius shook his head—he couldn't remember exactly. He took a final swig from the bottle of tincture, which still tasted bitter, like wormwood. Wrinkling his nose bad-temperedly he placed the empty bottle back onto the table. His thoughts had still not become any clearer. The memories of the last few days seemed somehow disconnected, displaced, wrapped in darkness and fever, beginning nowhere in particular, ending with nothing much, so that he couldn't be sure if they were real. He tried to recall the face of the young woman he had seen on the steps: she had been slim, with short, dark hair, and her skin was almost translucent. But he could see nothing clearer than that. The image may have been preserved in his memory from a dream or from real life, but it was weak. Then an image of someone dressed in dark clothes, with a crown on his head, came back to him.

"The king?"

He closed his eyes and tried to lie still for a while, as if hoping that that would help him remember what he had seen last night, but the hard bed and the cold seeping in through his cape drove away the last remains of sleepiness. The king, a woman? He couldn't remember exactly. The unheated room smelt musty; his clothes seemed to have soaked up the dampness from the surrounding air, and the bed boards underneath him were as cold as stone; his back was stiff all over. He remembered that the young woman had told him he should try to recuperate, but now he was sure his sickness could only get worse. And he had used up the last of his tincture.

He heard a clattering coming up the stairs, followed by a knock at the door.

"Come in," Laurentius called out, sitting up in bed and glancing round to check that the room was in a presentable state.

A pleasant-looking, plump-cheeked maid came in and stood there, staring at him. It was clear that she was unhappy about something.

"Good morning, sir," she said.

Laurentius glanced down at his naked legs with an absent-minded expression. This was definitely not the same girl he had met in the yard yesterday. The young woman standing in front of him had a ruddy complexion and puckered lips, and was clearly not yet twenty. Locks of blonde hair peeked out from under a blue, embroidered headscarf, and her white linen dress was held fast over her full, rounded breasts by a bodice. She was holding a clay mug in one hand, and resting on top of it was a breadboard containing half a loaf of bread. She bore no resemblance at all to the girl from yesterday evening.

"I'm sorry to bother you like this in the morning, to be sure, but circumstances are such that the landlady has asked me to pass on that we can't offer the breakfast which was originally agreed. That's just how things are, I'm afraid. Otherwise I have always made a point of providing meals for my tenants, and it is always decent food, not like elsewhere, where you'll get just bread and beer, to be sure," the maid explained to Laurentius.

She put the bread and beer down on the table with a thud. She was obviously very worked up about something, and her otherwise decent German sounded stiff and unnatural. "But now, I just don't know, all the prices have risen so much that if we had to cook meals here as well we simply couldn't manage, God help me. It's a good thing I got hold of that bread, otherwise we'd starve to death, just like those poor souls out there. I don't even dare walk down the street with a loaf of bread any more, in case someone nabs it from

93

me. That's to say nothing of what's happening beyond the city walls!"

Laurentius nodded. He had already realized that something was not quite right when he had gone to speak to the rector yesterday morning. The town seemed cheerful enough, but the people he saw were anxious, and even with the constant drizzle of rain there were hunched, hungry-looking peasants loitering about everywhere. Some of them were alone, others in groups, and their faces were stubbly and sullen, their hands clenched into fists. Together, the weather and peoples' miserable appearance made for a tense, ill-boding atmosphere.

"I fully understand; don't you worry on that score. I'll get hold of something to eat myself. I'm not normally very hungry in the mornings anyway," Laurentius said, trying to be polite.

The maid smiled gratefully.

"But may I have some wood for the fire?" Laurentius asked. "It's really damp in here."

"But of course," the girl exclaimed happily. "I'll make up the fire. The landlady will probably add it to your rent. The thing is, we don't have any spare logs for your room. The landlady did say yesterday that you will have to get hold of them yourself. There's plenty of people selling them at the Haymarket, down by the river. If you go down there and pay for them, they'll deliver the logs. Then I'll show them where to stack them up," the maid explained.

Then she started to leave, seeming to be in a hurry.

"By the way," said Laurentius, stopping the maid before she had managed to step out of the room. "Is there a daughter in the family, or some other girl living here?"

The girl raised her eyebrows in surprise. "No there isn't, there's no one… no one at all," she added after a brief pause.

"The man of the house left this morning, and the landlady's children have all been taken by sickness. For goodness' sake don't raise that subject with her."

She smiled a little awkwardly again, pulled the door shut behind her and clumped down the stairs in her wooden shoes. Laurentius watched her leave and nodded his head. He walked a few paces around the room to stretch his legs, which were stiff from the hard bed and his fever, and performed a couple of practice parries with his sword.

"Let us pray for a healthy body and a healthy mind," Laurentius declared.

Commentators were not unanimous on whether that meant that if the body was healthy then the mind would be too, or whether a good mental condition would ensure that the body was also in good shape. The different schools of medical thought seemed to focus on either curing the body or the mind, seeking to find the root cause of every illness in one or the other. But as far as Laurentius was concerned there was no difference between the body and the mind—the mind was the body's form, its shape, without which it could not exist. So he had to be sure to keep himself in good shape.

He put his sword back in its sheath and leant forward to take a slice of bread from the table. He wasn't very hungry, but he decided he should force himself to eat, since he hadn't had a single meal for longer than he could remember. He knew that it was important not to let the organism become too weak when ill… Moreover, the bread appeared to have been baked from good-quality flour, and it was still slightly warm, probably straight from the baker's.

"Damn!" Laurentius cursed out loud.

He stood glaring at the slice of bread in dismay. It was unexpectedly bitter and unappetizing, like eating hay or birch leaves, just like his fever tincture.

"I hope all the food here isn't like this," he thought to himself as he washed the bread down with gulps of weak beer. The tough bit of bread slid about inside his mouth as he tried to chew it, just as sodden leaves from a puddle stick to one's boots and clothes and are impossible to get rid of. It took him several more swigs of beer before eventually he could swallow the two slices of bread.

"Pah!" he muttered to himself. "It's a good thing that they don't provide breakfast here any more."

Either they had bought the cheapest bread made from some sort of dross, or the situation in town was already so bad that it was impossible to get hold of decent flour from anywhere. He hoped that it was the former.

"Now then," he told himself purposefully. "Time to get a move on."

He pulled on his boots, put his sword belt on and went out. There were still a few things he needed to get hold of to set himself up in his lodgings, but first he had to drop in at the academy and find out about the examinations. Otherwise there was no hope of being accepted for matriculation, and he could lose the first part of his stipend. He might also be able to find out if there was any laboratory equipment anywhere, so that he could prepare some proper tincture.

Laurentius adjusted his sword and took a deep breath of the chill air. His room had been cold and damp, but outside the fresh air had an invigorating and cleansing effect on him. The rainwater was already starting to drain from the pavements and he started to make his way to the academy, trying to step in the gaps between the puddles and glancing hurriedly at the people and houses on either side. He saw only ordinary people and nondescript houses, just like everywhere else he had been. But on the whole Dorpat didn't make a bad impression at all, if only it weren't for the constant rain. Walking on in the dim morning light he turned off Broad Street, got almost as far as the door of the academy, and came to a standstill. This was a more open spot, and the light seemed somehow brighter. He smiled to himself, and cocked his head back to view the grand, metal-plated spire. Due to the brownish-green tones of the roof, the church looked quite different to the other buildings, which generally had grey shingle roofs. Laurentius recalled how the innkeeper had spoken about this church spire with pride yesterday. It was indeed quite handsome, although Laurentius couldn't help feeling that it might be better if it were slightly slimmer.

He strained to look higher, and he noticed that the cockerel sitting on top of the stubby roof was almost touching the low clouds. The wind blew gusts of fine rain down at him, stinging his face and forcing him to screw up his eyes. As he tried to count the small figures on the facade, moisture collected under his eyelids and everything started to turn hazy. The clay figures started to look diffuse, as if they were papier mâché decorations. The foul taste of that morning's tough bread started to ooze back onto his tongue with the drops of rainwater, bringing back the rotten stench, the ragamuffin and his sickness with a terrible intensity. The mental images which were hazy and unreal when he woke had unexpectedly returned, and they were now clearer than the faces of the terracotta figures in front of him. His fleeting good mood passed quickly. The church spire now seemed strangely out of proportion and threatening.

Turning around and spotting a student hurrying in the direction of the academy, he stopped him and asked, "How might I find Professor Dimberg?"

"Professor Dimberg? If you want to talk with him right away, you're out of luck. He probably won't arrive until after lunch. He's currently receiving visitors at home," the student replied.

Laurentius said a quick thank you. By now, the foul smell swirling in his nostrils and the weakness in his legs were warning him that his fever could be flaring up again. Perhaps he shouldn't have gone outside so quickly, but lying there in his cold, damp room wouldn't have been any better for him. There was no sense in going back to his lodgings now, but he didn't feel like asking for Dimberg to receive him at home either. Unannounced visits like that could sometimes involve a lot of waiting, and he would probably have to exchange gossip and engage in empty conversation too. It was better to wait and see Dimberg at the academy, which meant that he now had at least two hours to spare.

He shook his head and set course in the general direction of the river, following the route the maid had explained to him. He had plenty of things to fill those spare two hours with. Looking down, he noticed some stone slabs which had been placed along the edge of the road for people to step on. They were poking out of the puddles, somehow contributing to the overall melancholy atmosphere with their distinctly medieval appearance. He started walking, thinking of nothing in particular, and looking at the shoeprints of other people who must have been there just before him. He pondered how these must have been preceded many years previously by Polish soldiers' boots, little children's loafers, monks' sandals, peasant women's slippers, handicraftsmen's brogues, paupers' clogs, beggars' and peasant folk's bare heels. So many footprints of differing shapes that now it seemed almost a privilege to be able to tread there in his boots as well. But how often do those very same boots, which wear away at the stones, take control of the person wearing them, determining his direction? For example, when boots start to chafe, and instead of walking one can barely hobble, or when one puts on a fancy pair, and can hardly bring oneself to walk through muddy puddles. Or the opposite situation, when one is clad in soldiers' boots and it is considered bad form to turn up at the opera. It may seem that the wearer has planned his route himself, but at some point the shoes take control and go exactly where they please, where it is in their nature to go. And then the wearer has no choice but to comply. The soldier goes to war, the peasant to the field, and death awaits them both.

Laurentius came to a standstill, looking annoyed.

No, he thought to himself. It is in people's nature to become themselves. Death is a state of not being and is therefore an aberration. Death happens, but that does not mean that all is finished. A person leaves memories, impressions behind him. Now those impressions had sunk into Laurentius' soul, pressing deep furrows into it, and everything else could do little more than scratch the surface.

"Clodia," Laurentius said.

Where was his parakeet now? Where was his companion, who could help him drive away his phantasms, or at least hold them at bay for a while?

He set off again, trudging determinedly, almost angrily out through the city gates, and then he stopped to glare moodily at the brown river water flowing past the low banks. He tried to concentrate on something other than the thoughts which were spinning round in his head, to find something to fix his gaze on. He had to try to think rationally. He had an examination to do; he could not let himself be distracted. But what should he do?

There were small boats bobbing about on the river, carrying wood to the opposite bank. He watched the little skiffs, knocked together from planks of wood, daubed black with spruce tar, and they seemed tiny from where he was. He tried to work out what the purpose of so much bustling activity could be. No one knew how cold the winter would be this year, but it seemed that people were trying to stock up on firewood just in case. Those who were able could earn their daily bread that way, and in current circumstances there was no shortage of people ready to do the work.

"Wood, of course." Laurentius awoke from his thoughts. "I need wood for the fireplace—that will help. And straw. I must get a move on."

WEDNESDAY NOON

T HE POND WAS FULL OF BULRUSHES, debris and weeds, and a disgusting smell was wafting out of it. The smell which had been swirling in Laurentius' nostrils since his arrival in Dorpat now combined with the choking, sweet stench oozing from the muddy riverside marsh, creating a mixture which was familiar and yet new. He stood still and tried to take in the view, which with the rain and wind looked almost like a scene from a painting. The path was just outside Dorpat, by the Russian Gate, but it seemed to be in the middle of a wasteland, somewhere far beyond any city or other human settlement, far away from anywhere. Behind him, across the river, were the town's outskirts, but he couldn't see a single house there now, and the city wall had all but disappeared into the twilight. From where he was standing the riverside bastion looked more like a hillock overgrown with grass. The path which led directly from the edge of the pond to the hillock had been laid with rounded birch poles and branches and then filled in with sand and stones, and now it was strewn with fallen leaves. The marshland reached right up to the city walls, and in the summer it probably dried up almost completely, but now, after several months of rain, it bore a closer resemblance to a small lake. The path passing through the middle now looked like a plank of wood laid down to cross a puddle, unstable and treacherous.

Laurentius stepped onto the boards of the bridge, which were slippery and sagging from rot, and looked around. Sinewy silver willows were growing along the edges of the riverside path, probably planted some time ago as reinforcement, to prevent the path, which had been built on such soft foundations, from disappearing completely into the ground. There was a twisted, tangled mass of broad roots trying with all their might to hold the clumps of earth together, but in places the water had washed the surface soil away, and some of the trees now looked almost as if they were growing in mid-air. This seemed to be the right place.

Laurentius had been directed there from the Haymarket, where after a little haggling over wood and straw he had managed to summon up the courage to ask for advice from one of the more friendly-looking tradesmen. Maybe Laurentius' money had helped to make the tradesman a little more favourably inclined, since judging by past experience he had paid an exorbitant price. But he hadn't thought it wise to argue too much and had given in pretty quickly—if only not to get himself too worked up ahead of the afternoon examination. Any kind of stress and exertion always made his fever flare up, just like strips of bark smouldering in the hearth when they are blown onto. Movement and anxiety were the very essence of the fever, so he had to try to balance them with stillness and calm. That was why it was so easy to develop a fever while travelling, and why people who had anxious dispositions were most likely to fall ill.

It was his fever which had brought him to where he was now.

He had started worrying about his tincture as he stood by the church feeling his fever rise. When he set out on his journey he hadn't thought it necessary to take much with him, but since the death of his parakeet and the moment when the stench had first assailed him he had used up an unexpectedly large amount of it. He had already delayed making a new batch too long.

Laurentius fished out a small knife and a piece of paper from his knapsack.

The tradesman had seemed oddly put out by his question, but after hesitating for a moment he advised Laurentius that the best place to find willow trees was next to the Russian Gate. But the friendly tone had quickly left his voice; his eyes had narrowed, and his command of German had seemed less sure. Laurentius had tried to explain that he needed the willow bark for medicinal and scientific purposes, but the look of apprehension and suspicion had not left the tradesman's face. It seemed he had a particular antipathy towards that part of town. He just shook his head at Laurentius' clumsy attempts to explain himself, adding in a scathing tone that no good ever came from what went on in those parts. Laurentius had tried to point out that he didn't plan to get up to anything untoward, at which the tradesman grew angry and started hurriedly trying to explain something to him. Swearing profusely, he told Laurentius that some sort of refuge for the starving had been set up beyond the outskirts of town, and that all sorts of odd people had started to loiter about. Then he had pointed at Laurentius' sword and asked scornfully whether he knew how to use it, should the need arise. He added that just the other day there had been an incident with an old man who turned out to be a cannibal, and had to be knocked down dead. He had been biting passers-by in broad daylight just like a dog, and he had even devoured a little baby whole.

"That old man didn't kill anyone," Laurentius had told the tradesman. "I happened to be walking past nearby at the time; as far as I could tell he didn't even manage to bite anyone."

"Well he was definitely on a bit of a rampage," the tradesman had muttered, shaking his head. But then he just made a resigned gesture and concluded, "What business is it of mine anyway? My job is selling straw."

Laurentius had thanked him and started looking for the gate to which he had been directed. He walked through the city outskirts, which were full of dilapidated buildings with children standing in doorways watching him unsmilingly as he passed. All of them were extremely thin, and they looked at him with wide-eyed, reproachful gazes. Laurentius had offered one boy a coin, and the boy grabbed it out of the palm of his hand and disappeared into the darkness of his house without smiling or uttering a word. When the other children saw that, they livened up and came running out into the rain, and started thronging round Laurentius and pulling at his clothes. He had felt like he was their quarry, and he flailed his arms around helplessly and quickened his pace before breaking into a run to get away from them. He had felt those looks on him before, and he had experienced what the children were feeling himself. That was how poverty and hunger felt. He breathed a sigh of relief as he got past the houses and arrived at an area of brushwood by the river.

"Now then," Laurentius said, looking around and taking in his surroundings.

He approached a suitable-looking tree, clambered up the roots and adjusted his grip on his knife. A couple of large pieces of bark should suffice at first, but they would have to be cut from a branch which was roughly two years old, where the bark would be most potent. Ideally he would have gathered it in spring, but there was nothing he could do about that now.

His godfather Theodus had been the first to teach him the art of preparing medicines and tinctures, and it was on his godfather's advice that he had eventually gone to Leiden to study. Leiden Academy was the leading centre of medicine at the time; it had the newest instruments and was up to date with the latest thinking in the field. It had been clear from the way his godfather had spoken that he regretted that his work had taken him away from his own studies. Theodus would smile wistfully and shake his head as he recalled his own university days. But he would always conclude his reminiscing by giving Laurentius an encouraging pat on the shoulder.

"Don't you leave your schooling unfinished like me. Make sure to complete it at all costs," Theodus had advised.

Overcoming his own regret, Theodus would begin enthusiastically explaining how to fight different ailments, and how to make one's soul stronger. He was clearly glad of the chance to share his knowledge. He had made great efforts to educate Laurentius and advise him which books to read. He would always say that the more education a person had, and the more he cultivated his soul, the stronger and more productive he would become. At first, Laurentius had not understood what his godfather meant. Melancholia and emptiness had already taken a grip of his weak soul, and he didn't know what to do—sometimes he dared not leave the house. The world seemed a terrifying place; demons lurked everywhere. Only by gradually learning more about himself and the nature of melancholia did he become aware of the relationship between his experiences and the bouts of sickness. The experiences and ailments would enter through his eyes, ears, nose, mouth and skin; if he wasn't careful they would build a nest inside him and flourish like samphire or mould. Various medicaments and procedures could be used to rein in the bad experiences, to hold them at bay, but once they had bored their way into his soul they were just like a bad habit, like drinking spirit was for some. Just one taste, and they could no longer control themselves: their addiction had them completely in its grips. Laurentius' melancholia was the same. Therefore the aim of his studies had been to reinforce good habits and experiences, and to avoid bad ones. And if he did not succeed in avoiding them, then at least they could be alleviated, soothed and subdued. The tincture had that effect on him, just as Clodia used to.

He hoisted himself up the gnarled roots of the willow tree, trying not to get his clothes dirty on the damp bark, and started looking for a suitable branch. Level with his face, he could see a number of notches which someone had made in the trunk. They had now healed over like scars, and taken on a grotesque rippled appearance. To Laurentius they resembled ineptly scrawled seals of Olympian spirits, or something similar. But right next to them he could see some branches of a suitable thickness jutting out, so he got down to work, whistling to himself. He gouged out a couple of large pieces of bark from the tree and wrapped them up in the piece of paper. That should be enough to start with.

"Now then," he said, turning round.

He nearly dropped the knife and willow bark out of his hand as he felt the fever, which he had managed to forget, come surging back like a rush of blood to the head. Struggling to support himself, Laurentius grabbed hold of one of the branches. Down by the base of the tree three stern-looking men were standing and observing his activities in silence. It looked like they must have already been there some time, watching what he was doing up the tree. Laurentius had not seen a single soul as he walked along the riverbank, and he hadn't heard any footsteps or the murmur of voices either. Maybe the men had been hiding in the shade of the high riverbank? But what did they want?

"I was just collecting some bark," Laurentius announced with no real purpose and making an awkward gesture.

The men spat over their left shoulders in unison and took a couple of steps to one side, but it didn't look as though they planned to leave. Shrugging and trying to feign nonchalance, Laurentius bent forward, put the knife back into his knapsack and placed the piece of paper containing the bark to one side of it. He had now become very aware of his sickness; the fever had started throbbing away in his temples again, and his head was spinning. The men were still standing there, heads cocked to one side, watching his clumsy movements. Laurentius remembered what the tradesman had said about this part of town. In alarm, he hurriedly placed his hand on the hilt of his sword. He was sure this wouldn't end well.

The oldest-looking man said something in Estonian and pointed in the direction of the tree.

Laurentius watched as the others clambered up the tree and started to inspect the spot where he had been cutting the bark. One of them explained something agitatedly and motioned to the others. It seemed as if he had angered them in some way.

Laurentius lifted his knapsack onto his shoulder and slowly started to leave, hoping that the situation might resolve itself. But the peasant man standing in his path wouldn't let him past. The man bowed politely several times and then started to explain something in a very persistent tone of voice, prodding his finger in Laurentius' direction as he did so. Laurentius cast his gaze downwards and shook his head.

"I don't understand what you're saying," he said.

The man's mouth twisted in a sneer; he snorted resolutely, and then he started talking again, pointing at the tree. He was standing in an awkward pose, sideways on to Laurentius.

Laurentius started to edge backwards, glancing at the men and the tree as he did so, and trying to make it clear that he couldn't speak Estonian, but it looked like the man standing in his way was not going to back down.

"Back off!" Laurentius shouted, trying to sound angry, and putting his hand on the hilt of his sword. The situation had already become uncomfortable and unpleasant—but he wasn't particularly surprised that it had come about. Everywhere he had lived the same thing had happened sooner or later. People started to suspect him of having the evil eye; gossip started spreading and before long the whole town knew about it. And even those people who wouldn't admit outright that they believed in the evil eye started to look at him differently and speak with him warily.

"What's going on here?" someone suddenly asked in Swedish.

Laurentius breathed a sigh of relief and turned in the direction the voice had come from. It belonged to a young-ish-looking student, who, judging by his walking stick and muddy boots, had already covered a long distance that day.

"Laurentius Hylas," Laurentius said, introducing himself. "These peasants clearly want to tell me something, but I can't understand a thing that they're saying."

"Peter Börk, from Dalarna," the young man said.

He started talking to the men, who pointed in the direction of the tree and at Laurentius and then spat over their left shoulders again. The young man grinned, shrugged and addressed Laurentius in Swedish: "It seems that there has been some sort of unfortunate misunderstanding. The men claim that you were engaged in witchery of some kind. They say that they saw you cut the fetters of some spirits which were skulking inside the tree. They are convinced that you have the evil eye."

"Well, that is pretty ignorant of them," Laurentius said, trying to laugh with Peter. "All I was doing was gathering willow bark for scientific purposes."

At that Peter raised his eyebrows, but then he turned and spoke with the men again, pronouncing every word slowly and carefully. They stood there and shook their heads with stony expressions on their faces, and they appeared to be insisting on some point.

Peter shrugged his shoulders and beckoned for Laurentius to come with him. "Let's get going; there's no hope of sorting out this muddle."

He shook his walking stick angrily a couple of times and took Laurentius by the arm. The peasants sullenly watched them leave.

"Easy does it," said Peter. "Don't look back now."

"Why?" Laurentius asked.

"These are troubled times; some folk have been completely driven to distraction. It's not worth getting them too worked up. They think that you want to put the evil eye on them," Peter explained.

As they walked off Laurentius could feel the men's glares fixed on the back of his head.

Eventually Peter turned to Laurentius and enquired, "But why were you gathering that bark there anyway? The way things are at the moment you can't do anything at all before people start thinking God knows what."

"It really was to prepare some tincture," Laurentius explained. "I fell ill recently and it's the only thing that will help with the fever."

Peter sighed. "You know, they're not easy to deal with, these peasants. Once they get something into their heads it's impossible to talk them out of it. They're very suspicious folk; they see witches wherever they look. It's a good thing our court system works so well, otherwise they would have slaughtered half the population of the villages by now. A while ago they burnt Võhandu mill down to the ground because they reckoned it was causing the cold weather. They're probably thinking the same thoughts about the bad weather we're having now, looking for someone to blame. These are very unsettled times," Peter said, shaking his head thoughtfully.

"I suppose that's just how things are sometimes," he continued, although he now sounded a little unsure of himself. "There are sometimes periods of history like that. John Napier made a mathematical prediction that the world will end in 1697. One is tempted to believe him, although the forecasters all mention different years and dates. Just this morning I was walking along the riverbank here, composing hexameters. I had been walking along for around an hour without seeing anyone at all. But then at some point someone comes up behind me; someone else appears from out of the forest, and then finally someone turns up on horseback." Peter looked at Laurentius' expression, clearly seeking confirmation that he hadn't veered too far off the subject.

"Eventually you all meet; you end up side by side on the same road, and it's cramped and uncomfortable… but then after that no one else comes for ages again. Things like that happen all the time now. It's just the times we're living in. One event tempts out another… and then everything happens all at once. There are lots of signs that the end is nigh, but no one really knows how to interpret them properly," Peter mused philosophically, swiping at blades of grass with his walking stick as he went.

"I subscribe to the view that the end of the world isn't located in some specific moment, but is personal instead," Laurentius countered. "A personal end, as the early theologians used to say. We all die, but no one knows when. It's the same thing as the end of the world; there is no significant difference."

"Indeed," said Peter with a grin, sending a yarrow flower flying with a whack of his stick. "But it still makes you wonder. When you see the misery and wretchedness of the peasants, you can't help feeling that the end of the world might actually be the best thing for them."

"But what did those peasants back there say about witchery?" Laurentius asked, changing the subject.

"Oh, some story about a willow king. That Old Nick lives in the hollows of tall willow trees. And that you can spot an evil witch by the look in their eyes. A very muddled story; I couldn't fully understand it either."

WEDNESDAY AFTERNOON

P ROFESSOR DIMBERG was leafing through Laurentius' thesis with a look of concentration on his face, nodding to himself from time to time.

"Not bad, not bad at all," he commented.

Meanwhile Laurentius was pacing slowly up and down the room, looking at Dimberg's measuring instruments and apparatus. His fever had risen again, and although he could still think quite lucidly, everything he looked at seemed to be the wrong colour. He had walked with Peter as far as the academy building, and Peter had then directed him to Dimberg. As he departed he told Laurentius that he should be sure to come to the banquet the next day, and the sly expression on his face had suggested that some full-scale revelry was in the offing.

He had given Laurentius a friendly pat on the shoulder and repeated, "Make sure to be there!"

Laurentius' fever had flared up again after the fright he got by the willow trees, and he could now feel it becoming more and more acute. He knew he should be lying calmly in his room, waiting for the maid to come and light the fire and stuff his mattress full of fresh straw, so that he could sleep, sleep for as long as he was able. But he had no choice: he had to take the examination without fail.

He blinked his eyes and rubbed his temples. The light glaring off the glass objects seemed too bright, and the reflection
from the brass ones was too green, like the colour of spring
grass. At the same time he could hear a ringing in his ears.
He tried to force himself to think calmly and work out the
purpose of all the instruments. It was clear that chemistry
and astronomy were of personal interest to the professor,
and Laurentius spotted several modern devices, including
a geometric astrolabe, and in pride of place an impressive
twelve-cubit telescope. He only had to hold out a little longer.

"It's just a shame that you haven't made use of the latest
research," the professor eventually said.

"I studied Frommann's tractate on the evil eye quite thoroughly, but I didn't think it necessary to address all of his
views," said Laurentius, trying to provide as full and clear an
answer as possible. But he was aware that his voice sounded
odd, as if he were talking through a tube. "In my view his work
is based excessively on popular conceptions of the problem; he
could have benefited from taking a more scientific approach."

He had read all of the available literature on the evil eye,
but had not reached a clear understanding of the phenomenon. In general, the authors had just presented separate
stories; not one of them had come up with a comprehensive
scientific theory. But what had been clear from his readings
was that eyes do not only communicate their own essence—in
that eyes could be seen as being just like all other objects—but
also transmit the whole being of their owner, his spiritual
condition. That explained the genesis of the saying that the
eyes are the "mirror of the soul". Through the eyes we see
the aspects of a person which may remain concealed on a
more superficial inspection. The literature claimed that the

most ferocious creatures could even kill with one look. Pliny the Elder wrote that there were women born in Scythia called Bythiae who were said to have two pupils in each eye, and that if they got very angry they could kill someone just by looking at him. One could conclude that the presence of two pupils was key, since it was the pupil which contained the *virtus visiva*, so the essence of the Bythiae's rage could be transmitted with much greater force than through a single pupil.

"Frommann is very thorough, but he does not provide a full explanation," said Dimberg in agreement. "I have just arrived back from England, where they are doing tremendous work in the field of occult forces."

"Oh really?" Laurentius said, relieved that Dimberg appeared to have understood him. Everything he looked at seemed to be shrouded in fog, and his tongue felt like it had been wrapped up in a rag.

Dimberg walked up to the distillation apparatus which was set up on one of the tables, gave one of the flasks a light tap, and with a ceremonial exhalation of breath he declared, "Corpuscles and vapours."

Laurentius could guess what path their conversation was likely to go down now. Frommann also spoke of vapours and miasma in the context of fascination. But it was of course impossible to fully explain such processes with the theory of vapours. In Laurentius' view Aristotle's theory of elements and form offered a much more satisfactory account, which Laurentius had corroborated with his own personal experiences, which had often been far from pleasant. But it would be highly inappropriate to start constructing a theory of fascination based purely on personal experience. If he went down that route he would be lucky to get away with wide-spread derision; in the worst case he could up in the dock. His defence of his thesis in Leiden had caused problems which had eventually taken on such proportions that Laurentius had questioned whether it would be wise to share his work with anyone again. Of course, there had been nothing written down in the thesis itself for anyone to latch on to—he had incriminated himself while debating with his opponent, during the disputation. It was exactly that kind of rashness which he had now vowed to avoid. He would have to learn to bite his tongue.

"I'd be interested to hear more," he said, prompting Dimberg to continue.

"Robert Boyle offers the clearest and most comprehensible solution here," began the professor, taking obvious pleasure in the opportunity to demonstrate his knowledge. "Corpuscles are transmitted as vapour from one being's organism to another, and they then infect it. For example, when someone is bitten by a rabid dog, the corresponding part of the body is infected—namely the head. And thus the corpuscles from the mad dog's saliva bring about a transformation in the person's mind. Certain types of corpuscles are capable of…" Dimberg's voice had risen, and he paused a while for emphasis.

"They are capable, I repeat, of using the principle of sympathy, to cause other things to change and become like them. The transmutation of metal takes place in just the same way, of course, as the Chemist himself has demonstrated. He compared this property to the way in which seeds grow—pay attention, now! Certain corpuscles are capable of seizing and carrying others with them. For example, when a tree grows from a seed, its matter does not derive solely from the seed;

it comes from the air, earth and water, but its shape and form are given to it by the spirit concealed in the seed."

Dimberg spun round theatrically and took a copy of Robert Boyle's *Sceptical Chymist* from the bookshelf.

"Have a look for yourself; it's a splendid work. I strongly advise you to acquaint yourself with it."

Laurentius nodded. Boyle's theory was pretty persuasive, although he was aware there were objections to it. "Sympathy is still a very vague concept; it is difficult to comprehend how it might actually operate."

Dimberg placed the book on the table and took a few paces backwards and forwards. "I agree. The theory has indeed encountered criticism, but it remains the most logical explanation we have. Of course, people have also challenged the theory of gravity because it describes a concealed and apparently occult force. Therefore it cannot be scientific, they say! Just think! But of course they cannot deny that it fits current mathematical models much better than any other theory. I am convinced that it is exactly those kinds of forces which operate between corpuscles. Antipathy, sympathy and gravity."

He slapped his hand down on the table to empathize his point, causing the flasks and measuring instruments to rattle.

Laurentius nodded. He neither wanted to nor was capable of arguing; Dimberg had stated his position, and was unlikely to back down from it now.

"Very interesting," he said to indicate his general agreement.

Dimberg smiled triumphantly. "Corpuscular theory currently has the greatest explanatory power. From spirits and souls, to cases of people rising from the dead—everything is explicable in mechanical terms. Absolutely everything!"

Laurentius smiled uneasily. Dimberg should have been asking him about his religious convictions, but Laurentius had the impression that it was the professor's own ideas which could give rise to questions. Mechanistic theory was not at odds with Lutheran orthodoxy as such; it was just some of the possible ramifications which gave pause for thought.

Dimberg was watching Laurentius, clearly trying to assess his reaction. "I assume you won't object if I hold on to your thesis for a while? I would like to have a more thorough read of it, and I'm sure that Professor Sjöbergh would like to have a look as well. It appears that you have quite a few interesting thoughts here, even if you do express them in a somewhat vague and muddled fashion. I would advise you to attend Professor Sjöbergh's private lecture on Friday morning; he is currently dealing with the subject of the soul. You may learn a thing or two. We have no lectures tomorrow owing to the banquet. You've been invited, I assume?" Dimberg paused for Laurentius to nod affirmatively. "Very well. But you should definitely be there on Friday. I understand that Sjöbergh is planning to present some new thinking on the subject. I just brought some literature back from England for him, the latest research!"

Dimberg stuck a single finger up into the air and paced around the room in silence like that for a few moments, clearly immersed in thought.

Eventually he came to a standstill and lurched towards Laurentius. "An exceptional pleasure," he uttered ceremoniously, and squeezed Laurentius' hand warmly. "You passed the examination brilliantly; welcome to the fraternity of Dorpat Academy."

Then he pulled his hand away with an equally abrupt movement and stood eyeing it thoughtfully. "Hmm. Your hand is hot. I conclude that you have a fever?"

"Yes," Laurentius agreed reluctantly. There was no reason for him to try to hide it.

"How do you treat it?" the professor asked.

"I try to counterbalance the hot and damp elements of the fever with willow tincture," said Laurentius, realizing immediately that he should have said something else, or nothing at all. The adherents of Boyle and Newton definitely considered the theory of the elements to be dated.

"Elements!" Dimberg squawked in amazement. "That is a completely false approach and will only make you more ill. You have to find the *spiritus* of the ailment. Boyle talks about that as well. The corpuscles which transmit the spirit of the sickness must be destroyed. There is no other way. Complete disintegration, *nigredo*, is what is required. Before that no change at all can take place."

Laurentius nodded. "I'm familiar with the basic outlines of that theory, but I must admit that such a view of spirits is not consistent with my convictions."

"You don't believe that substances and ailments have spirits?" asked Dimberg, raising his eyebrows. "Things have spirits, I tell you! They manifest themselves in many different ways. Fantasy even gives them a form. Next you'll be telling me that you don't believe that the soul exists!"

Laurentius shook his head. "Of course I believe in the existence of the soul. There can be no doubt about that."

Dimberg cast a suspicious glance in his direction, possibly recalling the rules for examining students and realizing that he hadn't checked Laurentius' theological views at all.

"And so that soul is immortal?" He asked a probing question.

"The posthumous existence of the soul is clearly explained in the Bible, and what's more it is scientifically provable," Laurentius agreed, offering the most conservative theological position he could. Some of the radicals in Leiden had been of the view that the Bible said nothing about the soul existing independently of the body after death. This question of the immortality of the soul was a popular subject of debate in more freethinking circles.

"Hmm? But how do things stand with spirits?" asked Dimberg, refusing to let Laurentius off the hook.

"As you said, fantasy creates them," Laurence suggested.

"You are mistaken there. Fantasy gives them form, but they exist independently of our fantasy or our sensory perceptions. A number of academics have researched the subject of poltergeists, and our very own Professor Michael Dau has written about them too," the professor said.

Laurentius bowed. "I confess that I am poorly informed on that aspect of the soul and spirits. But I am happy that it will be possible to receive such expert guidance on the subject at this university."

Dimberg was clearly content with Laurentius' last point, and he grunted approvingly. "I presume you are familiar with the lecture programme? This semester I will be speaking on Newton's mathematical principles and gravity, which are of course vital to understanding the question of the soul. I look forward to seeing you at my lecture next week."

Laurentius felt unable to continue the conversation much longer. He was sleepy from the fever, and his thought processes had slowed down. But he had heard enough to convince him that Dimberg's thinking was indeed rather modern and progressive. Laurentius had certainly heard about Newton's theories when he was in Leiden, but no one there had openly approved of them or included them in the official lecture programme. They favoured Descartes's philosophy there.

"I am most grateful," Laurentius said.

Dimberg smiled and started to rummage about in the stacks of papers which covered the table. After a while he fished out a sheet of paper and stood looking at it with a solemn expression on his face.

"On student life and habits," he informed Laurentius in an official tone of voice. "Make sure to acquaint yourself with it. It won't do to be lazy. But this evening you must treat your illness. You really must."

"Indeed I must," Laurentius repeated. "Would you be able to offer any advice in this respect?"

Dimberg livened up again. "Why, bloodletting of course! To start with you need to overpower the illness' spirit, to expel and destroy it. We have one barber here who does quite a decent job of that. The bad blood must be drawn out. But in moderation. As Boyle says, excessive bloodletting is not a good idea either. In moderation, do you hear? And following the procedure Boyle advises, take essence of gold, *aurum potabile*."

"And how could I get hold of some of that?" asked Laurentius, growing more interested.

Dimberg seemed momentarily lost for words. "Unfortunately he speaks in very general terms on that point," he added in a quieter voice. Then he turned to face the bookshelf and started inspecting the books, snorting gently to himself. "Very general indeed." Dimberg peered distractedly at the spines, and Laurentius got the impression that the problem of preparing *aurum potabile* had been a preoccupation of his for some time now. After rocking back and forth on his heels for a while he turned to face Laurentius again. "But bloodletting is the thing. Moderate bloodletting. That is what you must start with. Don't forget, *nigredo* is essential at all costs!"

WEDNESDAY EVENING

L AURENTIUS CAME ROUND THE BACK of the church of St John and out onto the main street, and then he headed in the direction of the town hall square. His face was burning from the fever and he felt as tense as a wound-up clock, ticking away as its spring uncoiled. At first he had reacted to Dimberg's idea of bloodletting just as he would to any other piece of casual advice, but then he realized, much to his own surprise, that he actually intended to go through with it. Tick-tock went the clock, and his feet carried him forward. Following Dimberg's directions he soon arrived at a building with a red-and-white emblem hanging from a pole outside it, advertising that it was a barber's shop. According to Dimberg the sauna keepers had recently started offering bloodletting services too, but their equipment was generally filthy, and there were repeated cases of them making their clients even sicker than they had been before. Such practices were therefore banned and the right to perform bloodletting and basic surgical operations was passed to the town's doctors and barbers. The sauna keepers anyway enjoyed an ill repute, and could often be seen walking about half-naked, and engaging in pandering quite openly. Dimberg had admitted to Laurentius with some regret that they had still not got as far as establishing a modern clinic in Dorpat, even though

Below, the professor of medicine, had repeatedly stressed the importance of doing so.

Laurentius took one more look at the scalpel and knife on the emblem, as if wanting to make absolutely sure that this was the right place, and then stepped somewhat warily in. The first things to catch his eye were the shiny polished floor, a dirty sheet with a dark stain on it which was pulled over the table, and the dour-looking man who was sitting there. He was wearing a long overcoat decorated with fashionable embroidery and an ostentatiously high wig, which was curled and powdered.

"Greetings," said Laurentius.

"Have you come for a wig?" the barber asked in a sing-song voice with an indeterminate accent. "Your hair is certainly quite unsightly; we will have to cut it all off. It just lacks the necessary refinement. My wigs are first rate—all the gentleman in town buy from me."

Laurentius bowed, making sure the whole time to direct his gaze downwards. "In fact, I came regarding bloodletting."

"Ah, is that so? Not today I'm afraid," the barber replied, sounding disappointed. "Now is a bad time. Mars is in an unfavourable position and brings sickness. But I can offer you an enema or cupping instead—they're actually better than bloodletting. They cost a little bit more, but it's worth it."

Laurentius stood there indecisively.

"It is in your own interests," the barber explained. "One has to be sure to observe the correct days for bloodletting." He jabbed his hand in the direction of a piece of paper on the wall. "I've got everything written down here; I had the mathematicians do it for me. It's very precise and reliable. But come on in; we'll get some cups on you right away. Now would be an opportune moment to do an enema too. One way or another you will have to empty your bowels before letting blood."

He clattered about in his cupboard and produced a sturdy-looking enema pump with a wooden handle. It looked worn out from repeated use, and didn't seem particularly clean either. The barber eyed it glumly as he made a few pumping movements, and then nodded in approval. What Laurentius took to be the musty smell of urine and faeces assailed his nostrils, but he found himself hoping it was just a figment of his overly powerful imagination. At that moment the possibility that this was the stench which was already in his nostrils, which came from his soul's black bile, seemed considerably more appealing than the other explanation. He shuddered and screwed up his face. Enemas were a common form of treatment, but he had always been wary of them. He purged his body in the natural way as often as he found necessary, and felt no need to assist the process artificially.

Noticing Laurentius' reaction the barber's expression became serious and he shook his head, causing his long locks of hair to flap about. "Don't you be so squeamish; the King of France himself has an enema performed on him regularly—you can't be more fastidious than him. First we'll scrub you clean and then we'll give you a good, proper enema."

"I've had hardly anything to eat all day; it's unlikely to be necessary for me," said Laurentius, trying to decline politely.

"Well, eating is one thing but purging the bowels is quite another. The ancient Greeks already knew all about cleansing—catharsis they called it. That is the whole point of the enema. We'll flush your intestines clean for you and then you'll be a new man," the barber persisted, slowly edging closer to

Laurentius as he spoke. Laurentius got the impression that he was planning to perform the procedure right there and then, without worrying too much whether he had the client's consent.

"That's true, but it was more in the figurative sense," Laurentius said, gradually backing towards the door. "At least, it certainly was in Aristotle's case."

"Oh, I've given enemas to everyone here: the rector, the professors, even their wives." A wistful note had come into the barber's voice. "And definitely not in the figurative sense. All of them got their catharsis, that's for sure."

"Professor Dimberg did advise me to let blood; I have to try to cure my sickness," Laurentius tried to object.

"I'm sure you do, but just you pull your trousers down and come and sit on this chair. We'll put a bowl underneath you as well," said the barber, showing no intention of listening to Laurentius' objections.

Laurentius glanced quickly behind him, groped the door open with his fingers, and with a forced smile on his face, slid out. "I may come back at a more opportune moment," he said hurriedly, before darting off down the street.

"Curses," he hissed through his teeth.

Laurentius sensed that he had just made a lucky escape. Experiencing a strange combination of euphoria and panic, he walked down the street towards the university, trying to gather his thoughts. What now? The idea of going to the next barber he could find to try to let blood seemed silly now. After that episode with the overzealous convert to catharsis he had no desire to entrust himself to the next quack he came across. Even thinking about it caused the stench in his nostrils to grow so strong that he had to stop and gasp for breath.

"Damn it," he cursed quietly to himself, and he leant forward with his hands on his knees and tried to calm himself down. His hair was wet from the endless spatter of rain, and he could feel drops of rainwater trickling down his collar. Dusk was gradually falling and the street already looked as if it were just waiting for thieves and cut-throats to arrive; it was the time of day which always brought an unpleasant edginess. If he still wanted to let blood, then the right thing to do would be to find someone who was properly educated and less in thrall to astrology, someone who instilled confidence that he had some idea what he was doing. But where could he find someone like that in this unfamiliar town? At the apothecary's? Although it was possible to find the occasional apothecary with a university education and expertise in his field, their shops tended to be dens for gambling and beer-drinking, and they were not averse to the stronger drinks either. In their eagerness to sell their medicaments they could forget they had ever learnt anything about medical science, and they would start trying to palm off all manner of dubious concoctions on you. Homemade salves, powders and poultices—and who knows what else. They would dream up overblown and unappetizing names for them such as "Rhazes' white pastilles" or "worm oil". For the most part these preparations were no use at all, but you could be sure of paying a handsome price for them. Laurentius decided it would be better to put off his investigation into the local apothecaries until a later time. He should anyway be able to manage a simple procedure like bloodletting by himself. He probably already had all the necessary tools; it would just be important to prepare for it properly…

"Yes," Laurentius said to himself. "Of course."

Feeling that he had arrived at some kind of decision, he headed off down the cobblestoned footpath. As he walked he noticed how the rain had washed out the sand from between the stones, creating a long, streaky pattern along the ground. There was rubbish lying about in the mud by the roadside, and he could see dots of yellow light reflected here and there in the puddles. They were the same flickering lights which illuminated the faded paintwork of the houses and the passers-by with their hunched forms and glistening overcoats. Directly in front of him he noticed a young man and woman walking unhurriedly, arm in arm, seemingly oblivious to the rain. Laurentius couldn't help thinking that there was something familiar about the appearance and gait of the young woman.

He slowed down a bit so that he had more time to observe the wet hair which was visible from under the hat, savouring the prospect that he might see a familiar face there.

"Her hair looked exactly the same..." Laurentius found himself thinking.

The appearance of this girl from out of the damp mist had an inexplicably uplifting effect on his mood. Could this be the same young woman who had been standing on the steps outside his lodgings yesterday evening, with whom he had spoken? Laurentius shook his head. He didn't want to be in too much of a hurry to find out. After all, he couldn't just walk up to her and start inspecting her face—that would be impolite.

"Of course, what's the reason to doubt it? It's quite possible that she is one and the same," he told himself.

Most probably the young woman lived somewhere nearby, and that was why he had now seen her twice in a short space of time. There was nothing unusual in that as such. But he couldn't shake the feeling that the first time he had seen her was in a dream, rather than real life. In fact he was so sure that she had been an apparition that it didn't seem possible that she really existed. What had she looked like anyway?

As he struggled to recall the vision of the girl, he glanced down at the ground. There, goggling back at him from the muddy road, was a dead jackdaw. Its wings were pressed flat against the sides of its body, and its legs were bent as if it were poised to take off from a branch, but one could tell straight away that the bird's body was already as stiff as iron.

"So then," thought Laurentius to himself, coming to a standstill.

The girl and her companion walked on, with the rain continuing to spatter against their hats and capes.

"So then," he repeated to the jackdaw in a sterner tone of voice.

"Yes, indeed," the jackdaw's gaze seemed to say in response.

Laurentius squatted down and prodded the bird cautiously with a twig. He felt uneasy about touching a dead creature with his hands—God only knew what it died of.

The jackdaw flipped over onto its other side.

"I should try to push it to the edge of the road somehow," he decided, remembering how the ragamuffin had come and grabbed his parakeet. It seemed the situation was a little better in town, otherwise someone would have already plucked the jackdaw's feathers and made a meal of it. Although it may have just recently fallen to the ground, so no one had yet had time to.

He shoved some sodden twigs under the dirty bird, planning to lift it to one side. But as was often the case with dead birds, its body turned out to be surprisingly light, and he misjudged its centre of gravity. He flicked it up to almost waist height before accidentally dispatching the wretched, floppy bundle of feathers into the nearest puddle.

"Damn it," he found himself saying, and suddenly he felt afraid.

The jackdaw's corpse fell into the puddle with a gentle splash. The stream of water which had accumulated after several days of rainfall took the bird's body with it, and it started moving slowly towards the small pool which had formed in the centre of the road, temporarily getting lodged against the various obstacles which it encountered on its way. Laurentius watched as invisible currents played with the dead creature and sodden maple leaves clumped around its tiny form.

"Whoa, whoa!" a voice yelled out.

Laurentius heard a clatter, and a carriage appeared, water splashing up from its wheels and the horse's hooves. He quickly hopped to one side, but he couldn't avoid getting his stockings wet. The driver flashed an angry look at him, and then the whole contraption was swallowed up into the dusk, like a demon disappearing into the night. The coachman's whoaing and the rattle of wheels rang out for a little longer, before silence descended again. The jackdaw had disappeared, perhaps pressed into the mud by the carriage wheels.

Laurentius shrugged his shoulders and looked about him. There didn't seem to be anyone at all around.

"Home," he said to himself.

At least he now had somewhere to go in this town, a place he could call home. Maybe once he was back there he would have a clearer idea of what he should do next. Feeling as if he had reached a decision, he lengthened his stride. Once he had got to the church of St John, he turned to walk past the university building again, and from there he headed in the direction of Broad Street. Having walked a couple of buildings past the university he came across a large group of students, standing in the dim light outside what looked like a storehouse, discussing something among themselves. Passing by quite close, he recognized Johannes, who greeted him with a friendly wave of his hat.

"Evening! What's afoot?" Johannes called out to him.

"I'm heading to my lodgings," Laurentius answered in a weary voice.

"We're going into town; perhaps you would like to join us?" Johannes suggested.

"I'm not sure; perhaps…" Laurentius answered with a sigh.

It might have been a good opportunity to get to know the other students a bit better, but he already had a pretty clear idea of what lay ahead. The German students could always be relied on to be good company—largely because they were better off than the Swedes, and they had a reputation for buying drinks for whomever they were with. For them it was a matter of honour to make sure that the table was always laden, and that people's hearts were always full of good cheer.

Laurentius had started to feel a vague sense of nervous anticipation in the pit of his stomach. Something was telling him that he should go, while also warning him that perhaps it wasn't such a good idea.

"Come on, come with us," Johannes said, trying to spur Laurentius on, and he grabbed him by the arm. It was clear that they had made a start somewhere, and the company already seemed nicely merry.

Laurentius warily let them take him along for a bit, listening to their jesting and trying not to stick out as a foreign element too much. They had already embarked on a philosophical discussion, evidently on a subject covered in a recent lecture.

"Plato provides a good example of the virtues in *Menon*," a young man with red-rimmed eyes proposed. "There are a great number of them, a myriad, just like bees!"

"Who? Bees?" Laurentius queried in surprise. "Actually, Plato wrote that the soul of a man who has lived a good life is reborn as a bee. Their souls are like bees."

"No, that's another dialogue! There are lots of bees, but they all express a single idea. The idea of a bee! It's the same with the virtues. There is really only one virtue," the young man insisted.

"But bees are born out of decay and putrefaction," Johannes interrupted. "Pliny states that—"

"That's a different subject—for God's sake don't get side-tracked again," groaned the young man who had started the conversation. "Virtues—"

"They really are born like that," said Johannes, refusing to back down. "They are born of death. And Porphyry says that they are eminently just and sober beings."

"Well, then you definitely aren't a bee," snapped the young man who had been trying to discuss the virtues. "It's just a metaphor. A figurative usage." And as if to reinforce his point he pulled out his sword and waved it in the air.

"A metaphor for what?" Johannes said in a slightly teasing tone of voice.

"For the most important thing," the young man answered.

"Because they gather honey? A metaphor for collaboration?" Johannes asked.

Laurentius realized that this was the kind of conversation which would inevitably go awry, and he feared that if he stayed with the students nothing but trouble would come of it. He had to somehow free himself of the tension which had built up inside him as a result of his autumn melancholy, the fever and fear over his uncertain situation. But he didn't have many options available. He either had to let blood, or he had to spend time in the company of people whose jollity might help to soothe his soul. He had to do something! But it wouldn't be a good idea to let himself lose control and drink himself drunk, even if losing control—oblivion—was exactly what he wanted at that moment. Tick-tock—his clock clicked on, but it was getting slower and slower.

"I really should go," he told Johannes. "I still have some matters to take care of today."

"A meeting, is it?" Johannes asked with a grin.

NIGHT

L AURENTIUS LAY THERE listening to the dripping of the rain outside. Drip, drip… It was the first thing to impinge on his waking consciousness. Like a perpetual clock, which measured out the days, hours and minutes of his heartbeat while he himself was absent. The kind of clock which did not need winding. Somewhere up above, almost invisible drops of water had started trickling downwards through the narrow cracks in the shingle roof. The droplets had slowly collected on the ceiling of his room, the surface tension temporarily giving them a nebulous spherical form, before they strained free from gravity's grip and fell with a gentle dripping sound to the ground. Drip, drip. They fell more and more frequently, until they had eventually made a blurry brown patch on the floorboards. He was pretty certain that it hadn't been there in the evening.

Laurentius was sitting slouched in his chair, staring into the distance with unseeing eyes, his gaze fixed on a point which culminated somewhere beyond the limestone paint, the plaster, the stacked stone wall, the hazy town air and even the sky above. Staring into nothingness. His eyes looked as if they had been painted onto the slack features of a madman, and his gaze was empty, unblinking, piercing into eternity. He might just as well have been dead. The dried blood on his forearm, which was resting in a bowl half-filled with a dark liquid, reinforced the impression.

Drip, drip.

The damp air felt chill against his sweaty forehead, but he didn't dare to move, even to wipe the sweat away. He feared that the slightest exertion would cause him to lose his senses, that he would fall forward and hit his head against the floor with a thud. His heart had almost stopped beating, out of fear that his muscles would stretch too much and grow limp; his blood was no longer circulating evenly throughout his body; his veins were filling up with salts, becoming clogged and unfit for use. All movement inevitably ends in destruction, and all things strive towards their final resting place. But what, then, was man's place?

Laurentius felt as if his body were that of a dead saint, inert and imperishable. But he knew that could not be, that it was impossible. The moment his body gave up on movement, on the breath passing through his nostrils, something would die within. That was how people always died. His brain, concealed within the hard bone of his skull, would give one final tremor and cease its activity, and his consciousness would disappear somewhere. All those things which had indisputably existed, which one could name and see, would be lost. But where did they go? Into nothingness?

The air had started shimmering before his eyes, and although it was yet to take on any clear form, it already had dimensions, and light was radiating from it. It was too bright for his eyes, which were used to staring into emptiness.

His eyelids closed reflexively.

It felt like he might gradually be regaining consciousness. He must have made some stupid mistake… what could it have been? Where had he been all that time? That which has no substance is impossible to conceive, because words can never capture it. Did I have consciousness? Am I my consciousness? Do we possess it, or do we embody it? No, Laurentius told himself. He must not allow himself to get bogged down in those kinds of thoughts: they would exert his brain, use up his energy, cause his body to release its warmth, out through his scalp into the chill of the room. He would have to try to restrain himself. To restrain himself from thinking, to restrain himself from speaking, the main thing was to keep hold of his consciousness. If he could eke out the breaths which he had been allotted, conserve the beats which that lump of gristle produced, then he could live. He still needed to live, for some reason.

The shimmering patch of air in front of him started to acquire clearer outlines, and through the unbearable glare he could make out an oblong human form. There was a chalk-white face, offset against the dark ceiling in the background, and long hair, flowing down onto the figure's shoulders. And through the gleaming light Laurentius could see a halo, slowly taking shape around the dark silhouette of the head. Flashes of light shot out intermittently from the shimmering image, piercing through his narrowed pupils and straight into his brain. His eyelids were flickering uncontrollably.

The moment he closed his eyes and saw darkness, the face appeared clearly before him. He had seen it somewhere before. Some time ago, a long time ago. Had it been a dream? He had been standing by the gallows, grass and sand underfoot. There had been silvery trees which looked like people: roots for feet, branches for fingers. Long, arrow-shaped leaves.

With a strain he managed to open his eyes.

The candles were burning balls of flame, which illuminated the outlines of baskets and bowls on the table in front of him. Was that food?

His recovery would require energy, and he needed food to restore it. He had to try to recover. Laurentius tried to control his anxiety and comprehend why he had been summoned from his dreamless sleep, why he could see a person standing in front of him, and why her clothes were brighter, much brighter, than he could remember from the previous occasion.

"The previous occasion?" the question flitted through his mind.

Now he could see that the young woman was clad in a long white robe, fastened around her body with green bands, and her hair was clasped with a strip of gold. Her hands were outstretched as if she were praying or proffering goods. He could see a large bowl of yellow honeycomb, baskets of oranges, shallow vases filled with yellow and red flowers, green apples, red tomatoes, pomegranates, a bright array of colours.

Laurentius involuntarily closed his eyes.

Damn it, he thought to himself, remembering what had happened. He had decided to let his own blood. That was why his arms were bloody, and why the phantasms had appeared, those hallucinations. The right thing to do would have been to wait until the morning, to overcome his qualms and go to an apothecary, or to try his luck with a barber again. He certainly should not have hurried, given the fragile state he was in. One had to be very careful when letting blood, since losing too much could cause fainting.

Laurentius snorted angrily to himself. "Sufficiently careful!"

He peered through half-shut eyes, and the table in front of him now seemed to be empty. But the room was still a strange shape, warped like an image viewed through a magnifying glass. His head started spinning, and he had to shut his eyes again.

Of course some doctors held the diametrically opposed view, believing that fainting during bloodletting was the most reliable indication that the treatment had actually worked. Laurentius had always been suspicious of the whole process himself. His teachers in Leiden had not favoured the expulsion of large volumes of blood from the body, asserting that due to circulation, a phenomenon which Harvey had recently confirmed, it wasn't really necessary. But Dimberg's view on the matter had been quite convincing, and if a sceptical authority such as Boyle was also an adherent, then it was at least worth trying. According to Boyle, blood carried corpuscles of sickness, and if they were expelled in moderation it was easier for the body to deal with the ones left behind. In any case, bloodletting was one of the most popular and widespread forms of treatment.

He tried to focus his gaze on something, but to no avail. What had actually happened earlier?

He had been sitting there in his chair, holding the incision in his forearm open with a small glass rod, and reading prayers to himself.

The blood had been dripping into the bowl, and it was already half-full—that was the last thing he remembered.

He must have fainted. The rod must have slipped out of his vein, and the flow of blood had eventually stopped, otherwise he would no longer still be there. Had he spent the whole night sitting in that chair by the table, staring out of the window like a corpse hung from the window hook? Had he in fact been dead?

And yet, and yet, he was sure there had been someone else there as well.

Laurentius made a great effort and managed to stand up. His ears were ringing, and he had to grab hold of the back of the chair for support. As he stood there trying to recover his strength, he peered around the room. It was empty; there was no one there. He stumbled a couple of paces towards the bed and threw himself down. His limbs were no longer stiff, but he felt light and fragile, like a dried-out leaf. He was weak, but his senses were somehow functioning differently from usual. Sounds seemed louder; the light was different in some inexplicable way, almost the same, but slightly altered nonetheless. Was this another result of his illness? He knew that sickness was the Devil, delusion and fallacy. Fallacy immediately caught the eye; madness could be spotted from afar—it caused fear; it stirred up memories and phantasms. The memories, the furrows scratched in his soul, were still there: he could still feel them inside him. But somehow they were shallower, much weaker than before, as if they had been forced open. As if someone had taken a sharp knife and scratched the horrific stories and degenerate images from the parchment pages of a book, and now the dark ink dust was floating about in his soul. Maybe if he coughed, then the corpuscles of his memories would fly out of his mouth, as little droplets.

Laurentius allowed himself to cough for a while. With every cough he felt healthier, revived.

Once the coughing fit had subsided he lay on his bed thinking, and he remembered that he had to go to the banquet later that day. Nearly everyone he met had invited him to it, so it seemed wrong not to make an appearance. He felt very weak, but he would have to try to get himself into a decent state, and he should probably try to eat something as well. He had agreed with the maid and turned down the breakfast at his lodgings, but that had been with good reason: he was sure that his stomach wasn't up to digesting that lousy sawdust-laden food; it might even make him faint again. He had to eat, but only good-quality food. Bread baked with decent flour, and even fruit, if he could find some. He remembered the basket of honeycomb and pomegranates which he had seen in the dim light of his room, and he swallowed. That was exactly what he needed.

"Yes," he said to himself, as if he had reached a decision.

There were two options available: he could eat in a tavern somewhere, or wait until the banquet. They were sure to offer the finest dishes in Dorpat there. He would just have to endure for a while longer and try to rest; the banquet was supposed to start at lunchtime. Laurentius lowered himself back onto his bed and lay there, thinking of sweet honey and fresh red apples.

THURSDAY

THE STONE HOUSE had been neatly painted with green and yellow limestone paint, making it stand out from the other buildings, which generally had dark-grey planks of wood for their exteriors. Hardly anyone painted their houses in these parts, and due to the weather they tended to turn various shades of dull grey—the newer ones a bit lighter, the older ones darker, even black sometimes. Colour was a mark of affluence.

There were dark, low-hanging clouds in the sky, and the candles in the stone house had already been lit. Their warm, flickering light shone through the windows, and inside one could make out silhouettes of people dressed up for a special occasion, walking around and conversing among themselves. They were like the silhouettes which artists sometimes drew, just as Butades' daughter had preserved the shadow of her beloved on the wall before he went to battle. The servants standing on the stairway landings were dressed in respectable black, and Laurentius could not help thinking that it looked like the wrong heads had been placed on top of bodies dressed up in fancy clothes. These were the faces of young boys: pimply, insolent, out of place. Just a little earlier they had probably been running about barefoot, dressed in baggy clothes, stacking logs in a yard or leading horses somewhere. The worst of the mud had been washed off them; they had been dressed up smartly, and sent to help at the rector's reception. The boys watched the university students and professors with expressions which conveyed mistrust mixed with disdainful obeisance. They knew that the lives they lived in the back-yards, out on the fields, were more real, more genuine. The students, done up in fancy clothes, some of them with wigs and overcoats embroidered with gold thread, were distant and alien to them. Like the shrieking white birds which flew across the gloomy autumn sky but lived their lives elsewhere, somewhere where the sun was shining.

"Maybe in a sense that is how things really are," Laurentius thought, watching as the servants lit the torches. Literacy, reading and the classics would always ensure that the students had a privileged position over the peasant boys—once they had learnt how to read the wax tablets then there was no going back. From then on their world had changed for ever, and it was impossible ever to forget the power of the writ-ten word. But peasant life was shaped elsewhere. Scurrying about in the cold mud, sleeping on hay in cramped, grimy rooms with animals grunting and children whining. And the swans flew over high above, stirring a dark yearning in the people down below. A long time ago, in the village where he had studied with Father Theodus, Laurentius had watched the swans with the same kind of longing. Theodus had tried to teach him how to forget, how to make his soul stronger, but in vain. Melancholy had left its imprint on his soul, and it was a burden he would always carry with him, which he could never forget. Only the company of others, their ideas, the books he read, and his fidgeting parakeet occasionally managed to distract his thoughts.

As if answering his wishes, someone standing by the doors with the large, opaque glass panels announced something in a high-pitched yelp, bowed, and pushed the doors open from either side. Two of the boys unrolled a wide, dark-red carpet down the stone steps.

Laurentius moved forward towards the unfurled red tongue with everyone else. He was now very aware of how weak the bloodletting had left him and he could feel cold shivers running up and down his spine, and cramp in his calves; maybe this was his fever flaring up again? He tried to focus on his surroundings. Who were all those unfamiliar people? There were a lot more of them than he expected to see at a rector's reception at a provincial university.

He coughed purposefully, adjusted the sword hanging from his hip and headed into the building. He felt a stabbing pain in his stomach as his feet sank into the soft red material of the carpet, which was spongy like a bog, like a sloping hillside covered in blood. Every step he took left a soft impression in it, like a stamp in wax, like a memory. Then the red carpet gave way to wooden floorboards. There was no dust or mud in there, and the air was acrid, thick from the soot of candle flames. The earlier stench had somehow got stronger again. Could it be the greasy candle wax, or maybe someone's musk-scented body oil, or the soap used to wash the floor?

Laurentius faltered slightly, but he allowed himself to be directed onwards. He was there now and there was nothing that could be done about it. He had to try to forget about everything which had happened.

"Thank you," he said politely as the servant took his coat.

The illusion of a modern European interior was almost complete. It was only if one strained to look up at the ceiling joists and the knobbly edges of the plasterwork that one could detect the evidence of hasty, sloppy decorating work. But down below, at the normal plane of vision, there were smooth walls covered with dark wooden panelling, which had tapestries with plant designs and pictures hanging on them, and there was even a cloakroom. People were handing over their capes, warming their hands on the light-green ceramic stove tiles for a moment, and then heading deeper into the building.

Laurentius positioned himself by one of the walls, looking slightly awkward. Fortunately the room was warm, which would assist his body's humours in their struggle with the cold and damp. He realized that he had become terribly hungry.

He watched the procession of young men as they entered through the open doors. Many of them were talking among themselves as if already well acquainted, and some of them were casting curious glances in his direction. He tried to locate Peter and Johannes among them, but the faces were all unfamiliar. It was quite clear that strangers didn't appear in those parts often, and the students who had been there longer showed undisguised interest in every new arrival. Maybe they had already heard about his examination?

"You must have arrived in Dorpat just recently?" a young man dressed in a fashionable overcoat and foppish wig addressed him. Judging by his extravagant and ostentatious appearance he must have come from a rich merchant family. The noblemen tended to be a little less attentive to their attire: they had titles to convey their importance, but the ordinary citizens sought to compensate for their lack of social status by overtly demonstrating their wealth.

Laurentius made a vague movement of his head. "A little while ago, yes."

"Magnus Lundgreen, at your service," the man said, introducing himself in the French manner.

"Laurentius Hylas."

"Have you already found yourself lodgings?" Magnus enquired.

"Yes, with Fendrius. It seems like quite a comfortable place," Laurentius answered.

"Ah, there. Yes, that's a nice place, to be sure. Although they ended up throwing out the last lodgers. There was a right scandal there. They were Germans," Magnus informed him.

"Really?" said Laurentius, unable to think of anything else to say.

"I hear that you came from Leiden—is that so?" Magnus continued in a light-hearted tone.

Laurentius nodded. Clearly news of his arrival had already spread.

Magnus' formal manner initially took him aback slightly. The use of the second-person plural was generally a mark of refinement, and it certainly wasn't widespread. Yesterday, Peter and the German students had addressed him in much more familiar terms. Laurentius preferred that kind of directness: there was something of the ease and clarity of Latin about it. When he was addressed in the polite form he normally opted to respond with some impersonal construction, which often seemed the only way to avoid offence. He spoke German and Swedish fluently, but trying to find the suitable form of address always had him in a fluster. It always depended on the context, but he normally assumed that his interlocutor knew which was correct. Right now he couldn't decide whether Magnus was mocking him with excessive politeness, or just making an effort to be friendly.

Before he had time to ascertain which it was, the guests were invited to the table, and he and Magnus went to sit at the places they were shown to. These kinds of events were always organized with great pomp, and there was normally not the slightest hope of speaking more freely or of leaving the table until at least two hours had passed. Whenever he found himself at such events Laurentius recalled the sad fate of the astronomer Tycho Brahe. At one reception he was forced to restrain his body's natural functions for so long that his bladder burst, and he subsequently passed away. At least, that was what Laurentius had heard in Leiden student circles.

"*Silentium!*" someone called out across the hall.

Professor of theology Olaus Moberg stood up and started to say grace. He warned of the hard times which lay ahead, and said a prayer for those who didn't have such sumptuous and inspiring food to put on their table that evening. Professor of philosophy Sjöbergh took his turn, speaking on the theme of starvation and the punishment of the Lord, which was intended to make people strive to better themselves. The Lord always meted out the harshest punishment to his chosen people, precisely to encourage them to be better. Sjöbergh added that as they witnessed death and starvation all around, they should always remember that in the deepest darkness light would appear.

"*Lux luceat in tenebris.* Let our university bring light to this dark land! *Vivat, crescat, floreat!*" Sjöbergh exclaimed.

Everyone looked very solemn for a while, but the mood soon became jolly again as the servants started bringing the food to the table. They served it in order of seniority, which meant that Laurentius had to wait a while before the first dishes reached him. By now he was very hungry indeed.

He nodded, raised his mug and smiled dutifully as the older students called out the traditional toasts. It was obligatory to drain the mug to the bottom, but thankfully the beer tasted surprisingly good.

Hearing out the latest of many long and convoluted toasts, his neighbour turned to him and enquired in a half-whisper, "I don't suppose you have plans for the evening?"

"Yes, Peter Börk told me there is supposed to be some kind of performance taking place," Laurentius answered, feeling some pride in being able to demonstrate he was so well informed. "But I've got a cold; I may not be able to come and watch it after all."

"Come off it. It's going to be a major event. About Dorpat, the Athens of the Emajõgi river, and the Muses."

Laurentius raised his head, intrigued. "Really?"

Laurentius had been thinking of the Muses when he eventually chose Dorpat over the other provincial universities. Dorpat had an ill-defined but indisputable reputation as a place where the Muses were most inspiring.

"What kind of play is it exactly?" Laurentius asked.

"Don't ask, you'll spoil the surprise. Better to wait and see it for yourself."

Laurentius nodded. "You're right, of course. But unfortunately I'm not sure that my health will permit me to come today."

By now he felt so frail from the bloodletting that he found it very hard to assess what kind of state his health was in. Sometimes he would feel fine, but before long his head started spinning and he began to worry that he might faint from the fever. But that may also have been the effect of not eating for so long. That always made his organism weak—just like a fire in the fireplace needed wood to burn, the human body needed regular nourishment. When he didn't have enough, then his flame would gutter and smoulder without giving off any warmth. He would start to feel the chill darkness creeping closer towards him.

Magnus flashed a brief smile at Laurentius, and then turned to gesture to the younger students to finally bring them some food.

Eventually a lanky young man made his way up to Laurentius and Magnus and, with tetchily pursed lips, he placed a rustic, blue-glazed clay dish down on the table between them. Presented with undeniable artistic flair, on top of it was the main course of the evening: pike baked in leaves, covered in a rich cream sauce. The skin had turned quite crisp from the heat and the edges were properly browned; a few peppercorns could even be seen floating in the white sauce. Laurentius helped himself to some.

"Doesn't look like the famine which Sjöbergh was complaining about has reached here yet. This food looks splendid," he commented to his neighbour.

Magnus was poking at his fish with a thin two-pronged fork. He raised his eyebrows. "Of course. We don't have any problems here; there are plenty of stocks. Everything has become very expensive, but we certainly don't have to worry about going hungry."

Laurentius broke off a piece of bread and started to pick the tender fish off the bones. He noticed that only a couple of people other than his neighbour were using forks; probably that level of refinement was not yet widespread in Dorpat. He was quite relieved about that—whenever he had to use a fork it somehow felt awkward in his hand. And after seeing the light-hearted way his neighbour had spoken about star-vation while waving his fork in his hand the custom seemed particularly unpleasant.

Laurentius bit into the fish and gulped some of it down. But it seemed that the appetizing roasted exterior had created entirely false expectations. The fish immediately disintegrated into a viscous mass in his mouth; the flavour was somehow muddy and tainted, and he had to restrain himself from spit-ting it out. Only after taking a deep swig of bitter beer, and chewing a piece of the dry, sour bread was he able to force down the insipid, slimy mass. It seemed to be the same kind of bread as yesterday morning, but it was still several times less disgusting than the fish.

"How is the fish?" he asked his neighbour after his third large gulp of beer.

"The fish is always very good here," Magnus said approv-ingly. "Especially the pike. But we don't get to eat it very often."

Laurentius looked around and noticed that everyone else seemed to be eating the fish with gusto; some of them were even licking their fingers clean. Clearly the problem wasn't the fish or the bread. The fish was good, or at least it was edible. That rotten, muddy taste must be coming from inside him. Ever since Clodia's death everything had smelt and tasted disgusting.

"So you reckon there is no threat of famine here in Dorpat?" Laurentius asked his neighbour.

"I'm sure of it—we've nothing to worry about here, as I already told you. Especially in the city itself. The military keep their grain stocks here. Don't worry, just eat your fish," Magnus assured him.

But by now Laurentius was feeling vile. "As I mentioned, I've got a cold. It's ruined my appetite."

"So you'll let me have your fish then?" Magnus asked, and before waiting for an answer he lifted the fish from Laurentius' plate onto his own, just as if they were already on familiar terms.

"Please, be my guest," Laurentius said, watching as his neighbour got stuck into the fish. "But one could get the impression from what Sjöbergh said that the country folk are suffering pretty badly. I saw plenty of starving people myself as I arrived."

"True, the situation is pretty bad," his neighbour said with a nod. "But what are we supposed to do about it? We can't just produce extra grain for them. As far as the peasants are concerned, His Majesty issued a decree repealing serfdom two years ago, so they'll have to get by on their own now. They'll survive the winter somehow. They always have something put aside; it's never as bad as it seems." For some reason a remorseful tone had crept into Magnus' voice. "If you want to talk about wretchedness, then it's the young farmhands and the girls whose existence has become really miserable. They definitely won't survive the winter. The situation has already turned quite nasty."

"That's how it seems to me as well," Laurentius agreed.

"The city even put up some sort of shed for them. Before that they were just hanging about outside the city walls and wailing all the time. It was a horrible sight. Every morning some citizen would find a young child or woman outside his door, starved to death. The ones that are close to death have such a craving for bread that they start wailing in that ghastly way, begging for so much as a pin-sized crumb. But you must never give them any. As soon as they get their hands on a bit of bread and eat it, they drop down dead. I've been horrified to witness a twelve-year-old lad chewing greedily on his own fingers and moaning: 'Oh, I'm so hungry, so hungry!' When I eventually gave him a bit of bread he grabbed hold of it like a crazed thing, scoffed it down, and then collapsed onto the floor and passed away, just like that. That sort of experience gives one quite a fright, of course. I think the most wretched cases get food tokens from the city, and they're not allowed within the city walls any more," Magnus explained, pushing the long locks of his wig back over his shoulder as he spoke.

"Tokens?" Laurentius asked.

"Anyone who is entitled to support from the city gets a tin token which they can exchange for bread. Of course, no one wants to see women and orphans suffering. But I've already heard stories about the stronger lads stealing the tokens, and some people are even saying that they're being forged. It's a really nasty business. Strapping big men beating up women and threatening their children. Those food handouts are a bad idea: they just bring more beggars and villains here—the city can't feed all of them anyway. Who knows what will happen next? They might start rioting, or even bring the plague with them."

Finishing his explanation, Magnus shrugged his shoulders and carried on picking fish off the bones.

Thursday Afternoon

T HEY ENTERED A ROOM which was almost as bare as a barracks. At first Laurentius thought it might be a hay barn or a storeroom, and it took a few moments before he realized that they had entered an ad hoc theatre, which had been set up in a converted inn room. It clearly had no hopes of competing with Bollhuset or the London theatres, but it nevertheless seemed to aspire to being a theatre of sorts. There was a handsome carved music stand, and some chairs for the musicians positioned in the centre of the room. Two large candelabra, each with a number of arms, were positioned either side of the stage, casting a honey-golden glow around their vicinity. But the guttering light of the smelly tallow candles only reached as far as the front rows, and towards the back of the room the light was dim, so that one could only just make out people's faces and the glint of the occasional wig, propped up high on their wearers' heads. Laurentius found himself a place in the almost pitch black of the back row, and stood and watched as the young men in embroidered overcoats entered and inspected the handwritten programme nailed to the door, trying to keep their fancy clothes as far away from the walls as possible. At shoulder height there were stripped logs with planks nailed to them, and they had turned dark and smudgy from the smoke coming from the fireplace, which

vented straight into the room. There was evidently a crack
in the roof somewhere, as rainwater was seeping along the
rafters and dripping down onto the earth floor. Although the
earth itself had been trampled hard, the straw covering it was
wet and slippery in places. The innkeeper was seeing to it that
everyone had a large tankard of strong beer to drink, almost
forcing the mugs into the students' hands. It may have been
a theatre, but that was no reason to miss an opportunity to
make some money. Laurentius had taken a mug of beer along
with everyone else, and now he was trying to read the sign to
try to work out what kind of performance was in store. But
he couldn't recognize a single name.

"Are they local composers?" he asked his neighbour.

"Why do you ask?" his neighbour queried.

"All the names look unfamiliar to me," Laurentius said.

"Are you serious? You don't know anyone at all?" His
neighbour sounded surprised.

"Should I?" Laurentius asked.

"Well I don't know…" His neighbour tailed off.

The performers arrived in almost complete silence, looking
slightly nervous, and sat down on the chairs placed against the
wall, their backs straight, their hands on their knees, staring
straight ahead, seeming somehow lifeless, like sculptures.
Laurentius recognized Peter as he stepped out in front of
the audience and made a toast to the performers and visitors, which was followed by a long verse in Latin. Laurentius
guessed that it must have been Peter's own work since the
imagery was quite laboured and seemed to follow assiduously
a formula learnt at university. But there were nevertheless
a couple of witty wordplays in it, and a rather neat verse
structure, which together made for a fairly pleasant, refined

result. Laurentius laughed along with the others and waved his handkerchief in the air to show his appreciation. Peter gave a nod of acknowledgement to the audience, and briefly introduced the plot of the play. It turned out to be an allegorical piece: Orpheus loses his beloved to the underworld and returns to the land of the living, downcast and lonely. He starts to follow the god of art and learning, Apollo, which angers the bacchant followers of Dionysus, who set upon him and tear him to pieces. The Muses appear; they gather up Orpheus' limbs and bury the poet in his beloved Leibethra. In death, Orpheus is finally reunited with his wife Eurydice. The audience was evidently supposed to understand that the plot represented the academy being shut during the war and then reopened as home of the Muses. But it could also have been an allegory on the theme of moving the academy to Pärnu because conditions in Dorpat were unamenable, due to the constant conflicts with the local soldiers.

Laurentius smiled at the comparison of His Majesty's soldiers with the rowdy bacchants. It certainly wasn't very patriotic, but unfortunately it was often close to the truth.

The conversation in the hall died down, and people started looking expectantly at the performers. The compère made a gesture and one of them stood up and walked confidently but a little stiffly to the centre of the stage. He looked at the sheet music for a moment, and then lifted a lute up to his chest and started playing. Laurentius was pretty sure that he had not heard the melody before—it was old-fashioned, but distinctive and harrowing. He wasn't particularly knowledgeable about music, but he guessed the piece had been influenced by the works of Dowland. It bore some similarity to the *Lachrimae pavane*, and was intended to convey Orpheus' melancholy and sorrow. Everyone listened attentively, raptly even. But as the act went on and on Laurentius started feeling strangely distant from it all. The music seemed to grow quieter and quieter just as the stench in his nostrils grew ever stronger. The bitter beer had not washed away the vile rottenness of the fish, and now it seemed as if the music had somehow revived the taste and was drawing it from his tongue deeper into his nose and his head. He felt sleepy from the loss of blood. Clearly the bloodletting had not been a good idea at all.

"Hopeless," he whispered to himself.

The candles were starting to gutter and give off dark smoke; it was getting harder and harder to breathe in the low-ceilinged room, and he could feel a scraping sensation at the back of his throat. As Laurentius struggled to control another fit of coughing he cursed himself and mechanistic philosophy. It looked as if no good had come of following that advice about bloodletting; it had only caused his fever to flare up again. But now he had to try to focus.

After the act had finished two students went round trimming the wicks with long scissors, but the candles carried on smouldering. It looked like they must be the cheapest sort available. The musicians left the stage, and three young men appeared in front of the audience. One of them started singing jauntily, while the other two performed a dance in unison. It was clear that they were trying to present an operatic scene in the spirit of those staged by Molière and Lully in France. The scale was of course several times smaller, but one could not deny that fashionable theatre had reached these parts quite quickly. It was certainly not what Laurentius was expecting. Whenever anyone elsewhere spoke of Dorpat they would always mention that the town was on the distant periphery of the Swedish empire, that the locals were uneducated and ill-natured, and that they spoke a language which was incomprehensible to anyone else. And the situation at the academy was not supposed to be much better.

"Just the place for someone like me to come and lie low for a while," Laurentius had thought to himself at the time.

So when the Swedish state had granted him a stipend to come and study in Dorpat, the decision was made. This was the best place for him to wait quietly for the scandals to blow over before going back to Leiden.

But now it turned out that Professor Dimberg had read Newton and Boyle, and the students were even staging an opera. One could assume that the music he heard at the beginning was written locally or at least somewhere in the neighbouring region, but it was in no way inferior to the English original. He tried to immerse himself in the scene in front of him.

The dancing students seemed to have a significantly worse mastery of their craft than the musicians. In the flickering candlelight the young men's jolly prancing seemed somehow comical and frivolous. Laurentius assumed that they were supposed to represent Orpheus' male lovers, with whom he had his fun after he lost Eurydice, his true sacral love, to the underworld by looking back and killing her with one glance. Succumbing therefore to carnal love. But no, thought Laurentius, shaking his head. That would definitely have been too bold, and not at all in the spirit of the Lutheranism which was supposed to hold sway in the Swedish universities.

It was quite possible that the dancing men were supposed to represent the friends and companions who had tried to console Orpheus after he lost Eurydice, but one couldn't help suspecting that an alternative interpretation was also being suggested. Homosexuality had become almost fashionable in both the English and French royal households, and Laurentius was pretty sure that if the opera had already reached here, then those kinds of influences would have done so too. In any case this was yet another indication that the place was not nearly as provincial as he had thought. In some of the German universities, theatre was banned outright.

He stood up on tiptoe and looked around the hall. The other young men were standing and watching the play with appreciative looks on their faces, and there was almost no one chatting or being rowdy. There were a couple of students sitting at a table right at the back of the room and playing dice, but even they seemed somehow quiet and well behaved.

Laurentius took a swig of beer. He was finding the whole experience genuinely interesting.

The performers swapped round: some of the audience members clapped; others waved their handkerchiefs approvingly, and the conversation picked up a bit.

Laurentius could not help acknowledging the effort that had gone into putting on the performance. The result was in the spirit of English theatre, where Apollo and Hyacinthus' or King William of Orange and Arnold van Keppel's unconventional relationships were often made fun of, but never maliciously or moralizingly—more in a gentle, light-hearted vein.

He smiled and clapped with the others. But his body was racked with fever, and anxiety was welling in his chest after having gone so long without food. His forearm was aching where the blood had bled from him. He had to try to put those things out of his mind. The beer was good, and the mood of the company was contagious. Theatre was also known to be one of the best cures for melancholy. He had been to the theatre in Germany, Holland, Sweden, and seen plenty of performances which were far inferior to this one here in Dorpat.

"Encore! Encore!" he called out with the others as the second act came to an end.

In the midst of the hubbub Peter stood up on his chair, and the hollering got even louder.

"It's still early for an encore; the story is not yet finished. Our hero is lonely and despondent; he is yearning for his lover. But it's no good for a man to be alone: only wretchedness and despair can come of that. This was just a start, a foundation, from which we will now move on."

Peter gestured for everyone to quieten down, and then read out a hexametric poem in Greek, taking great care over the scansion. From that it became clear that now was the turn of the maenads, whose grisly task it was to rip off the poor bard's head. The musicians started playing again, but more vigorously this time, and together with the lute one could now hear a flute and even bagpipes. The wild, low-pitched droning sound suited the impassioned rage of the crime which was soon to be committed.

Some figures wrapped in white robes, with long flapping skirts, rushed onto the stage, and Laurentius leant forward to see them better. These were the younger students, and their childlike features were tensed, their cheeks were daubed black, and they had tangled old wigs fixed on their heads. Their bare feet stepped across the straw which had been strewn over the earth floor, and they thronged around Orpheus, whirling about and crying out. There were wreaths of woven willow twigs in their hair, which given the local climate were probably the closest available substitutes for olive branches.

"Come, come with us," they sang. "Leave your cold, stern Apollo behind and return to Dionysus. Only with him will you experience true joy and elation."

Laurentius watched them, feeling cold shivers run down him. The young men seemed very familiar, as if he had seen them somewhere before. They were dressed in rags, and they moved about jerkily, supposedly depicting crazy Greek women, although they bore more of a resemblance to starving peasant girls or witches. Their hair was hanging loose, and they had crazed looks in their eyes, as befitted the role.

"They look like vagabonds, don't they?" Laurentius commented to his neighbour.

"They certainly do," his neighbour mumbled in response. "But those are still the bacchants; you're yet to see the Muses. They are definitely more respectable-looking."

Laurentius nodded. He knew that the Muses would bring Orpheus' dismembered limbs to Leibethra, at which point the nightingales would start to sing overhead. That could be seen as an allusion to Dorpat's Emajõgi river, which was famous for its nightingales.

"I have always found the maenads rather horrific," Laurentius answered with a grin.

"Those vagrants?" his neighbour said, waving sceptically in the direction of the young men jumping about on the stage, and feigning surprise. "Come off it."

"Not necessarily those ones. In general," Laurentius answered.

His neighbour shrugged. "To be honest we've got more of those tramps and vagrants than we can cope with. The outskirts of town are completely full of them now, and the guard has been reinforced at the gates, to stop them coming and loitering about town. But they still get through somehow; I just don't know what should be done about it. Anyway, as far as I understand, Peter couldn't persuade a single woman to take on the bacchant roles. It would have looked a bit more respectable, I suppose."

Laurentius nodded in agreement as he watched the prancing ragamuffins, feeling detached and intoxicated from the effects of the beer and his fever. He imagined one of them holding the cage with his dead parakeet in it as they danced clumsily around. Bowing and singing, long willow branches flailing in their hands.

Laurentius rubbed his forehead and his temples, and tried to focus on the maenads. They had started whirling around Orpheus and clawing at him like dogs setting on an elk. All the stiltedness and silliness of the scene had gone. The ragamuffins clustered closer together; an old fencing dummy appeared from somewhere, and then they started to rip off the head which had been sewn onto it.

"Hey!" the public yelled animatedly.

The ragamuffins lifted the head up high, and the brown, curly wig which was supposed to be Orpheus' hair looked chillingly real and abject in the dim light of the room. Laurentius recalled the executions he had witnessed. The executioner had eventually lifted the head up so that everyone could see the face of the despised person whose soul had just departed, together with the blood which was trickling down the green knoll. But what happened to the body? Orpheus' body was ripped into pieces; the intoxicated women gorged on his flesh; the blood flowed down their chins and onto their chests, and they washed it down with red wine.

Laurentius had seen bodies being tossed into heaps and burned, the flesh charring and the hair smouldering in the flames. And he could remember the stench…

Laurentius started coughing; his shoulders shook; he felt a stabbing pain in his stomach.

Thursday Evening

O NCE THE PERFORMANCE WAS OVER Magnus offered to introduce Laurentius to the actors. After the last scene had been repeated twice and the final ovations had died down, they approached the motley band of young men sitting at one of the tables. They were dressed in jackets, without neckerchiefs and with open shirt collars, clearly trying to imitate the style of dress common among English actors, and they were discussing something heatedly among themselves, gesticulating wildly. They smiled in response to Magnus' convoluted introduction and patted him on the shoulder as they acquainted themselves in a disorderly fashion. Peter shook Laurentius' hand amiably and, evidently for form's sake, enquired how his examination had gone. Laurentius took the pale, long-stemmed clay pipe which was offered to him, and started puffing at the tobacco together with the others. Smoking was generally seen as a vile habit, and students with Pietist inclinations would be likely to make their opposition known to it at every opportunity. But in this company it seemed to be just another part of everyday student life.

"I'd like to work it up into a proper full-length tragic opera," Peter started to say. "Add some Monteverdi-style opening scenes, and of course the final part with the Muses needs to be better brought out."

"You and your yearning for Italy! No one puts on Monteverdi these days. English comedies are far superior, that's for sure," someone objected. Laurentius recalled that he had been introduced as Matthias. "The cathartic effect of comedies is significantly greater too. Of course I mean decent comedies—we can't include those German fairground farces in that category."

The company burst out laughing, and Laurentius recalled what the barber had said about catharsis. "I think comedy is actually a pretty complicated affair. It's easy to find that the deeper meaning of a piece is replaced by below-the-belt burlesque. Many contemporary English comedies are extremely coarse," he said, butting into the conversation.

"That is often the case," Matthias agreed with a vague wave of his hand. "But I'm talking about the basic principle. As we know, in comedies everything tends to go badly for the protagonist in the beginning, but it all works out in the end—that kind of development purifies the soul and leaves the audience with a nice uplifting feeling. Tragedies, however, make one gloomy."

"Tragedies are instructive," Peter explained. They remind us that even when someone is experiencing life's greatest happiness, fate can lead to his ruination. The purpose of theatre is not to create pleasant feelings, but to educate the public."

"But how are all those gloomy stories about the underworld and maenads supposed to educate people?" asked Matthias, unable to resist challenging Peter. "What's more, there is so much wretchedness and strife all around us these days that it's hard to see why it needs to be depicted on the stage as well."

"Matthias, you rogue!" Peter exclaimed. "Resorting to such underhand tricks to make your case! Well, all right then, I'll give you an answer. There is indeed a lot of wretchedness and strife in the world, but it has no broader meaning to it. It is just chance, unrelated episodes. Only the theatre, and tragedy in particular, is capable of binding these episodes together. Just as a book's cover binds the loose leaves into a single whole." At that Peter jumped up onto his feet and started to declaim in a loud voice:

> "In its depth I saw ingathered, bound by love in one single volume, that which is dispersed in leaves throughout the universe: substances and accidents and their relations, as though fused together in such a way that what I tell is but a simple light."

The others nodded and chuckled knowingly, and even Matthias smiled.

"Of course you know that Dante, whom you are quoting, named his work *The Divine Comedy*?" Matthias said.

"Touché," Peter exclaimed affectedly, and rolled his eyes. "But today all the divine comedies have been replaced with human ones, and only tragedy has the depth and the scope to rise above the buffoonery."

At that the academy's French and dance teacher Mr Bazancourt, who had been sitting quietly with them up until then, livened up and started cursing his pupils. "Too little attention is paid to French in these parts. And no one wants to study dance either—they're all too busy fencing!"

"Exactly!" Matthias agreed emphatically. "In order to stage an opera properly there must be movement. Dance can lighten the burden from our souls and transport our thoughts to other places."

The company then started a muddled discussion on the good and bad aspects of contemporary playwriting and the lousy French skills of the students at Dorpat. After that, the conversation moved to the classic question of the unity of place, action and time. And this inevitably led to a discussion of opera as a total spectacle which was capable of uniting all other art forms.

But all those words just slid past Laurentius' ears. He sat there for a while longer, watching the students arguing with a sleepy expression on his face, but eventually he made his excuses and got up to leave. By now the stench of sooty candles and the bitter tobacco burning in the clay pipes had become so strong that he couldn't stay in the room any longer. No one had trimmed the candlewicks since the end of the performance, and now they were smouldering like shoemaker's thread dipped in pitch. The smell mixed with the rotten stench which had already been wafting into his nostrils, creating a hideous new combination which he could no longer stand.

"Oh, in my view song is even more important—don't you think so, Laurentius?" Peter yelled after him.

Laurentius managed a quick wave in response before stepping out into the damp darkness. "Music is the true art form of the Muses!" Peter called out.

Outside, it was still raining and the lamp above the inn door was casting long shadows against the dripping trees. Laurentius sat down on a bench under the eaves of the building and stretched his legs out in front of him. The fresh air outside made him feel dizzy and light-headed. He rested his head against the wooden wall and closed his eyes, and he could make out indistinct sounds coming from inside— bursts of laughter, and the chinking of beer mugs. Drops of rainwater were trickling down from the eaves, forming puddles round the building, like a small moat. The cold wind blew his hair onto his face, but he didn't raise his hand to push it aside. Laurentius was thinking of Orpheus' hair, and how the maenads had tousled it. He remembered how they had ripped off his head and gnawed his body into pieces. In what had otherwise been an endearingly amateur production this episode had succeeded in being gruesomely true to life, and had caught him completely off guard.

Laurentius shook his head and shifted his legs restlessly. He felt sick and on edge again. He should be inside in the warmth, but he knew he wouldn't enjoy the chatter in there; he wouldn't even be able to focus on it properly. He probably would have just got caught up in something silly. The most sensible thing would be to go to his lodgings, but he felt strangely listless and apathetic. As he coughed, recent images appeared in his mind, which combined with the apparitions which his fantasy created. He tried to think about his parakeet, but that just made him grimace. Instead, the image of the cage and the ragamuffin reared up before his eyes.

That old man had been storming about just like those maenads. Starvation had caused him to bite people, tear at their clothes and leap about all over the place. If there had been more of his sort about maybe they would have ripped the tanner's lad to bits and gobbled him down too, gnawed his limbs and his head from his body. Laurentius started to think that despite his odd views on witchcraft and familiars, the tanner may have been right about the old man. It was a good thing that the lad had managed to strike him dead with his pole. Who knows what could have happened otherwise.

But had he really been responsible for that old man's death? He had already been behaving oddly up by the barn, so he may have just been crazy from hunger, in which case Laurentius would have had absolutely nothing to do with what followed. Had the old man really eaten his parakeet? Did he really pluck out her feathers and gobble her down like that?

Laurentius couldn't bear thinking about it any longer.

He tried to imagine the Muses dancing at Leibethra, the nightingales singing, and greenery all around. That had been the final scene of the performance. But it had been much weaker theatrically, and much less realistic than the frenzy of the maenads. An image of a clearing with brown grass and a low, grey sky appeared in front of his eyes. He was twelve years old, dressed in worn-out breeches, with no boots of his own to wear. He stood there barefoot on the cold ground, and a man in a black robe approached from amid the sinewy trees. He was wearing a greyish-white crown on his head.

Laurentius had looked in the man's direction, his eyes full of turmoil and shame. The executioner had wiped his sword on some blades of grass, and the court attendant said something. He had looked into those eyes for some time, and he had seen madness and grief there. The fever had been washing over him in waves, just as it was now. Someone had grabbed him by the shoulders; he had resisted, and one of the peasants had slapped him in the face. His lip had started bleeding. The blood had been red, like pomegranate juice.

Laurentius started coughing and he felt a grating pain in the back of his throat. His stomach was contorted with cramp; he had a sour taste in his mouth and stinging pain on his tongue. He needed something to eat; he was so hungry. And something to drink, to rinse the taste away.

He remembered the basket of fruit, the bread and the wine from that morning. Had it been a vision? He had told Dimberg that he did not believe in spirits and apparitions, but the images had seemed so real. The food and drink may have been nothing more than a muddle of wishful thinking and the phantasmagorical visions of his weary, feverish brain. He had to try to stay lucid. But it really had seemed as if someone were there in the room with him. He had seen a face with a bright white halo around it…

"Eh?" a voice asked from directly above him.

Laurentius came to with a start, and looked up in amazement. Standing there in front of him was a woman whom he had never seen in his life before. A moment earlier he seemed to have been looking at a very different scene. A pallid face, black hair, translucent skin. A basket full of honeycomb and fruit. He had seen it all very clearly in his mind's eye, just like that morning. If a similar sight had appeared from the darkness right now it wouldn't have surprised him at all. He had been expecting that, maybe even hoping for it to happen.

"Eh?" Laurentius blurted in response and he gawped at the dirty, flushed face looking down at him.

With her rough cloth skirt, which was sodden from the rain, her bare feet, her tangled hair and the wild look in her eyes, the woman didn't resemble his phantasm at all. Laurentius was so amazed that he even forgot to avert his gaze, and he just sat there gawping at the woman.

"Eh?" the apparition said in response, and she beckoned him over with her finger.

Laurentius stayed sitting where he was, smoothing his hair with one hand, unable to think of anything to say. Then he realized that he was still staring straight into the woman's eyes, and he quickly looked down.

"Damn," Laurentius hissed between his teeth. That was not meant to happen.

"*Fucken,*" the woman proposed in broken German. "*Das he fucken?*"

"I'm sorry," Laurentius muttered, still confused. "Please go away."

The woman mumbled something in a plaintive voice and tugged at Laurentius' overcoat again.

"No!" said Laurentius, who was angry by now. "What sort of liberties do you think you are taking?"

"Come, come," she said, continuing to tug at him.

Eventually Laurentius stood up and followed the woman. He wasn't sure why exactly, although it may have been because he felt guilty for looking into her eyes for so long. They walked across a muddy square, past some stone houses, and left the town through the Russian Gate. The guards seemed to pay no attention to them at all as they passed. The woman had a fiery look in her eyes, and her movements were stiff and jerky, but she walked on with a sense of purpose. She clearly knew exactly where she wanted to go. Walking briskly, they arrived at the riverbank fortifications. From there a path laid with birch planks led across the blackened lowlands. Laurentius had already been there yesterday morning, and he recognized the willow trees which he had climbed to gather bark. That was the spot where the peasant men had been standing, watching him.

For some reason he felt he needed to explain something, to justify himself to the woman. So he pointed in the direction of the willow trees and said simply "fever".

But the woman didn't stop to look; she just beckoned Laurentius on, and they headed deeper and deeper into the shabby outskirts of town, moving inexorably onwards, as if in a dream.

Laurentius tried to focus on what was happening. Yesterday morning… yesterday morning Dimberg had told him to familiarize himself with a note about student life and customs, from which he had learnt that it was compulsory for all students to be in their lodgings by nine in the evening, otherwise the soldiers were entitled to escort them to the detention cells. That would certainly be an unpleasant experience, which he had to try his best to avoid. Laurentius attempted to come to a standstill, but as was often the case when he was dreaming he couldn't control his limbs; it was as if his legs were obeying the woman, not him.

He rummaged in his breast pocket for his watch. There was still a little time left before nine.

"*Fucken, fucken,*" the woman repeated, and beckoned him on.

He made another attempt to stand still, but the creature tugging at him was unexpectedly strong, and nearly succeeded in pulling him down to the ground.

Laurentius shoved his hand into his breast pocket and pulled a small coin from his purse.

"There, have that…" he said to the woman.

But she took one look at the money and burst into tears. Then she fell onto her knees on the muddy ground, and grabbed hold of Laurentius' high boots, sobbing uncontrollably.

"Now, now," Laurentius said, trying to console her.

Evidently this was one of those girls who had been let go from the farm where she worked. The girls were taken on to gather and thresh what was left on the fields after the rotten summer, but the miserable harvest had resembled caraway seeds or mouse droppings more than grain, and the farmers could hardly hope to feed their families through winter, let alone the farmhands too. So she had been forced to come to town to look for food.

"That's enough now," Laurentius said, hoping she would calm down.

The woman jumped up and started tugging him again. They walked along the riverbank and Laurentius looked up at the dark clouds, noticing how they collided and intertwined with each other as they rolled past.

"Wait," he said. "Stop. I'm not coming any further. I don't know why I came with you in the first place, but this is far enough now."

The woman looked straight at him, ran her hands through her hair, and burst out crying again. She may have been beautiful once, but now she was ravaged by hunger, her cheeks sunken and her skin cracked from the cold and damp. Laurentius helped her up from the ground, and her bony frame turned out to be unexpectedly light, even for him.

"Child," the woman started wailing. "My child. She is ill."

Laurentius started looking in his pocket for another coin, but he couldn't help thinking that if the other beggars found out then he would have no respite from their scrounging. Although there wasn't actually anything unusual about the situation. A woman had a baby and was sent packing. Most likely no one even knew who the father was, or he had refused to recognize the child as his own. In times of famine there wasn't much left for those sorts of women other than a whore's life. But that was probably not enough to keep body and soul together, and winter was fast approaching.

"Take it," Laurentius said. "Take it, and lead me to your child."

He remembered the times he had been ill, how he had waited for someone to come and care for him, but in vain. He broke into a fit of coughing, and the woman looked in his direction, seeming slightly alarmed. It was the first time her face had expressed anything other than emptiness and despondency.

"I have fever," Laurentius whispered by way of explanation.

They walked on a little further and eventually came to a large barn, which, judging by the groaning, sniffling and hawking sounds coming from it, was quite full of people. It appeared to be some sort of temporary dwelling place, and Laurentius recalled how Magnus and the hay trader had told him that the city had established a refuge for the starving women and children arriving from the countryside. There were initially more of them than men, since the men who were fit could always put themselves to use in return for something to eat.

Laurentius peeped in across the threshold. There was a rancid stench coming from the cold, damp interior, the kind of smell one would normally encounter at a cesspit.

At first he couldn't see anything at all, but then clearer outlines gradually started to take shape from the darkness. He guessed that the small humps by the walls must be children. Women were sitting on the bare earth; just a couple of them had bundles of mouldy straw underneath them, probably scraped together from some barn floor or sodden haystack, the kind which was no longer fit for fodder. Laurentius knew very well how difficult it was to get hold of decent straw in Dorpat—he had paid an arm and a leg for the straw for his mattress.

He cautiously stepped through the doorway, but no one paid him any attention: they were weak and listless from hunger and the chill damp, and they kept themselves to themselves. One old crone looked up and glared at him ill-naturedly.

"Good evening," Laurentius said, addressing no one in particular.

The woman he had come with squatted down by a small figure covered with an old cape. A head covered in blonde hair could just be seen poking above the grimy collar. Laurentius bent down next to them and touched his palm onto the child's forehead. Even with his fever he could feel the heat against his hand.

"She needs plenty to drink," he told the woman, glancing in her direction. It was not clear if she had understood him, but she nodded and said something to the cross-looking old woman in their language. The old woman groaned, pushed herself upright, and went outside.

Laurentius looked at the child. He could hear her breathing, hurried and husky. Her fever must have already been very high; maybe it was close to the stage when the blood became viscous and stopped circulating. Looking concerned, he reached into his breast pocket and took out a small package containing the pieces of silver willow bark which he had gathered the previous morning. Despite Dimberg's advice about corpuscular medicine, he had held on to them. They hadn't yet dried properly, which meant that their effect would be very weak, but it might still be enough for the child.

"We need some water. Boiled water," Laurentius said without looking up.

The woman nodded.

Laurentius gave her the package and tried to explain what to do with the strips of bark. The woman's knowledge of German was clearly limited to one or two words, and she didn't understand much of what he said. But Laurentius eventually managed to explain with gestures how many times a day and for how long she should administer the powdered bark, and a smile appeared on her face.

Laurentius tried to smile as well, but he only managed to raise one corner of his mouth. He couldn't be at all sure that the child's fever would not rise again later: there was too little bark to treat her properly. But he felt it would be unchristian of him not to give his last medicine to the little girl.

He pushed the sleeping child's hair off her face, and he touched her forehead again. At that she woke with a start, opened her eyes, and looked up in surprise. Her cheeks were gaunt, and her eyes seemed abnormally large in her narrow face.

"*Kuningas*," the child said, clearly and audibly.

"What?" said Laurentius, failing to understand the Estonian word.

"The king," the woman repeated in German.

He laughed and shook his head. "I'm no king. I'm just a university student."

He gestured to the woman. "Tell her."

The woman said something but the child continued looking about with wide, staring eyes, and then she pointed with one finger towards the open door, somewhere into the distance, and repeated.

"The king."

Laurentius looked in the direction she was pointing, but he couldn't see much through the darkness and fine mist of rain other than some distant trees swaying in the wind.

Thursday, Late Evening

B Y THE TIME HE ARRIVED back at the city gates the damp of the muddy road had already started seeping in through the tough leather of his boots. The rain had become more violent, and he wrapped his coat tightly around himself and tried to position his hat so that it would protect his face from the raindrops which the wind was hurling at him. That was the moment when he heard the rumble of drums and the yells of the sentry. This was swiftly followed by the sight of a storm lantern dangling on the end of a halberd, and then the uniformed guardsmen appeared from around the corner. The tiny lantern cast a weak yellow light, and the sentries had to lower it towards Laurentius, until it almost touched his face. They inspected him curiously.

"Are you a stranger in town?" one of them asked.

"No, I'm a student; I have just arrived," Laurentius replied.

"Well, Mr Student should get himself to his lodgings right away. It's already nine o'clock. You must have heard the drums just now? That's to let everyone know to stop loitering in the streets. Or are you hard of hearing?" one of the soldiers said in a tone of voice which would have suited a fairground brawler. He stood there looking straight at Laurentius, waiting for an answer.

Laurentius turned his head to one side and made a vague gesture with his hand. He didn't feel the need to get offended; he was anyway too tired by now.

"I'm already going," Laurentius said.

"And that's the law!" another guard added in a slightly disappointed-sounding voice before turning to leave. They may indeed have been disappointed that they hadn't managed to wound Laurentius' pride and start an argument. It was safe to assume that evening sentry duty wasn't the most pleasant of activities, and taking a student to the detention cells would at least have provided a bit of variety.

"Be sure to mind your step!" another guard shouted by way of farewell.

Trying hard to force a smile, Laurentius walked on. Before he was swallowed up by the darkness again he managed to spot the sentries peeking in through a door and rattling their ancient halberd around inside. Given how wet the weather was there was no point in them carrying their blunderbusses. Laurentius wasn't anyway sure whether there were enough firearms in those parts for all the sentries to carry one. The soldiers in Dorpat were mostly Swedish peasants who had already lived there for years, and they constantly got into rows with the students. The trouble had apparently started because the town dwellers, who were mostly of German origin, and those students who came from the local nobility treated the newcomer Swedes with suspicion and disdain, leading to much mutual offence, brawling and rancour. The city's inhabitants accused the garrisoned soldiers of picking fights, thieving and drunkenness, and normally with good cause. The conflict had originally come about on national grounds, but over the course of time it had spread from the students of German origin to include all members of the academy. By now this class divide was firmly entrenched and seemed impossible to resolve—there was no will on either side to do so. In this context the soldiers took particular pleasure in enforcing the law which required all students to be in their lodgings by nine. The belligerent zeal with which they performed their duties could be quite amusing to behold.

Laurentius shrugged his shoulders and hurried off in the direction of home. His legs were damp and cold; his forearm ached where he had cut himself with the scalpel the previous night, and his veins felt as brittle as glass. But hopefully he had expelled all the bad blood from them now.

Now he just needed to walk a little further down Broad Street, and then just before he got to the university's main building he would have to turn off down the narrow Cloister Street. There, a little before the Gustav I bastion came into view stood a house which had recently been repaired and painted with white limestone, where his lodgings were. He hoped the maid had already lit the fire for the evening, so that his room would be warm. Maybe the straw had been delivered by now as well. Then, for the first time in ages, he would be able to sleep in a warm, soft bed. He hadn't enjoyed such comfort for longer than he could remember. The long journey, the uncivilized guest houses and the constant rain had left him exhausted. On top of that he had spent the first night at his lodgings feverishly tossing and turning on the hard wooden bed boards, and the whole of the following night was passed sitting in his chair with his arm resting in a bowl of blood. He felt cramp in his stomach as he thought about it. By now he was very tired.

"Like a living corpse," he couldn't help thinking.

He turned the corner and entered the muddy yard at the back of his lodgings, placing his hand against the wall for support as he tried to avoid the larger puddles. That was when he noticed someone standing there, under the awning by the back door. He felt a hot flush of alarm slowly rise up his body, and he groped instinctively for his sword. But then he just shook his head and smiled ruefully to himself. He was feverish and worn out. Too tired to be properly shocked, too feeble to be capable of any vigorous movements.

"Hello," he said wearily.

He was so exhausted from going to visit the sick child that nothing could surprise him now. Somehow he had even been expecting to see the young woman there again. After the events of the morning the encounter seemed almost inevitable. Laurentius walked up to the steps and leant against the handrail. His boots left muddy prints on the wooden boards, and water was dripping from his hat. But the girl was standing there barefoot, clad in only a thin white blouse, just like the day before.

"I…" Laurentius started to say.

It was clear that the combination of seeing the delirious child and his own fever had caused the levels of black bile in his body to rise. It seemed that the bloodletting had not helped at all. All these unexpected encounters, the damp climate and being out at this late hour could only make things worse. He tried to smile, and awkwardly tried to find the right words. But what could he possibly say to her?

He had felt a similar disquiet and unease back at the barn, and in the end he had just silently put on his hat and left. He hadn't been able to think what to say then either—the sick child's mother had turned her back on him and started whispering something in a soothing voice to the girl, who had still been talking deliriously about seeing a king.

"Do you…" Laurentius started to say, but he failed to start a conversation once again.

Laurentius was a foreigner in that town, and he felt like an outsider standing in that doorway, just as he had at the barn. By now his fever was running high again, and the hot blood circulating round his veins made him sleepy. As often happened when he was ill, he felt as if half of him were situated in some other place. Somewhere where waking and sober people never went. That was why the sight of the trees had made him so anxious and frightened as he left the barn. He was afraid that he might see something amid them, some movement aside from the rustling and swaying branches and the dripping rain. The child had pointed towards the trees, after all. It was true that children would often rave when they were sick, but they could also be much more receptive to phantasms and spirits than adults. Sick people could often look beyond everyday objects and see things which healthy people could not. Laurentius always turned his gaze from such things, out of fear.

Healthy souls were often jaded and dulled, but sick and dying people's souls were fixed weakly to their bodies and could be as responsive as a lute string. They could see demons, sometimes even angels. As he had walked along the riverside path, through the scrubland, Laurentius had looked anxiously about, afraid that his sickness and his melancholy might cause him to glimpse a crown and cape somewhere between the trees. Or there above the sluggish dark river, edged with silver willows, he might see a darker patch of mist, clothes and a face… As he passed the trees where he had cut the bark he almost broke into a run, stumbling on smooth branches and slipping on long, arrow-shaped leaves. He had kept his eyes fixed rigidly on the puddles, watching the soiled toes of his boots as they hurried homewards, feeling a deep sense of unease writhing in his stomach like a snake. What would he do if he too were beckoned? If a hand appeared from the shadows and gestured for him to come? Now that he had looked the woman in the eyes, did that mean that the king and his entourage had already arrived?

He shook his head.

When he heard the clanging and prattling of the guards at the gate he had felt some semblance of courage return. But as soon as he set eyes on the young woman standing in the dim light on the steps, his first thought was that the king might be lurking in the shadows behind her. That was what he was expecting to see, and he was afraid.

"Did you do anything to treat your illness, as I advised you?" the girl eventually asked, clearly deciding that she would have to get the conversation started herself.

"It appears that I did not. I went to the banquet instead. In the circumstances I couldn't refuse the invitation," Laurentius said, finding himself giving a surprisingly logical answer. But he could not ignore the strange feeling that he was standing behind someone's back, and that that person was speaking on his behalf. As if he had no influence on what he said. "It was a magnificent event."

"Was it a pleasant repast?" the young woman enquired.

Laurentius tried to work out whether he could detect a note of irony in her voice.

"Yes," he agreed. "Indeed it was. But I have had no appetite recently. I couldn't eat a thing."

"No appetite?" Now he was sure he could hear a ring of irony in her surprised tone. "These days that really is an uncommon complaint."

Laurentius smiled despondently. "I know. But everything I eat tastes like mud; it just clogs up my mouth and makes me feel sick."

"Maybe my bread and wine won't make you nauseous? Perhaps you would like to eat something right now?" the girl said, looking at him coyly.

Laurentius turned his gaze downwards. He felt extremely weak, and had to support himself on the stair rail. The day had been too much of a strain for him. He was tired, and still intoxicated from the fever and beer. He gazed down at the wooden boards dejectedly, remembering the basket of fruit and honeycomb he had seen the previous night. But no… he had to try and be rational.

"I'm sorry…" he mumbled, and sat down on the steps. "I have a fever."

"Oh, no need to apologize to me. I'll see you to your room," the girl said sympathetically, and gave a friendly nod.

At first Laurentius thought he should turn down her offer and explain that he could manage on his own, that there was no need for her to help, but he felt so tired. So he supported himself on the girl's outstretched forearm and tried to smile.

"You are very kind," he said.

They walked up the dark staircase, and in his feverous state the young woman's arm felt stone cold against his.

"So do you live here as well?" Laurentius asked, for the sake of conversation.

"I sometimes come here, yes…" the girl answered somehow absent-mindedly, leaving the sentence tailing off. They walked on, accompanied by the creaking of the wooden staircase. Laurentius could feel a shooting pain in his legs, and he was grateful he had the young woman to support him. Arriving upstairs at the door of his room they came to a standstill, and Laurentius took a deep breath, trying to think of something to say. The situation felt awkward, and he needed to find a polite resolution.

"If there is anything you need, then let me know. I can make you something to eat as well," the girl said, filling the silence before Laurentius could say anything.

"Goodnight," Laurentius said with a smile, relieved that he had at least said something.

"Goodnight," said the girl, and she handed him a small bread roll.

Laurentius took it without thinking. The bread was warm, as if it were fresh out of the oven. Hot like his fever, he thought. The girl turned to leave, and Laurentius watched her silently descend the stairs.

"What is your name?" he said in the direction of the shadow, which was still visible through the dim light.

"Clodia," he heard from downstairs. "Goodnight."

Laurentius drew breath sharply and grabbed hold of the door frame to steady himself. He knew this feeling very well. He had felt it before. Just a moment earlier everything had been disintegrating around him; all had been disparate and purposeless; the days had been passing by like clouds in the sky, wreathing in and out of one another, devoid of any meaning. But then suddenly, unexpectedly, a purpose had appeared, a story with a beginning and an end. All those disparate elements were now inextricably linked, no longer just separate episodes which one had to struggle to piece together. The clouds looked like birds and animals; they all had sense and meaning, a destination which they would eventually reach. He smiled, pushed the door open and sat down on his soft, straw-filled mattress. He slowly lowered himself onto his back. The room felt warm.

"Clodia."

He was so tired that he fell asleep in an instant, before he had even managed to read an evening prayer.

NIGHT

I INSPECT THE FOLDED PIECE OF PAPER in my hand.
Maybe it will be of some use, although I don't know for
sure. But what else can I do? I have to try something. I go
outside to fetch some water, and the night air is cold and
damp. It's suddenly become very quiet. I lean against the wall
to listen. Drip, drip, followed by a splash, as the water trickles
off the eaves. The pail underneath is already full to the brim,
and now and again some water spills out onto the ground;
a large puddle has already formed around it. I bend down,
scoop some water from the pail into my mug, and I drink. I
should brew up some of the medicine right away, but I will
have to go to the cave to do that—there is nowhere to make
a fire here. Outside is too damp.

I shove the piece of paper under my clothes and run quickly
across the wet grass in the direction of the cave mouth, down
between the trees. There were once sand quarries down there.
No one knows for sure when they first started to dig, but a
great many caves and passages were burrowed out, some of
them narrow, some wider, branching off in all directions. Some
of the other women once went a bit deeper to look around,
but I didn't dare. It's dark down there; there's something
eerie and menacing about it; mothers frighten their children
with stories about the cannibals who live down there. Just a

couple of days ago someone scratched out some odd-shaped bones from the ground; they looked just like the bones of some evil spirit. They're just stories, of course, to stop the little ones from hanging around down there and getting lost in the caves. It's creepy down there—but there's nowhere else to make a fire.

My hair is wet from the rain; the water is seeping through to my scalp, making it tickle and itch. There's a damp tobacco smell wafting off my clothes, and the rain is spattering constantly outside the cave mouth. The fire has almost gone out now; there are just a couple of gnarled logs smouldering. I'm not sure if there is enough charcoal to get it going again. I pour some water from the ladle into the pot and throw some of the thinner, dryer-looking branches underneath. Earlier that day someone dragged a big pile of kindling there, hoping that the fire would dry it out. But then kindling is just kindling: it burns up fast without giving off much heat.

I shove some twigs and dry blades of grass between the branches and blow. The straws start to glow; they blacken and buckle; the fire catches for a moment, but it goes out again. The flame gropes its way along the thin blades of grass, trying to find its way. A thick plume of grey smoke starts to rise from the fire and move slowly out through the mouth of the cave, and it seems to be glowing greyish-yellow like fever. A gust of wind blows the smoke back into the cave and the acrid fumes make me choke. I stoop down close to the ground and blow onto the straw, and it starts charring again, but the twigs still won't catch. My head starts spinning from puffing so hard, and the smoke starts suffocating me. I lower myself down onto my stomach and continue to blow. Then the pile of kindling blazes up with a crackle, and the flames singe my hair and face.

I turn aside and lie there on the damp ground, and the smoke starts to thin out as it billows out of the cave mouth. Now I can sit up again. I wait for the water to boil, but I can't tell if the hissing is coming from the burning wood or the water in the pan.

"Oh Lord," I say under my breath.

I take the disc out of my pocket, the one which Maarja the witch gave me. The reverse face feels smooth; there is an outline of a pendant cross on it, etched with great skill—it's a fine piece of work. But that's only one side, on the other there are inscriptions. Those are used to capture disembodied souls. The witch said that all of the seals of the sylphs are there, and that with their help I can do whatever I want. I don't know how well they have worked before now, but I have no other hope. So I shake the long strips of bark out into the palm of my hand and twist the disc into them. Let it grind the strips into dust, medicine made from powder, flour to bake the bread which will make my little girl well again.

I throw the dust into the water and make the sign of the cross over it with a stone. The pieces of bark float there without sinking to the bottom, suspended in the dark water. It has to be stirred.

"Damn," I whisper, and I spit over my left shoulder.

The witch's brew must be stirred with fingernails, but mine are broken from all the hard work. Proper witches don't work, so they can keep their fingernails long. But maybe half a fingernail will do.

"Pain to the crow, sickness to the magpie. Amen, amen, amen."

That's how she taught me. Not that I have much faith in this witchery—I didn't really want to go to see her in the first place. They say she is in cahoots with the Devil himself, that he will be sure to take her dear soul with him eventually. But what's that to me? It's not my soul he's going to drag off. Although I would be happy for him to take mine, if he left my poor little girl's alone.

The water starts to bubble, and I try to remember how long it was supposed to boil. For as long it takes to say the Lord's Prayer ten times slowly. I start to recite it in a low voice.

"Our Father who art in heaven. Hallowed be thy name. Thy kingdom come…"

I hear a rustling sound from somewhere nearby. I jump up with a start.

"Who's there?"

No answer—just the roaring wind and the crackling fire. But it looks like there is some kind of bird out there, flapping its wings against the backdrop of rain and sky, a dark shadow hovering on the border between darkness and light. Is it a magpie? A crow? I can't see properly. I lift the pan off the fire and walk a couple of steps away from the ring of light, trying to get my eyes accustomed to the darkness. It's pitch black outside; I can't make out a single thing. I stand there for a while, feeling the warmth of the fire on my back and the cool night air against my face. Contours slowly start to form, a large tree with drooping branches and long, arrow-shaped leaves. There is a shadowy figure standing beneath it, a wide cape on his back, eyes glowing like stars. Or is that just the reflection of the fire? I notice an odd-looking bird perched on his shoulder; then suddenly it flaps its wings and comes flying straight at me. It grips hold of my face and my hair with its talons; it starts clawing at me. I cry out.

I try to tear the bird off, but I can't get hold of it—my hands just grasp at thin air. I hear some frightened voices yelling, crying out. It sounds like they're up near the barn.

"Over here," I scream. "Over here, help!"

The black bird claws at my hair.

FRIDAY

L AURENTIUS WAS OVERCOME by a fit of coughing, and his stomach was knotted by cramp. He could feel a grating sensation at the back of his throat, and a pain in his chest. He swallowed to try to get rid of the sore feeling, to soothe the pain, but to no avail. His head was spinning, and he was short of breath. It was a big strain just to try to breathe evenly.

"One, two; one, two," he repeated to himself.

Eventually the painful irritation in his throat passed, and he pushed himself onto his knees to look at his pillow. Was that blood? Fortunately, he couldn't see any dark stains there, although the pillowcase was a little dirty in places and would need to be washed. He shook his head and tried to concentrate, but his thoughts were still blurry.

Just a moment earlier he had been dreaming. But there was nothing resembling a narrative left behind in his memory, just a vague sense of guilt. But guilt over what? Over what he had done that evening? Irresponsibly going off with that woman to the refuge, giving her his medicine, and with it hope? He knew very well that giving someone hope also meant taking on an obligation. A person who is hungry, alone and in distress—tormented—eventually comes to a resigned standstill. He gets tired of running; he just waits for it all to be over. But if you give him hope, he will hang on to you for support with all his weight. What is the right thing to do in those circumstances? The world is full of people like that, man cannot bear their weight on his own. But God is distant and alien to those people; they prefer to see the Devil and evil spirits wherever they look. Maybe it would be better for them to seek help from medical science; it might be closer to them than God.

Laurentius nodded. Science was probably the best thing for them; they would always sully faith with their superstition, turn prayer into witchery. He could share his medicine for example; it was not much trouble to prepare some more.

He read out a morning Psalm: "The Lord sent them a lamp so that they would not get lost in the darkness or stumble on the rough ground…" But now he had to go and study, to let the light of learning illuminate his path. He made sure to mention the academy in his intercessory prayer, as well as the starving peasants and his parakeet.

"Clodia… Clodia…"

He repeated the name that was so familiar. His parakeet had always been by his side, soothing his melancholy. But what about that girl? He had been so tired yesterday evening that he had dared not think too much about what happened. But today? No, he still couldn't allow himself to think about it; it was impossible to know what to make of it. He had to focus on curing himself. His supply of tincture had run out, so he would need to prepare some more. But yesterday he had given away all his willow bark, so he may have to try some other medicine. Perhaps he should try the gold tincture which Boyle had mentioned?

Laurentius pushed himself up into a sitting position and, groggy from sleep, started to try to make himself more presentable. His fever seemed a little lighter now. Sleeping on a soft mattress with fresh straw filling must have helped a bit. And now that the room was warmer his pillow had even lost some of the mustiness from the journey. Maybe that was why the rotten smell in his nostrils was a little weaker too. His head still hurt slightly, but that may have been from the beer at the banquet. The thought even brought a faint smile to his face. A hangover was a sure sign that he had been initiated as a full and equal member of the student community. Which also meant that he would have to attend his lectures. Of course he would! Professor Dimberg had strongly advised him to go to Sjöbergh's private lecture on the soul, and given the circumstances it seemed like the right thing to do. What's more, he had read in the student guide the day before that all students were obliged to attend university according to the timetable, and to study with diligence and application. He planned to follow those rules to the letter.

"Diligence and application!" Laurentius repeated to himself.

Maybe yesterday's bloodletting had been some use after all? He tried to recall the theories he had read on the subject. He knew that bloodletting was supposed to weaken his sickness, but it could weaken his organism too. It was therefore essential to begin restorative treatment immediately afterwards. He had to be surrounded by other people, to gain succour from their joy and happiness. Loneliness could only make the sadness worse: the soul starts aching and memories dig themselves free. New experiences help to fight melancholia.

"So," Laurentius said, jumping purposefully to his feet. He had to banish everything other than the upcoming day from his thoughts, act according to a rational plan. He took a few steps in the direction of the wash bowl, planning to clean himself, but nearly fell flat on his face. His head was spinning.

"Of course," he said, feeling annoyed with himself as he groped for the bed behind him and sat down again. He could see a shimmering haze in front of him; all the objects in the room looked somehow transparent, intermeshed with each other. He gradually managed to focus his gaze again, and found himself staring at a small bread roll on the table in front of him.

Ever since the episode on the way to Dorpat, when the carriage had collapsed, he had felt nauseous if he tried to eat anything. There was a constant rotten smell in his nose and mouth, which made all food taste disgusting. That was why he had hardly managed to consume anything over the last few days. A lack of appetite might be a good thing during a famine, but it was true that hunger would not help his health at all. He had to eat something.

Clodia had given him that roll yesterday. He had been a little bewildered, dazed by all the bizarre events of the day, and had been unable to decide what to do with it, so he had put it on the table by his bed. It looked quite appetizing, but he was convinced it would taste the same as everything else. And he had nothing to drink, to wash the taste away. But what had Clodia said yesterday evening? "Maybe my bread and wine won't make you nauseous?" It was just a shame that she hadn't had any wine…

"Very well," Laurentius said to the roll.

He decided to take it with him; maybe he would even risk eating it later in the day. He rose to his feet again, this time very slowly, and carefully started to get dressed. Yesterday his veins had felt as brittle as glass, and now that same fragile feeling had spread to all of his limbs. He glanced round to give the room one final check, and then went downstairs. Outside, the cold rain was still drizzling, making ripples in the puddles. He noticed the maid bustling about with some logs near the awning.

"Good morning!" Laurentius called out to her. Then he remembered the logs in his room. "I see they eventually brought those logs yesterday; looks like I didn't waste half of my allowance on them after all. And thank you for lighting the fire. The room was pleasantly warm when I got back."

"Oh, but I didn't light the fire!" the girl replied, sounding a little taken aback. "The landlady called me to help with something, and I'm ashamed to admit that I forgot all about it. Please forgive me, I'll go and do it right away."

She grabbed a couple more pieces of kindling and, gripping them close to her chest, clattered upstairs. Laurentius stood and watched her as she went.

"Strange," he thought. "Did I get things muddled up, or was it her?" Maybe he had been tipsy from the beer yesterday? Laurentius shrugged his shoulders and set off into the light morning rain, in the direction of the academy.

As usual the lecture started with a prayer, which was fol-lowed, as Dimberg had promised, by the autumn semester private philosophy lecture. Professor Sjöbergh had announced that it would be a continuation of the general philosophical discussions from the previous year, and that it was intended as a supplementary lecture for those students who had to prepare for their disputation. It was not compulsory, so only a few of the more senior students had turned up; the younger ones were either still in bed, or had already headed into town to drink beer. Despite the small audience Professor Sjöbergh was in an enthusiastic mood, and it quickly became clear that he took the subject of the soul very seriously—it seemed to be of personal interest to him. He noted that one only had to go out into the street to be confronted with the question of how people's souls stayed fixed within their bodies. Dorpat was full of people whose souls were already teetering on the brink, and no small number who had completely failed to keep body and soul together. During the lecture it also became apparent that he was very interested in the new ideas regarding the nature of the soul which were doing the rounds in the academic correspondence. Sjöbergh had a wide circle of correspondents, and kept himself abreast of the new directions of thought. There were philosophers from Germany and England among his contacts, and he even received letters from Italy now and again. And Dimberg had just brought him some of the latest books back from his travels as well.

The students listened to Professor Sjöbergh's introductory words with a modicum of interest, but did not seem to be overly enthused by the lecture. Notwithstanding the innovative new thinking he made reference to, he hadn't changed the structure of the lecture very radically, and the students were forced to continue the discussion of Aristotle's treatise *On the Soul* for the fourth semester in a row. Lectures on the subject of the soul had started with this text since the Middle Ages, and the majority of students now reacted to it with a degree of sceptical disdain. They knew very well that contemporary philosophy had overturned all of Aristotle's positions, and that he was now only of historical interest.

It was only at the end of the lecture, when Sjöbergh referred to the anatomical theatre which Professor Below was planning, that the auditorium livened up again.

"This year we plan to do things differently. Our aim is to gain a better understanding of human anatomy, which should be instructive in our wider studies. Many questions pertaining to the soul should become clearer to us. We shall proceed with the dissection as soon as the city provides a suitable corpse, possibly even within the next few days."

The students were clearly excited by the prospect. Elsewhere, dissections were already a standard teaching method, but in Dorpat there was yet to be a single examination of a human corpse. Professor Below planned to conduct an initial trial, with the aim of subsequently securing official support from the city. He hoped to satisfy public curiosity by making the dissection open to all, as had already been the practice for several years in Leiden and Uppsala. Up until that time mostly only cats and dogs had been dissected for the edification of the students and amusement of the citizens, although a dead horse was once dragged onto the dissecting table too. But this hadn't generated as much interest as might have been expected. There weren't many students of medicine in Dorpat, and the other students weren't particularly drawn to looking at animals' internal organs—they could anyway see them at the market every day. But a systematic dissection of a human corpse was something altogether different. The university would be able to charge the citizens to watch it, so the whole enterprise might even end up turning a profit.

One of the students raised his hand to ask a question, his voice stammering from excitement. "Sorry, but will we be discussing the circulation of blood? And what is your position on the location of the soul? Will we cover the subject of blood as a substance which carries the life force around the body?"

For a moment, Professor Sjöbergh appeared to be lost in thought. But then, seeming to ignore the student's question, he turned to Laurentius and asked, "You're from Leiden, aren't you?"

"Yes," Laurentius replied, with a nod.

"Then you will definitely be familiar with the idea that the soul is located in the pineal gland?"

"That is the Cartesians' view, yes. But I am sure that it is a mistaken one."

"So you are a Platonist, then?"

"No. I am indeed an adherent of the Philosopher," Laurentius conceded, realizing that this would put him in a rather difficult position. From the way the auditorium had responded to the lecture it was clear that no one had much respect for Aristotle in these parts any more. His advocates tended to be old-fashioned bookworm types who had been educated in the old style and could not countenance the experimental method at all. Laurentius knew from his own experience in Leiden the kinds of disputes this question could provoke.

"Ah, so do you believe that he is correct to posit that the soul is the body's form?" Sjöbergh enquired in a slightly mocking tone.

Laurentius had a quick glance around and started trying to defend his position. "Is the soul not the actuality of the body? That is why we do not find the soul when we dissect a person's body, because a dead body is no longer an actual person. We can slice the body up into lots of little pieces, but we won't find the soul, because it simply isn't there any more.

But anyone who is alive experiences an aching within his soul sometimes, does he not? We are alive, and can therefore feel our souls inside us."

Peter took his turn: "I'm sure that the anatomical theatre will illuminate this matter for us. Perhaps Master Hylas has already sliced up lots of corpses and is therefore fully convinced of his positions, but experience teaches better than words, and experience is precisely what we need. After all, what else is theatre but an experience?"

He bowed, and then turned to Laurentius and smiled, making it clear that his interjection shouldn't be taken too seriously.

Professor Sjöbergh turned to the student who had initially asked the question. "I am sure that we will be able to discuss those questions during the disputation." He nodded in Laurentius' direction. "Perhaps Master Hylas could produce an overview of the relevant theories? But be sure not to leave the problems of blood and the pineal gland unaddressed, otherwise your fellow students may ask you some very awkward questions."

Sjöbergh's request was not in itself unusual. Students who had arrived from further afield often had to establish their reputations—by proving their debating skills and their knowledge of Latin, for example. Laurentius' educational background certainly played a role here—being from Leiden he was expected to be better versed in some matters than the other students, who were mostly from the provinces. But the decisive factor was probably that Dimberg had shown the other professors his disputation, 'On Fascination'. Sjöbergh clearly thought that Laurentius was competent enough to present the latest views to the other students. In any case, a trial disputation of this sort normally only consisted of an overview written by the presiding professor himself, words which he had put into the student's mouth. Sometimes that could be the only way for the professor to express radical ideas which might conflict with those generally accepted at the academy.

"I would be happy to write on that subject, presuming of course that I can have recourse to Professor Sjöbergh's personal expertise, and of course his excellent library," replied Laurentius, accepting the proposal.

"Naturally," said Sjöbergh. "Come to see me at lunchtime today and we can discuss the matter further. But you should bear in mind that you will have to cover the printing costs yourself. We shan't be able to make any exceptions in your case, especially given current circumstances."

Friday Lunchtime

IT WAS NOW RAINING SO HEAVILY that none of the students dared to venture outside, and they had gathered on the ground floor of the academy, where they were busy talking among themselves.

"I don't know; doesn't look like it's going to ease off any time soon," said Peter with a sigh as he looked outside at the river of rainwater flowing down the street. "If we just stay here waiting for it to stop then no one will get home before evening."

Laurentius shrugged his shoulders.

"There's a decent tavern across the street, right behind the church—we could go to have something to eat in there, and they serve coffee too, or at least they did yesterday. We could all do with some of that now," Peter continued with a knowledgeable air. The others nodded before rushing en masse through the door, holding their hats firmly pressed onto their heads with one hand. They splashed through the rainwater with their capes flapping behind them, round the corner and straight through the door of the first building they came to. Laurentius ran with them, pushing the large door of the tavern open to arrive in a warm room which smelt of coffee. In this town of tall, narrow, medieval buildings nearly every staircase led to some sort of tavern. Some citizens had also obtained a brewing licence from the city, and sold food and drink from the ground floors of their own homes. Peter explained that there were yet to be any proper coffee shops in Dorpat, but there were certain places where one could drink it. Laurentius was not overly surprised to hear him speak of Dorpat coffee culture. If opera had already arrived there, there was no reason why coffee should not have too. In any case, it was a welcome discovery, as he had already grown accustomed to drinking coffee back in Holland, and he had been expecting Dorpat to be a much more provincial kind of place.

Laurentius gave his face a quick wipe with his wet hands, and sat down at a table by the window with the other students.

"One pipe and a coffee, please," he said to the girl who came up to the table. "…with sugar," he added after pausing for thought. The others ordered themselves drinks of various descriptions, shouting rowdily over one another, and a long discussion ensued over what they might order to eat.

Laurentius sat looking out of the window, waiting for his coffee to arrive in trepidation, unsure what it might taste like in Dorpat. In Holland they tended to make coffee in long-handled cups, Turkish style. But there was scope for a lot of things to go wrong during preparation: it was important not to let the fine powder boil for too long, for example. In any case, he had decided it was safer to order his coffee with sugar. It might make it cloyingly sweet, but it would at least hide any unpleasant taste resulting from deficiencies in preparation. He was also afraid that otherwise it might taste disgusting, like everything else in Dorpat.

Peter and the short student sitting next to him had started arguing about something, switching smoothly over to the

Elfdalian dialect of their home region, which Laurentius only understood a few words of. But he got the impression that they were discussing financial matters. He tried to follow the conversation for a while, but eventually turned away to look out of the window again. Rainwater was streaming down the thick glass windowpanes, but he could just about make out the hazy forms of people on the street. They had their dark rain capes pulled tight around them, the hems flapping in the rain, which seemed to be even heavier than before. They were stooped forward as they struggled against the wind, hurrying to find shelter, to reach their destinations, wherever those might be. Yesterday evening, when he met Clodia, Laurentius had also had a goal. He had truly felt that he had his own will, that he could strive for something, desire something. Achieve something. But now that feeling had gone, and his thoughts were again in total disarray.

"Who ordered the pipes?" the waitress asked.

Laurentius smiled at her, gripped hold of his pipe, and took a deep puff. The tobacco was acrid and bitter-tasting, but he carried on smoking nonetheless, hoping that together with the warmth of the room the hot smoke might hold his damp sickness at bay for a while. There was no sense in ordering anything to eat as he was already quite sure that he would not be able to swallow a single mouthful.

"Thank you," he said to the waitress.

He had worked out his plan for the day as soon as he woke up, while he was still capable of thinking clearly. He had to apportion the time available to him rationally before the bile of his sickness started to rise again. There could be no risk of deviation; everything had to be predictable, certain and clear. All chance meetings and unexpected invitations would only cause more confusion and worsen his condition. He had to make a strict plan and stick to it. This was exactly the kind of forward planning which Spinoza referred to in his *Ethics*—the predetermined, unerring execution of local motion. Science, in other words. It was how an arrow must feel as it flies from the bow, straight to its target. The wooden stick was lifeless and lacked a soul, but forward momentum took it inexorably to the point at which it was aimed. One could determine the precise spot which the tip would pierce in advance—the arrow's own will had no influence on that at all. But yesterday evening he had had his own goal. He had been more than just a mechanical force set into motion, like Kircher's automated organ. He had really felt he had his own free will; he had experienced a feeling akin to freedom. Was it possible for the arrow to come to a standstill in mid-flight, to snap in two from the strain and lose its grey goose-feather tail? To waver, to veer off course, to do something other than arrive unerringly at the predetermined target? Yesterday evening he had felt that it was.

"What do you think of the disputation topic which Sjöbergh proposed?" Peter asked, apparently having successfully concluded the argument with his neighbour.

Laurentius shrugged his shoulders. "I've actually written a number of disputations already—not for assessment, just for practice. But I've no idea how good his library is. It could be difficult to produce an overview of the latest trends in thinking without access to the right literature."

"As far as I know he's got a good selection of the latest writing," Peter said. "But that Sjöbergh of ours is secretly a dedicated Cartesian... You'll see that for yourself shortly—he's sure to have all the books you need."

"So does he lend out his books?" Laurentius asked in surprise.

"It has been known," Peter replied.

That certainly improved the situation a little. Given the state he was in, Laurentius found the thought of trying to work at someone else's house a little daunting. All the more so if the household was a large one. It could end up being more of a social visit than an opportunity for academic research. There were some students who deliberately used that kind of research assignment to set themselves up in the professor's home. At least then they didn't need to worry about where their meals were coming from.

"Where does he live anyway?" Laurentius asked.

"Right here behind the academy. Lunch tends to be pretty good at his place; I've been there a few times myself," Peter replied.

He then started to divulge his knowledge about which of the professors had a reputation for feeding their students. He had already been in Dorpat for a while, which meant that he was already well informed about the various local characters. He knew which of the professors stubbornly maintained a distance from their students and never invited them to their homes, making it clear that they would never be seen in such dubious company. And there was another category of professors who occasionally invited people to their homes, but provided scant food and nothing more than weak beer to drink.

"You can sometimes even get wine at Sjöbergh's, if he happens to have any in. In any case, definitely best not to order anything to eat here," explained the young man sitting next to Peter. Laurentius noticed that although his boots were falling apart, with their heels worn crooked, he was wearing a well-cut overcoat. His hat was also fashionably narrow-brimmed, folded and pinned at three points, and there was even a sodden feather poking out from it. It seemed he belonged to that band of students who spent all their state stipend and the allowance from their parents on fancy clothes and revelry, and were then forced to scrape by at their friends' or even their professors' expense for the rest of the year. Laurentius was sure that Peter and this student had been arguing on that very subject. Those sorts would normally end up working as private teachers. Decorum was a relative concept for them, which meant that they had a knack for getting on with people. Laurentius liked those sorts much more than the ones who abided obsessively by the rules of propriety—they were normally unjustifiably full of themselves and would brandish their swords about at so much as one wrong word. Unfortunately, however, those kinds of students made up the majority.

He smiled and nodded in gratitude. Now, however, he had started worrying about what might happen should the food at Sjöbergh's taste as bad as everywhere else, and how he could then maintain a polite demeanour and avoid doing anything untoward.

"I don't particularly enjoy going to lunches," Laurentius explained. "I hope he won't be offended if I go to visit him after lunch instead."

"Well, I don't know… Why should he be offended? I think he probably invited you more out of politeness than anything else. But it would still be best to let him know that you can't go," Peter advised.

"It would be a little odd for me to go and announce on my own behalf that unfortunately I can't come," Laurentius said sceptically.

"I can go!" announced the student in the fashionable hat, perking up. "Maybe he'll invite me in to lunch instead?"

Peter gave him a slap on the shoulder. "You, Jonas, are just too sly."

Laurentius shrugged his shoulders. "Of course, why not? Tell him that I feel lousy and had to go home with fever. It's true anyway. If it weren't raining so hard I would have gone back to my lodgings by now. Tell him that I'll come in the evening instead."

Jonas began to drain his mug of beer in large gulps. "But what do you have against the food here anyway, if I may ask? Magnus said that you didn't eat anything at the banquet either?"

"Really?" asked Laurentius in surprise.

"Yes. We happened to be discussing your good self. Are you in training for winter? As far as I know all other creatures prepare for winter by eating as much as they possibly can. Or maybe you are showing your solidarity with the peasants?" Jonas asked, and burst out laughing.

Laurentius forced a smile. "As far as I know fasting has never been considered a crime. But if I remember rightly, gluttony is one of the seven deadly sins. I don't know, is it better to prepare for winter or for death?"

Jonas stopped laughing and shook his head. "You know it's one thing to take care of your soul. But if that soul is no longer there inside you, then you have nothing left to care for, do you?"

At that they all fell abruptly silent. They sat looking out of the small window at the peasants with ragged beards and shabby hats, plodding barefoot down the wet street. Notwithstanding that the guards had been ordered not to let any more ragamuffins through the city gates, there they were, shuffling along in the rain with slow heavy footsteps, hands pressed together as if in prayer, their gazes downcast. They probably hoped to find work so that they could earn enough money to buy some bread and somehow keep body and soul together. But the prospect seemed unlikely given the wretched condition they were in. Laurentius recalled the peasants he had seen who had fled starvation, and were now sprawled across the mouldy hay in the barn, waiting for food from the city. He thought of the girl whom he had given his last fever medicine to, and of her mother, who had tried to sell her body to earn money for food.

"Yes, quite hopeless," Laurentius said in agreement.

He found himself wondering whether there would still be any of the medicine left, and whether it had been of any help. He would now have to go to the apothecary's again to get hold of more medicaments. After all, he had finally given the girl and her mother hope. He should go to the river to gather more willow bark; then he could go to the barn and see how they were. By going there the previous evening he had taken on an obligation. But for some unknown reason he had been feeling guilty ever since, as if he had done something wrong— committed a bad deed rather than a good one. So he had to go back. Given the weather the prospect was an unpleasant one, but there was nothing else he could do. Even if he wasn't sure he would be able to find the right building again.

"Incidentally, who is responsible for that barn which was set up for the peasants? I understand that they're not normally allowed through the city gates?" Laurentius asked.

"That's right, they're not allowed! But then look at this lot here!" Jonas exclaimed. He finished off his beer with a disgruntled look on his face, as if he were personally offended that there were hungry peasants loitering in the streets.

Peter shook his head. "But I don't think there's more than a couple of soldiers on duty; they can only check the barn from time to time. It's not as if they don't have enough to worry about. Just this morning I heard from my landlady that they plan to start transporting grain from here to Sweden soon. The situation could start to turn very nasty indeed," said Peter, sounding genuinely concerned. There were fears that if the number of starving peasants continued to grow, then the city would have to start using soldiers to restrain them. In those circumstance there was the danger of plague breaking out, and if plague reached town, it would spare no one. No matter whether student or peasant. "That barn is actually pretty far from town, Aruküla way, so they're not likely to end up here just by chance. The city probably hopes that if there is an outbreak of disease, at least it won't reach the citizens straight away," Peter added.

Friday Afternoon

H E COULD REMEMBER THE DARK, high walls, the moaning of hungry children, the muddy road. They had gone out through the Russian Gate, crossed a rotten bridge over a river edged with willow trees, and then taken a turning off the road. That part had been straightforward.

He stood looking at the trees from which he had cut the bark a couple of days earlier. He remembered how the peasants had appeared as if from nowhere, and instinctively his hand reached for the hilt of his sword. But right now there was no one to be seen. The river looked safe and tranquil; the road seemed in a better state than he remembered—even the shabby houses across the river looked more inviting than before.

"Now then," he said. He went up to one of the trees, swiftly cut a few strips of bark to take with him and hurried onwards.

There was a strange silence hanging over the dilapidated hovels which made up the outskirts of town. Occasionally someone would appear and cast a sidelong glance at Laurentius, and wide-eyed children stood and watched him from the doorways just as before, but this time he steeled himself not to show any concern. The buildings all seemed unfamiliar, so he carried on walking in no particular direction, occasionally peering beyond the houses to see if he could spot anything resembling the barn. But he could no longer remember which way he and the woman had gone. Peter had mentioned that the barn was situated somewhere in Aruküla, but since he was still unfamiliar with Dorpat geography he only had the vaguest idea where that might be. Wherever he looked there were just low houses and small outbuildings, nothing which tallied with his recollection of where they had been.

Ever since the memory of the sick girl had come back to him as he sat in the coffee house, he could think of nothing else. Had his powder been of any use? Had there been enough? Had her mother managed to administer it properly? Maybe it was because he was sick himself that he was worried about the girl, that he could empathize with her. Maybe he sensed that if she got better, then he would too.

Laurentius hurried onwards without bothering to think if he was going in the right direction.

He had sat in the coffee shop talking with Peter and Jonas for a little longer before telling them that he needed to get some medicine and heading to the apothecary's. The apothecary had seemed surprisingly well educated, and demonstrated some expertise in his field, speaking at length and quite eloquently about various treatments, and employing plenty of learned Latin terms. He took obvious pride in showing Laurentius a list of remedies which he had got printed at the Dorpat press. On hearing that Laurentius came from Leiden, he started telling him all about the situation in Dorpat, in particular about the climate, which he believed was particularly conducive to certain types of ailments, especially melancholia, and he had added that the nearby marshes also played their part. Laurentius even started to regret that he had been so wary of seeing an apothecary before letting blood. This one didn't seem like a quack at all. It was only when he pulled a cunning expression and started to justify the local population's fondness for the bottle that Laurentius realized that something was not quite right after all. A weakness for the tipple was known to be the second vocational malaise of apothecaries, after quackery. The apothecary had then all but forced Laurentius to take a small bottle of medicine made to his own personal recipe, at which Laurentius had hurriedly tried to explain that he only needed some ordinary fever medicine. He had tried to explain to the apothecary that one should take great care when preparing tinctures, since too much spirit could do more harm than good, making the sick soul even less receptive to treatment. But the apothecary would have none of it.

"Pure drivel," he had said. "It's scientifically proven. The stronger the spirit, the more powerful the tincture. I've also got something with an adder preserved in it here. I use it myself; it's a most effective remedy, in particular against curses. You rub it onto your neck like this, back and front."

Laurentius politely declined the adder tincture and bought a small bottle of ordinary spirit instead. To make a proper tincture he would need to distil the extract of the willow bark, but if he soaked the bark in spirit and used it carefully it should still help to restore the child's fragile constitution. If he could teach her mother how to administer the medicine, then she should be able to manage the child's treatment herself. Although given what the apothecary had said about the local people, there was always the danger that she would just drink it.

The town outskirts came to an end; the road started winding uphill past a small pond, and then Laurentius recognized where he was. He could see the same narrow footpath which he had walked down yesterday evening. This was the spot where he had been startled by the vision of an elf king, hovering above the river. Now he just smiled at how superstitious he had been.

He pushed on, struggling across the patchwork of muddy fields and occasionally passing the odd tree, until eventually he spotted a building which resembled the barn, standing alone, deserted on the hillside. There were no guards there; nor were any of the former inhabitants to be seen. The large double doors were wide open, and the space where dozens of people had been lying packed tightly side by side was now empty. There were some tattered bits of clothing strewn across the floor, but otherwise very little which would have suggested that people once lived here. Some wisps of straw, some square patches on the earth floor, but otherwise emptiness. Laurentius started to suspect that the city had finally decided to shut down the refuge and ordered the soldiers to send everyone packing. But then he noticed that at least one person was still there, hunched in the shadows to his right, peering at him hostilely.

"Hello," blurted Laurentius. "Where are the others?"

The question was met by a shake of the head, from which Laurentius concluded that the hunched figure probably didn't understand German. But he decided to try again.

"The others, where?"

The old woman continued to stare up at him, gesturing somewhere into the distance. Laurentius turned his gaze away.

"Soldiers?" he asked.

The old woman waved her hand towards the forest again, and when Laurentius looked he could indeed make out a vague, bluish object against the dark grey strip of forest which ran along the riverbank. It may have been a soldier, but it could just as well have been a tree stump or a large boulder.

"Thank you," Laurentius said.

He hurried on with an anxious look on his face. A large number of people had evidently gone that way before him, since the grass had been trampled and the road churned into mud. Once he got closer to the bluish-grey form it turned out that it was indeed a soldier. Laurentius came to a standstill and stood there awkwardly. What should he say?

"It certainly is raining hard," he observed by way of a greeting.

The soldier raised his hand in a friendly gesture, having evidently established from Laurentius' dress and his sword that he wasn't a peasant. "It's pouring fit to wash the teeth out of your mouth!" the soldier replied.

"Has the refuge over there been shut down, then?" Laurentius asked, trying to make his question sound like nothing more than passing curiosity.

"Oh no," the soldier seemed happy to inform him. "Most of them are here in this cave."

Only then did Laurentius notice that he was standing very close to the mouth of what looked like a man-made cave. Inside he could make out people's backs and their hats, and there were children standing at the outer edge, pressed tightly against their parents to shelter from the pouring rain.

"So what's happening then?" Laurentius enquired.

"Well, this morning we heard they were scrapping here overnight. It was a right muddled story; they mentioned some sort of willow or alder king. In any case, they battered one of the women with cudgels and dragged her into the caves. When we arrived for the morning watch she was already half-dead.

Now they're going to take her away on a stretcher; Pastor Mellinck is here as well," the soldier explained.

As the crowd parted and two peasants carrying a stretcher stepped out from their midst, Laurentius felt a cold shudder run down him. The scene reminded him of watching the ragamuffin being lugged off after the tanner's lad had knocked him dead. He didn't need to ask who was lying there under the sodden cloth. The pastor was walking behind the stretcher, dressed in a broad black robe, talking to the soldier beside him in a serious tone of voice. The soldier was nodding, distractedly fumbling with the hilt of his sword as he went.

"Have you found out who is guilty?" Laurentius asked, struggling to hold back a powerful wave of nausea. A rotten stench was wafting up from somewhere nearby.

"How could we hope to now? They all claim to have seen nothing. There are plenty of incidents like that these days. The city gives the women tokens to exchange for food, then the lads come and take them off them. If the woman has any sense in her she gets away with her life, but if she puts up a fight, she'll get a whack. That's how things are round here, see," the soldier explained, sounding like he knew what he was talking about. "We have all kinds of bother here, but we don't have enough men to enforce the law."

The peasants huffed and puffed, cursing to themselves as they carried the stretcher past, and Laurentius stared down at the ground, trying not to look at it. He could see long, brownish grass, wet with rain, and the muddy path ahead. The men were walking briskly, and the load swayed slightly in time with their footsteps. They quickly came up alongside Laurentius, and started to descend the slope. Then one of them slipped on the wet grass and nearly fell over, and the other one staggered about as he tried to maintain his balance. The cloth which had been placed over the stretcher slipped to one side, and a bony leg clad in torn leather foot straps was left dangling over the edge at an odd angle.

"Curses!" exclaimed one of the peasants.

The soldier leapt towards them and grabbed hold of the stretcher. "Nearly went for a tumble there!" he announced jauntily as he placed the leg back onto the stretcher.

The crowd started clamouring noisily. Someone started addressing them in an authoritative-sounding voice, while others mumbled angrily. Some of them were pointing their fingers in Laurentius' direction.

"What's wrong with them?" he asked.

By now the pastor and the soldier accompanying him had arrived alongside Laurentius. The pastor lifted his hand and lightly touched the brim of his hat, smiling broadly. He was around fifty years old, with a full beard, and his hair was cut short like a Pietist or English Roundhead. Laurentius cast his gaze downwards. "Good afternoon."

"Greetings. Jacob Mellinck, shepherd of souls. What brings you here?" the pastor asked cheerily. "Were you out having a walk?"

"Laurentius Hylas—I matriculated just recently," Laurentius announced in a sheepish-sounding voice. "I was indeed walking nearby; I'm acquainting myself with the locality. I gather that there are a lot of marshes here, and I have heard talk of healing springs as well. I understand there have even been balneological investigations conducted?"

That had been one of the many pieces of local knowledge which the apothecary had shared with Laurentius. He had

told him that one Professor Micrander (his personal acquaintance, no less) had conducted investigations into the healing
properties of the waters near Dorpat.

"Yes indeed," the pastor replied. "I have even been involved
in that myself—the springs here produce a slime which is very
easily absorbed into the joints and can drive away serious
illnesses. But there is less and less time available for research
these days. You can see for yourself what I have to deal with
on a daily basis—the ignorant masses."

Mellinck gestured towards the rowdy crowd of women
and children. The children appeared to be trying to explain
something to their mothers, worriedly shaking their heads.
They were dirty and unruly, and the pastor's description of
them as ignorant seemed quite a charitable assessment.

"What happened? What are they so worked up about?"
Laurentius asked.

"Just now? Well, look, the corpse started bleeding. They're
saying that the blood starts flowing when the corpse is carried
past the murderer. But it's just silly superstition, of course. The
soldiers moved the woman into a different position—that's
why the bleeding started."

"Ah, really?" said Laurentius, unable to think of anything
else to say. He could see bright-red blood trickling down the
blades of grass, mixing with the rainwater, and viscous brown
streaks had formed in the pools of water collecting in the
men's footprints.

"Is she dead, then?" he asked the pastor.

"Yes, she died before I arrived. It was an ugly scene, to be
sure. At first I thought that it was because of those tokens—we
have had a lot of trouble with those here; it would have been
better if the city had found some other way of tackling the

problem. But it seems that it was in fact the same old witchery story. They were talking about a king appearing from somewhere and giving the woman some powder, so that she could go and worship Satan. Normally they just come and complain to us about it, but in these troubled times they have started taking justice into their own hands."

Laurentius barely managed to nod. He should have known that this would happen. He felt tears welling up as the shame and remorse overpowered him. Maybe there was some truth in what they said about the corpse bleeding in the murderer's proximity, even if the phenomenon had been found to have no scientific basis. In any case, he was the one who had given the child the medicine, so he could be seen to bear direct responsibility for her mother's death. It had never occurred to him that people might think it was some sort of witch powder. But the way things were, only the slightest excuse was needed to accuse someone of occult activities. He shook his head despondently, unable to think of anything to say.

"Yes, that's a familiar story round these parts," the pastor eventually said. "I am constantly trying to tell them witchery is just a figment of the imagination, that it is caused by melancholy, but just you try explaining anything in rational terms to this lot! They simply won't listen. They'll insist that they consort with Satan and fly through the sky on goats, and all manner of things. One old man once stubbornly assured me that he was a werewolf, and that he frequently visited hell to fetch grain. The court dismissed the case twice, but the crazy old man wouldn't drop his story. It's as if they're troubled in the head or something," Mellinck said, sounding as if he were seriously vexed by the situation.

Laurentius smiled ruefully. It was clear that the pastor's views on the subject came straight out of Johann Weyer's work on the illusion of demons.

"In my view *De praestigiis daemonum* provides a very balanced explanation," Laurentius said, just to say something, anything at all, to hide his grief and despair. He had used that very book to try to understand his own condition better, to try to find a cure.

"Oh, you've read it?" asked the pastor, livening up. "It's a most sensible text. I have been referring to Weyer for some time to try to make clear that witchery is a sickness of the mind rather than something based in reality. But we still have all sorts of trouble with it. Since you are new in town I should warn you that folk are very superstitious here. They see spirits and demons wherever they look. They have listened to just enough of the teachings of Christ to use the Bible in their spells. Forselius and I even started running schools for the country folk, to try to tackle the terrible ignorance and superstition which prevails. It's a great shame that Forselius met his demise like that. But fortunately new schools are being established all the time, and I believe that the situation is slowly starting to improve," said Mellinck, gazing thoughtfully into the distance as he spoke.

"That's good to hear," Laurentius agreed distractedly. "But that woman... did she have any kin?"

He didn't dare to ask directly about the sick girl, in case that aroused further suspicion. But nor could he just forget the matter.

"Any kin?" the pastor asked, a note of surprise in his voice. "If she had any kin, then she probably wouldn't have got into this mess in the first place. It is the ones who have no one at all who have it the hardest. In these parts they send off their elder children to go to work for strangers as early as ten, and then when the hard times come they have no one left. There are plenty of orphans round here."

Laurentius was already familiar with that sad state of affairs. At one time he had even roamed around like those children himself. He had been sent away from home at the age of eight, and now he could remember nothing at all, not even his mother's or father's face. He had been forced to find work on the farms, to live among strangers, surviving on scant pickings, crying himself to sleep every night. All the time he had yearned to go home; once he had even tried to run away.

"This one had a child too," the pastor continued. "Most probably begot with some stranger in the village, and then both mother and daughter were sent packing. The wretched little thing is still there in the barn. She appears to be sick."

Laurentius and the pastor headed to the barn together and looked in through the door. The old woman peered at them suspiciously from the corner again, but when Mellinck addressed her she directed them to the back of the barn, where they found the girl sleeping under an old soldier's cape.

The pastor scratched his head thoughtfully. "I'll take her into my household for now, until it's clear what will happen next. That is if she survives, of course: no one can know that yet. But she will be sure to die if she is left here."

Laurentius squatted down to look at the small sleeping figure. The girl opened her eyes slightly and sighed.

"The king," she whispered barely audibly.

Friday Evening

T HE COLD HAD ARRIVED SUDDENLY, and by the time
Laurentius arrived at Sjöbergh's the earlier rain had
given way to fat, wet snowflakes. At first they melted as they
touched the ground, forming a thick, dirty sludge under
people's feet and the horses' hooves, but as the weather got
colder and colder the snow coated the mud in a thick white
layer. The wind had picked up and was rattling the windows,
blowing white flakes against the panes, down people's collars
and into their faces.

Laurentius pushed the basket of wood closer towards the
fireplace and tossed a couple more logs onto the fire.

The wood smouldered and hissed as it released its dampness into the room. The languid flame didn't give off enough
heat to be felt more than a couple of steps from the fireplace.
But when Laurentius squatted down in front of the hearth,
shaking from the cold, he immediately started to feel hot
and uncomfortable. He could hear the stone chimney breast
crackle, and the thick grey smoke and warm air disappearing
up the chimney with a whoosh. As he bent down to position
the logs so that they would catch better, he felt his face flush
bright red like a drunkard's and his skin smarted, although
that may have just been his fever rising again. The tempera-
ture in the room oscillated continually between hot and cold.

The warmth spread outwards from the fireplace in concentric circles, like ripples around a stone tossed into the water. They grew weaker a couple of steps from the centre, forming little ringlets as they collided with various obstacles, covering the small floor space of the room unevenly. The external walls of the building should have held that warmth in, deflecting it back into the room, coddling it, nurturing it. But they did not. They were made of plaster, powder—dust which had set firm. They were a bridge between warmth and cold, a bridge between inhabitable and uninhabitable spaces.

Laurentius rocked backwards and forwards on his heels.

He had lit the fire himself, without calling for the maid, struggling with the birch bark kindling with hands which were stiff from cold, growing gradually more frustrated with how long it was taking. But calling for her would only have made things worse. He would have had to make conversation, exchange pleasantries. He had no time for those kinds of formalities now.

Laurentius sat down at the table and rested his head in his hands.

As soon as he had seen the woman's corpse on the stretcher by the caves he had been sure that his melancholy would deepen. He had felt fear, almost panic. Looking at the corpse he had realized that he was no different to those people who lived in irrational fear of witchery, who were gripped by the talons of crazed superstition, who could only be saved by education. He had been one of them once; he had also been afraid. As he stood there by the cave he had sensed that they were being watched by a king, wearing a crown and a cape. And all the people there had looked as if they were painted onto paper: in small, two-dimensional, unnatural colours. As if he were looking at a picture of which he was also a part. Only the king had seemed real.

Blood had been dripping onto the blades of grass. But then Pastor Mellinck had arrived and spoken about writers, debated theories and methodologies, and complained about financial strictures. He had provided a logical explanation for everything, proved that there was nothing unusual or supernatural going on. And he had added that due to crop failure Forselius' noble initiative might come to nothing. Laurentius had nodded, and as they shook hands Mellinck had said that he should come to visit without fail. Laurentius had felt like he was at a Sunday service, where the priest had given his benediction after Mass. He had felt his anxiety slowly subside, giving way to a momentary shimmering in front of his eyes, before clarity had dawned. As he had headed towards town it had started to snow. He knew now that only study could save him. He proceeded to Sjöbergh's house hurriedly, even eagerly. Almost joyfully.

The housekeeper had directed him up the steps to a slightly overheated study. All the books had matching leather binding, with raised bands visible on the exterior, and there was a piece of parchment stuck onto every spine. The abbreviated titles of the books had been inscribed onto the parchment in handsome uniform handwriting. In the case of the multiple-volume works this was a fairly long sequence of letters. There may have been as many as two hundred books on the shelves which lined the walls of the room, mostly fairly modern publications. Sjöbergh had regarded him thoughtfully and even apologized, after a fashion, for his behaviour that morning. He had explained that excessive acquiescence could kill a discussion dead, and that he was expecting the disputation to provoke a stimulating debate. He had no doubt that a well-educated young man like Laurentius was capable of writing a very good thesis, and he planned to give him a fairly free hand.

"Cartesian interpretations accommodate our contemporary understanding of physics much better; Aristotle is outmoded now," said the professor with an expression which suggested that he regretted that fact. "But Descartes's theories of the soul have received a great deal of critical attention. Make sure to address them also."

Laurentius had nodded. After some brief discussion with the professor and having listened to his advice he decided to take just three books with him. The first one was naturally Aristotle's *On the Soul*; then the second volume of Alsted's encyclopaedia, which dealt with pneumatics and psychology in general, and the third book was Descartes's *Passiones animae*.

He had been quite determined to start writing his disputation that very evening. Full of nervous excitement about the prospect of getting home and starting it, he was already drafting arguments and planning the structure in his mind. It might be what he needed to finally comprehend his own condition. Maybe it would even give him some sort of explanation for everything else which had been happening. He had bid a polite farewell to Sjöbergh, trying not to reveal what a hurry he was in, and stepped outside, straight into a gust of white flakes. It was a fine, fresh autumn evening, and there was a whirling flurry of snow falling. He took a better grip of the heavy tomes which he had bundled in cloths, wrapped his coat around him and hurried homewards, feeling happy. He had the books, now he wanted to get down to work. Now he had a clear target in sight, like an arrow fired from a bow.

His head had first started spinning when he squatted down in front of the fire, hurriedly trying to get the hissing logs to catch. As he snatched up the logs he had grazed his knuckles against the stone fireplace, drawing blood, and now he felt a stinging pain. The fire seemed not to want to light, and as much as he blew and blew, the logs would not catch. The acrid smoke reminded him that the vile, rotten stench had still not gone anywhere. He saw the scene from the cave, the episode from his dream, where he had been squatting down in front of damp logs, trying to get them to light with wisps of straw. There had been a crow there, or maybe a magpie… For some reason he started worrying about the sick girl again. His fever stealthily started to rise, and he grew ever more anxious.

"No, I must get down to work!" he told himself.

He grabbed hold of one of the books determinedly, and pulled it towards him. Alsted's encyclopaedia provided a good overview of the relevant theories; it was systematically organized, and quite well written too. He decided it would be worth his using a similar structure. Laurentius found himself a sheet of paper to make notes, and tried to concentrate. The book was large and heavy, but the script itself was tiny and faded, and it hurt his eyes to read it, as if his eyeballs were being scratched with a rasp. Scraping, irritating, distracting. The printer had clearly tried to fit as much text onto each page as possible, but due to the small typeface all the details had run together, and the text was quivering in the flickering candlelight, making it even harder to read. Laurentius shook his head in frustration, and leant closer towards the text. But the words and characters remained distant and disjointed, as if he were looking at them through a fog. Sometimes they were blurred, but then suddenly they would come swimming towards him from out of the whitish mist, acquiring razor-sharp definition. Despite all his efforts the sentences simply would not come together into a single whole; they were empty, voiceless, hollow phrases which were devoid of any meaning, and they just kept slipping out of his grasp. The yellowed, porous paper of the encyclopaedia started glowing in the candlelight, dominating his entire field of vision with its luminescence; then his eyes started smarting, and he had to close them. He was aware of a low humming sound, a strange unsettling drone, breaking the earlier oppressive silence.

"Hopeless," Laurentius said to himself.

He put the volume to one side and looked out of the window, but he could still see the lines of text quivering before his eyes; he could almost make out some of the individual letters. He could see white snowflakes whirling through the night air. He breathed in. Then once again. In and out. His breath almost looked like a fog floating in front of him. He noticed a bad taste in his mouth again. The snowflakes were striking the windowpane with a gentle pinging sound, and the window frames were rattling in the draught.

"What's going to happen?" Laurentius asked himself.

The feeling of uneasy torpor was becoming more oppressive. He felt completely alone, helpless and vulnerable. His earlier enthusiasm for the disputation had totally disappeared.

"Clodia…"

Laurentius felt as if he were no longer quite present in his room, as if he were physically located in his lodgings, but somehow differently from usual. Almost as if he were dreaming and separated from reality, lying with his eyes shut, surrendering to oblivion. Was his consciousness no longer capable of distinguishing between reality and imagination?

All the colours in his room seemed very pale; even the candle flame was somehow a cold, sterile white colour. Was that reality? Then, out of the corner of his eye, he noticed something black moving across the pale wall. A spider. He watched it, thinking that it must have been crawling there for some time already, behind his back, beyond his field of vision. It occurred to him how often that must happen. Things are right there, all around, but you do not perceive them; you are completely unaware of their existence. You only notice them when they make themselves known, when they start moving, buzzing and hopping. But where were they the rest of the time? Did they actually exist? When my head is resting on the pillow and someone comes to stand beside my bed, watches me and pats me on the head so tenderly that I do not feel it—has that actually happened? If my eyes are closed, then I do not know.

Laurentius went up to the wall and observed the spider. It was moving somewhere, towards an unknown goal.

"This is now the company you must keep," he whispered to the arachnid. "Cold and black."

Or maybe it was just a mechanical being, of the sort that Descartes had described. A being which had no free will, no soul, no humours, just an impulse for forward movement. Which felt no pain, which knew nothing of good or evil. An arrow fired from a bow. He watched the spider busily going about its affairs, and he hoped that that was indeed how things were. But the insect didn't care what he thought; it just continued on its way, eventually reaching the window and crawling onto the window frame. There beyond the window he could see an expanse of darkness. Cold and black.

Laurentius shook his head. No, that spider was no company of his. The company he would keep were the birds up in the sky, light and radiant.

He pushed the window open and leant out. The crisp, cold air helped him to focus his thoughts, and he gulped down lungfuls of it. It was slightly acrid, but still damp and fresh.

He had to balance the heat of his fever somehow. He watched as puffs of steam flew from his mouth, confirming that he was still breathing, still alive. He stood in complete silence, slowly inhaling the cool air, watching the little shreds of mist flying from his mouth and then dissipating, disappearing together with the soft glow of candlelight into the promised land of darkness beyond.

Was his breath like that spider scurrying across the wall? Always present, but seeming not to exist until the moment it made itself known. A moment earlier the very same breath which had disappeared into the darkness had been inside his lungs, in contact with his blood, animating his body. That breath would now be absorbed into the damp air of night and became a part of it; it would continue to flow in and out of his lungs even as his spirit and his reason became more and more dulled by the advance of evening. Even when he had collapsed into bed, when he had fallen asleep, into the void of memories. So was the breath which flowed in and out of him life itself, that which made him human? If one raised a mirror to it, the glass surface would display the condensed vapour, the warmth of his body, its damp humours. That was life, ever present. Like logs hissing in the fireplace, demonstrating the existence of something intangible. In the same way that the reflection in a mirror represented the existence of a person, a painting represented a person's face and body, and the letters on the paper represented the voice. Some form of existence was being realized. Always alien to itself, always uncertain.

Laurentius could see some lone lights flickering faintly in the darkness, candles which people had lit to mark their homes. To guard their warmth, and keep strangers at bay. He felt very acutely that he was a stranger in this town. Everyone was a stranger there.

He sighed.

The fever was to blame for all this. He had to try to get better, to keep his reason clear. There was nothing left for it but to take the spirit he got from the apothecary and the willow bark he had gathered by the river. He could not allow his fever to get any worse, and the willow bark and the spirit were now the only remedies available to him. Maybe what he really needed was *aurum potabile*, but even Dimberg didn't know how to make that.

"Where is one supposed to find it?" he mumbled to himself. But he knew that it was just the unattainable dream of alchemists, not a remedy tested by medical science.

He found himself thinking about the sick girl, and the vision of the king. He picked up his knapsack to look for the bottle of spirit, and as he rummaged through his things he came across a slightly dusty, worse-for-wear bread roll lying at the bottom of the bag. He smiled involuntarily.

"Of course," he said to himself.

It was the roll Clodia had given him. He had not eaten properly for days now, and as a result he had been weak from hunger the whole time. There was no way that he could recover his health while he was in such a feeble state. He would have to force himself to eat, whatever the food tasted like. Bloodletting had broken down his body's defences; now he had to rebuild his organism afresh. How had Dimberg explained the chemistry behind it? Laurentius picked up the bread roll and tossed it in the palm of his hand.

"Very well," he said, and bit into it.

It was no surprise that it tasted as bitter as wormwood. But he managed to swallow down a couple of large mouthfuls, if only to get the unpleasant substance out of his mouth as quickly as possible. After he had swallowed it, however, it brought a sweetness to his stomach. As if he had just eaten honey.

NIGHT

EVENING HAS ARRIVED AGAIN. The snow has melted, leaving puddles of muddy water behind. It is a foggy, rainy evening, as always in these parts. I am travelling by carriage with my godfather, and we are sitting looking out of the window in silence. The window shutters are almost closed; the windows are smeared, grimy with soot, grease and condensation from the warm breath of the passengers. I have no idea where we are. But the road somehow feels very familiar. I have been here before. The carriage rattles on; fewer and fewer voices are audible from outside, and there are no longer any buildings for the pounding of horses' hooves to echo back from. Then, suddenly, we have emerged into grey, open land, and we trundle on in silence. Eventually the carriage comes to a stop; my godfather opens the door and I get out. Before me is a painfully bleak expanse of land, the focal point of which is a single house, a few trees with tangled branches growing around it. The house is made of wood, and it is long and narrow like a coffin, with a low roof. The absence of any sign of human activity around the house is unsettling. No cinders marking where fires have burned, no laundry hung out to dry, no barking dogs, no prowling cats, no horses. None of those everyday things which are inextricably part of human life, without which we cannot survive.

I can see sinewy willow trees and sandy knolls with hollows, passageways and caves burrowed into them. As I get out of the carriage my shoulders shudder from the chill air. I feel a little afraid, but I struggle to suppress that feeling. I walk on down the wet gravel road. Thin streaks of fog slide past the knolls, descending down-valley; I feel my bare feet and my trouser legs getting wet as they brush against the blades of grass. No one knows me in these parts, even though I have visited here many times. It is just a place where I come in my dreams again and again. I walk down the weather-worn road which leads directly to the house. There are small puddles of brown water here and there, and in places the carriage wheels have left slimy tracks on the gravel. The sand crunches under my feet as I walk on, trying to avoid the puddles and glancing occasionally at the yawning cave mouths and burrows to my right. I look up at the sky, and the stars are tiny piercing dots, pulsing with the movement of the air, and there are light shreds of cloud stretching across the dark backdrop. The house in front of me is entirely unremarkable: grey walls, which have started to rot, and darkened windows. I walk up to it and stoop to enter through the low doorway. The walls are made from wood shingles, covered in streaky stains from many years of rainfall; the roof is made from branches, and in places flashes of dark-purple night sky are visible through the gaps. I can see a corridor, and either side of it are camp beds made from rounded wooden poles the thickness of a forearm, where people are lying in silence. But I know that without looking. Young and old, men and women. I quietly approach one of the figures lying on the plank bed, and stand there beside him. The man has long grey hair which is falling onto his face; his breathing is regular and stable like someone sleeping, but his eyes are wide open. He looks straight at me, but he says nothing. I smile at him. I know this place. This was how the barn near Aruküla looked, the place where people took refuge from starvation, the building which I once visited in real life. A woman is lying quite close to the man; her face is cut, but she has a smile on her lips. Her foot straps are torn. I know everyone here. I bear the blame for their deaths. I feel such terrible remorse, but there is nothing I can do. Whatever I try to do is overshadowed by a curse which I cannot comprehend, by a nightmarish feeling of guilt about what has happened. I want to be free of all this, but I know very well that it is not possible. I will bear this burden for the rest of my life. I have murdered many times. And not a single person knows.

I want to rush up to them, to beg their forgiveness, to explain everything.

"I didn't know..." I whisper under my breath.

All those years ago, when I watched that witch—that woman—being executed, because I had named her, I was terrified by the power of witches. Just like everyone else, always like everyone else. She struggled; someone had grabbed hold of her, and the sword struck her neck. And I had stood and watched that woman whom I pointed the finger at. Only then did I see that there was no malice or strength in her gaze, just grief and sorrow. I could see the black bile of death in those eyes. Fear and ignorance had sealed the fate of all those people, my own fear and ignorance—those tools of the Devil, those demons. I am to blame, because I was that superstitious child who had no idea what he was doing. I condemned them; I pointed the finger; I said the word.

"Witch!" I shouted out.

That woman is also here now, on one of the beds at the back. But I will never find her. These men and women were killed because I accused them of witchery. They were taken to the hillside, their heads were chopped off, and the ground was mired in blood. I have had to see it again and again in my dreams. Bodies and heads thrown onto the flames, lying amid burning branches. The peasants were hanging around the execution site, heads hung low. They came to slit my throat while I slept. I woke up screaming, and I fled. They would have caught me and killed me if I had not managed to run to the church. There was no one in there: the dark space was empty apart from a few chickens wandering across the flagstones. The men came through the door, knives in hand. Behind them, the sky was growing lighter as dawn broke. That was when the pastor came and saw what was happening.

"Be on your way," he had said. They turned round and walked away, and I was left alone with the chickens. The next morning the pastor took me to the execution mound and spoke about superstition, about the black bile and about phantasms. I realized that the only way I could survive was to give up believing in witches, to recognize that witchery was just an apparition, an illusion. But it was still not over. The horror of what happened remains in my soul; I have to bear it wherever I go. It is there in my eyes for all to see.

I turn round, close the door and leave the building. The trees—dark, nearly black, dripping with water—press in on me. As I walk on they gradually become lower and lower, eventually giving way to dark-green bushes and undulating meadowland. I watch a parade of glow-worms crawling along an invisible blade of grass—not just lone dots, but a whole constellation of them proceeding through the damp autumn night, hundreds of shimmering lights. It is as if those lights mark a boundary between two different worlds. And I am standing there between them.

Someone is approaching across the dark meadow, but the cold light of the glow-worms is too weak for me to see them properly. The figure gets closer; it comes right up to me, and now I can feel someone's breath against my face.

SATURDAY

A KNOCK AT THE DOOR. Complete darkness apart from a few coals smouldering in the fireplace, glimmering like glow-worms. Laurentius sat up and looked about in confusion. The fire in the hearth did not properly illuminate the room; it just shaded it lighter in places, making it possible to make out the depth of some of the objects. The knocking at the door continued, but it sounded more enquiring than insistent in tone.

"Wait a moment!" Laurentius called out.

He pulled his cape round him, stumbled sleepily towards the door, and yanked it open, looking annoyed. Standing there in the wavering candlelight was the maid, dressed in a nightshirt, her hair down. She was looking straight at him with an alarmed expression on her face.

"Was that you, yelling?" she asked.

"Me, yelling?" Laurentius didn't at first understand the question. He had to stop and think for a moment and ask himself if it had indeed been him. He had been told that he moaned and groaned in his sleep several times before. That hadn't been a surprise to him, since his dreams were often troubled, and took him to places from which he had to flee. He had decided that his dreams needed to be scientifically investigated, and he had always written them down, categorized them and analysed them, but he hadn't achieved much clarity. Although it was widely believed that dreams were divinely inspired, or that they revealed future events, Laurentius was convinced that they were nothing more than random thoughts, traces of memories left behind in the brain. They accumulated on top of each other, intertwining and combining in the most astonishing of ways. If they did provide a view of the future, that was only because the future was potentially present in everything he saw. Every image, every act, potentially contained its own final purpose, its eventual actuality.

"Yes, I heard someone yelling," the maid explained. "I'm not sure why, but I decided to come and have a look. These days there is always some sort of trouble occurring. People moaning and groaning out on the streets, women giving birth too early. Some people fear that the end times are nigh, that at any moment the horned beast will come to rule over us all. I've also had some dreams recently which just don't bear thinking about. I wake up, and my body is dripping wet all over, like I've been to the sauna, and all manner of ghoulish monsters are chasing me. I can't even bring myself to talk to the pastor about it," she said, blushing in embarrassment.

Laurentius tried to smile reassuringly. "I'm sure it is all just a coincidence. I've always been a pretty poor sleeper; I have all sorts of odd dreams. But I am confident that they don't have any particular significance."

"Oh really?" said the maid, seeming to take childish cheer in that. "Our pastor is generally very concerned about dreams. He says that they are often meant to show us things to come."

"That's just idle chatter; these days no one actually believes that dreams warn us of future troubles," Laurentius said dismissively, but then it occurred to him that it probably wasn't appropriate to contradict the maid's pastor like that. "It may sometimes be true, but the majority of theologians are of the view that prophetic dreams are actually very rare."

Laurentius felt some relief at being able to speak so openly. There was something down-to-earth and sensible about this girl, which had a calming and reassuring effect on him. He groped in his cape pocket for his watch and had a quick glance at the time.

"Dreams are like hallucinations; they are the fruits of our imagination," he started explaining hurriedly. "The things which occur in our dreams are caused by phantasms, the images which come from inside us and are linked to our own fears and yearnings. Let us suppose, for example, that we see something really awful happen in real life. That image is then preserved inside us, and it may combine with images from previous days, or with previous experiences we have had. Often the things we see and do in our dreams aren't actually our own actions at all. One might ask, therefore, whether we have freedom of action in our dreams or not."

Noticing that the girl was not responding in any way, Laurentius nodded and continued expounding. "The majority of us have had dreams where we find ourselves doing things which we would consider improper if we were awake. If we have freedom in our dreams, should we feel guilty about these things? Are we even free when we are awake? Granted, when we are dreaming we sometimes don't know what we are doing. But sometimes we do things which we do know to be wrong. In those cases, are we free or not? It may seem to us that we are. But if we really are, then should we be held responsible for the things we do?"

Laurentius noticed the growing look of incomprehension on the girl's face, and realized that all his arguments had been intended more to convince himself. He decided to leave his last theoretical question unanswered, and stood there rocking back and forth on his heels awkwardly.

"Forgive me, but I don't even know your name," he eventually said, deciding to change the subject.

"Madlin," the girl said with a nod and a smile.

"You know what, Madlin," Laurentius began. "Perhaps you could light the fire and then bring me a mug of beer? I don't think I will go back to bed now; best to get on with the day. It's nearly five anyway."

"Yes, it does look like it's nearly getting-up time. I will go and fetch the logs right away. Master Laurentius should wait here."

Laurentius watched as she left. For some reason he was in a cheerful, light-hearted mood. It even occurred to him that he could start work on the main theses of his disputation.

It was as if the girl's sensible and down-to-earth demeanour had made his troubles seem less serious, had eased them. He realized that he really did need someone by his side, someone to talk to. Perhaps he should have rented a room with someone, rather than relying on the maid to keep him company. People might draw all sorts of conclusions about that, and as things currently stood he didn't want to attract any bother. But it would be a lot of trouble to find someone to move in with now, and he couldn't be sure it would help.

Laurentius sat down at the table and lit the candle. The Alsted text was now much easier to read, and he soon started making notes. By the time the maid had arrived back with the breakfast and beer he had already managed to write the first draft outline of his disputation.

"There we are," said Laurentius happily. "I've done a good part of the work already. Come and sit with me to eat."

"I'm not so sure. The landlady wouldn't like it if she found out. I could get into all sorts of trouble," the maid replied.

"It's not as if I'm asking you to come to bed with me," Laurentius tried to joke, but he only succeeded in making himself blush. "I just want you to keep me company for a while; it's boring to eat alone."

The girl positioned herself warily at the foot of the bed, and sat there tense and upright.

"I'll sit here for a little while then, but I really can't stay for long," she said.

"Very well," Laurentius said with a nod, and he took a bite of the bread which the maid had brought. But he stopped dead in mid-mouthful. The taste was unbearable. Yesterday's bread roll had tasted much better, even if it had been in his bag the whole day and was rock hard and covered in dust. It had still been quite appetizing.

He put the half-eaten piece of bread down onto the table and sighed. "Actually, I don't think I want to eat now after all—maybe you would like this instead?"

Madlin shrugged her shoulders. "I suppose I could take it with me. It would somehow be strange to start eating it in front of you."

"Don't worry, it's quite all right by me," said Laurentius, trying to help her overcome her shyness.

The maid seemed reluctant, but she got up and took the bread out of his hand. With a barely suppressed sigh, she hesitantly started eating it. Laurentius watched as the bread crumbs dropped to the floor, and he realized that he was in fact terribly hungry. But he was quite sure that he couldn't eat another mouthful himself. He might be able to force down a swig or two of the sour beer.

"By the way, I'm quite sure that I saw another girl here earlier," he said to break the silence, which had started to become awkward. "She had black hair. I assumed that she must live in this house as well. She said her name was Clodia."

Madlin stopped eating for a moment. But instead of answering she just shook her head, and carried on chewing.

She eventually managed to swallow the mouthful of dry bread. "I don't know anyone by that name. But these days all sorts come loitering around here. We should probably lock the doors at night—anyone could get in. I occasionally hand out leftover food to the starving folk who have started wandering about, purely out of Christian compassion. But I'll make sure that nothing like that happens again, don't you worry on that account."

The maid was evidently a little flustered, but she didn't seem particularly surprised by Laurentius' question.

"She gave the impression of being a most pleasant and well-educated young lady," Laurentius continued.

Madlin shrugged her shoulders. "I have no idea… but I will make you an infusion; I'll put some raspberry twigs in hot water—that works very well for over-arousal." She gave Laurentius a friendly smile, cleaned up the breadcrumbs from her lap, and got up with a purposeful look on her face. "And I'll make a fire, a nice big one—that should soon warm the place up. Don't you worry. Just try to stay calm."

She slipped out through the door, leaving Laurentius sitting there, confused. He had not been able to deduce anything at all from her expression, but he was pretty sure that Madlin knew who Clodia was. She knew, but for some reason she couldn't tell anyone. Maybe Clodia was the landlady's daughter, but she was a weak-willed girl who had to be kept in her room? Maybe there had been some love story which had gone awry and she was banished from the public gaze until the gossip subsided. It might even be possible that the former tenant had made her pregnant (some scandal had been mentioned, after all), and now the family was waiting for the child to be born in secret, trying to keep the shameful truth hidden. But she hadn't looked like she was pregnant, Laurentius pondered. And her behaviour had been pretty bizarre—maybe she was just mad? Maybe there was another reason altogether why she had to hide herself away? Could he even be sure that she actually existed?

Laurentius shook his head and sat down at the table again, trying to calm himself down as Madlin had advised. He picked up the sheets of paper and started to examine the theses he had written for his disputation systematically. Then he selected some suitable citations and started to make footnotes for them. But the sound of people bustling about and talking in the kitchen below prevented him from concentrating. He tried hard to make out the individual words, and he even leant down towards the fireplace, in the hope that he would be able to hear what was being said through the chimney. But to no avail. He turned back to his text, rested his head in his hands, and focused his gaze on the sentences, trying to push his way through them by force—but the words just seemed hollow. Something was bothering him about the conversation which had just taken place. Maybe Madlin really did know something? And who was she talking to down there?

He stood up with a determined look on his face and went downstairs. It was still pitch black outside, and he had to feel his way along the corridor and grope for the door. It looked like Madlin had indeed lit the lamp in the kitchen, but the light didn't reach the yard through the windows or the chinks in the door, and there seemed to be no other lights shining nearby. The wind was howling, and blowing wet gusts of rain into his face.

"Good morning," someone said from somewhere very close by.

"Morning," said Laurentius, looking round in agitation. There, standing on the steps a couple of paces away from him, was the girl with dark hair.

"You again," said Laurentius. "Who are you?"

"You were right, I do live here," said Clodia. "But you have to promise that you won't tell anyone. And don't trouble Madlin with your questions any more; she has nothing to tell you. You're just tormenting the poor girl for no reason."

Laurentius looked straight at her and immediately felt that he had nothing more to ask.

"Very well, I won't ask you anything more. But I would like to meet you again all the same. The bread roll you gave me yesterday was the only thing I have been able to eat over the past few days. It tasted like honey; everything else I eat just tastes rotten."

Clodia smiled. "I will bring breakfast to your room."

SATURDAY MORNING

"A<small>CCORDING TO ARISTOTLE</small> there are three forms of the soul: the vegetative, the sensitive and the rational. Vegetative and sensitive souls exist in all living things, but the rational soul is found only in humans."

Laurentius was writing. The words were coming easily, and he only had to stop to reflect when it seemed that his arguments were in danger of conflicting too much with Platonist and Cartesian positions. After all, Luther himself had been opposed to Aristotle and warned against taking his philosophizing too seriously, demonstrating that Platonism was in every respect superior to Peripatetic philosophy. Descartes had in fact been of exactly the same view, and had eventually arrived at philosophical positions which were almost pure Platonism. Aristotle had been highly regarded at the beginning of the century, but by now, as the century drew to a close, attitudes had changed completely. In any case, Laurentius needed to be careful not to contradict contemporary philosophical views excessively.

"Although man is indeed alive and capable of sensation from the moment of his birth, his rational soul is actualized over time."

That was the thesis which always caused the most problems, because it suggested that there were people who lacked a rational soul. Of course that was wrong—every single person had a soul, even as an embryo, but it was yet to be actualized. Just as tomorrow follows today: it may not yet exist, but it is inexorably in the process of coming into existence, subject to what happened yesterday and today.

Laurentius paused to think for a moment. Perhaps that wasn't such a good analogy? He made a mark in the margin and wrote "check later" next to it.

For the first time in several days he didn't feel hungry at all, and his reason, that which constituted his soul, was capable of apprehending the surrounding world, making connections, and putting them into words. He was happy, happier than he had been for years. The black bile which had been sloshing around inside him, the stifling smells and his sickness seemed to have disappeared. He felt like a different person. It was as if Clodia had brought him ambrosia, the food of the gods, which made them immortal. *Aurum potabile.*

After meeting Clodia by the steps Laurentius had obe-diently returned to his room. He had sat there and waited in the dim light, with the candle burning on the table and Alsted's encyclopaedia open in front of him, and he had stared blankly at the text, thinking about Clodia, unable to decide what to do. What should he make of what had happened? How should he act?

When she eventually came, entering without knocking, Laurentius couldn't think what to do other than to greet her with a nod and a smile. He felt awkward, as if someone of high standing had graciously started to serve him for no apparent reason. The situation even seemed dangerous, as if a single wrong move could unleash chaos, destroying the fragile bal-ance which had miraculously maintained. It felt like a lion licking his fingers, wonderful and terrifying at the same time, but he dared not pull his hand back, nor reach out and stroke the beast on the head. So he stood and watched in silence as Clodia placed a loaf of bread on the table, covered it with a white cloth, and put a clay jug down next to it. She straightened her hair and smiled slightly mockingly at him. "I hear that you have some interesting views on the subject of dreams."

"Me? Well, it's not that I think dreams are unimportant, rather that they tend to be interpreted wrongly," Laurentius blurted.

Clodia took a step towards him. "Do you actually remember your dreams?" she asked.

Laurentius stopped to think. It was true that he sometimes woke up sure that he had dreamt about something important, but was unable to remember what it had been. Sometimes a vague feeling would dawn on him later, often in a completely different context, that he may have already experienced something in his dreams. But these were normally just separate details, images detached from any whole. The dreams which he remembered clearly, the ones which he had dutifully written up, were mostly of a trivial nature.

"Sometimes," Laurentius replied.

"And what did you see this time?" Clodia asked.

Laurentius tried to remember. Madlin had told him earlier that he had cried out in his sleep. What had he been dreaming about? Sandy knolls, glow-worms. Someone had approached from across a meadow and stood very close to him. It had been Clodia.

"You," he said. "I saw you in my dreams."

Clodia took another step towards him. "Are you certain that it was me?"

Laurentius laughed uncertainly. "Actually, I am not. It was dark, and you were walking across a meadow."

"But I was there?" Clodia asked.

"I heard you breathing," Laurentius replied.

Clodia came up very close to him, so that her hair almost touched his face, and he could smell the scent of flowers and the night. He could even hear her breathing, like a low humming.

Laurentius felt at a complete loss. He stood there staring straight at her, unable to turn his gaze away, unable to say or do anything. Eventually she smiled, turned round, and left the room.

"Enjoy your food," Clodia said from the doorway.

Once the sound of her footsteps going down the stairs had faded, Laurentius slowly sat down at the table. Then, with a ceremonial air, almost as if he were performing some kind of ritual, he started to eat the food that had been laid out. He broke off some bread and poured himself some wine, almost as if he were an actor on stage being watched by an audience of hundreds, or a priest leading Communion before a full congregation.

This bread tasted of honey too, almost as if it had been made with honey. Maybe that was the answer? Maybe mead and honey bread were what he needed to cure the surfeit of black bile in his body? The medicinal properties of honey had been known since time immemorial, after all. Honey could be used to preserve and to protect, and it could even cure melancholy. After his death in Babylon, Alexander the Great had been brought back to Greece embalmed in soft, sweet honey, bound with beeswax twine.

"Beeswax," said Laurentius, interrupting his own train of thought.

Of course! He nodded affirmatively to himself, trying not to let his thoughts run away with themselves, worried that they might upset the calm, ceremonious nature of the occasion. He would have to write all of this down later; for now he would just try to commit it to memory.

He slowly ate every last mouthful of the bread and drained the jug of wine dry; then he folded the white cloth down the centre, and placed it over the crumbs which had fallen onto the table. The cloth felt stiff in his hands, as if it had just recently been woven and pressed flat with a hot iron.

Only then did he get up and go to his writing desk. As he moved across the room his body seemed foreign to him; his limbs even seemed to be behaving strangely; he had to tell his arms and legs what to do, to give them clear instructions so that he could move forward. His thoughts were racing; he could see bright flashes here and there, like the spring sunlight reflected off river waters. Everything was clear, lucid.

He hurriedly sat down and started making notes. There was no longer any question in his mind as to how he should take on the Neoplatonists or the pantheists influenced by Spinoza. According to contemporary thought the soul was some sort of innate substantial idea; some people even believed that it didn't exist at all in the individual sense. But Laurentius was sure that the soul was an image, a phantasm, a figment of the imagination, just like light or a reflection. Similar to an encaustic painting, a drawing on wax. The soul enters from without, and it continues to exist both inside and outside us, like the breath we exhale, like the bees when they leave their hive to gather pollen. It arrives like a swarm of bees; then it fills the empty hive full of honeycomb, and stores the honey there. And it leaves the body just as bees leave the hive, a swarm departing suddenly one hot day, headed somewhere else.

He scribbled a note to himself in the margin: "Our experiences and our actions are etched onto our soul as if it were a wax board. Just as a picture does not exist until someone has painted it, our soul does not exist until we have experienced the world. Our soul and our very identities come into existence by virtue of our activities, through our apprehending the world and engaging with it. Otherwise we are just a husk, a blank slate, a *tabula rasa*."

Laurentius wrote the words onto the blank sheet of paper. If he had not been writing on it, it could have been used to compose a poem or draw a picture—all manner of things. It could just as easily have wrapped a piece of fish at the market or had the most rousing of love poems written on it. Or even both of those things.

He located Aristotle's treatise on the soul and wrote out a thesis from it: "Suppose that the eye were an animal—sight would have been its soul, for sight is the substance or essence of the eye which corresponds to the formula, the eye being merely the matter of seeing; when seeing is removed the eye is no longer an eye, except in name—it is no more a real eye than the eye of a statue or of a painted figure."

Laurentius added a reference to Aristotle in the margin, and started to write a commentary.

"To hold something in one's sight and to observe the world is an action, an intervention, which demonstrates that we are alive. Thus a carriage gains a purpose and a life when people enter it: those people constitute the soul of the carriage. The carriage moves and acts according to those people's will. Just like a birdcage, the essence of which is to contain the bird. If there is no bird inside it, then it is a cage in name alone. Just as the soul of the beehive is its purpose, to contain bees."

Having finished the sentence, Laurentius lifted his pen and wrote a reference to Virgil in the margin. According to Virgil, bees could sometimes carry sickness into the hive. They would take off from the mouth of the hive, come into contact with poisons and sickness, and then come back and infect the whole community. The infected hive can seal off the poisoned honeycombs with wax, but they inevitably leak, and over time the whole hive falls sick and itself becomes a source of infection. Similarly, people who bear too many terrible experiences and too much melancholy in their souls can seal it off and hold it within themselves for a while, but it will inevitably leak out. They start to radiate melancholy from their eyes, just as a candle radiates light, and they infect others with it. Laurentius found an exemplum on that subject: "When a crow alights upon a dead animal, it first gouges out its eyes, and from there its brain. Thus Satan catches a person's eye with his gaze and draws out his brain, leaving him witless." Whether we like it or not all the activities we engage in, even the simple act of looking at something, always bring about some sort of change in ourselves and our environment.

Laurentius recalled the tale of Orpheus and Eurydice which Peter staged. When Orpheus turned to look at Eurydice he sent her back to the underworld through his own actions.

There was a knock at the door and Madlin came in without waiting. She was carrying a pile of firewood, which she silently placed in front of the fireplace. Taking a quick glance at Laurentius' breakfast she clattered off back downstairs.

When she came back, carrying a smouldering piece of coal, it was clear from her expression that she was unhappy about something, but she remained silent.

"Clodia was here," Laurentius said to break the uncomfortable silence, although he was sure that Madlin already knew.

"I don't want to know any more about it. But if anyone asks, then I haven't seen or heard anything. Don't you worry, I'm not going to start blabbing your secrets," Madlin said bad-temperedly, and she knelt down in front of the fireplace with a purposeful look on her face and started blowing on the piece of coal, trying to light the fire.

"But I haven't done anything," Laurentius blurted defensively. "I don't see why you are so annoyed."

Madlin stopped what she was doing and stood up. "There's sure to be trouble from this. Big trouble, I can tell you. The landlady has forbidden lodgers from bringing strangers here, and you can tell me all the stories you want but I'm not totally simple. I know very well what people get up to and talk about behind my back."

Laurentius nodded. He had hoped that everything which was happening to him would eventually come to a natural conclusion, one which was both logical and comprehensible. But for now it seemed that the explanation remained stubbornly beyond reach.

"Very well, I won't ask you about it any more," Laurentius assured her.

"It's me that should be asking you the questions," Madlin said, scornfully throwing his words back at him. "But I'm not going to. I don't want to get mixed up in all that business." She stood there with her hands on her hips, looking angry.

"And I would prefer it if you stopped bothering me about it," she added.

Laurentius nodded again. He didn't plan to pursue the matter any further. He was all too familiar with the tales which warned the hero against being too curious. Some things in life were best left hidden; if they were dragged out into the light of day they might perish like a plucked flower. If he could just maintain his current lucid state and carry on writing, then he wouldn't need to ask any more questions.

"I promise not to," he said.

Madlin's expression had softened a little, and she even smiled, barely noticeably, as she left. Laurentius sat looking at the door for a while before turning back to his text and quickly running his eyes over what he had written so far. He would need to make some corrections in a few places, but he decided to leave that dull work for later and get down to the next thesis right away. It was essential to act while he was still experiencing the feeling that he was flying. Just as in a dream, the rational side of him knew that his body could not really be that light, but the air was somehow still holding his weight. As he looked down, the tops of the trees and the buildings all seemed very small, as if he were viewing them from a church spire. The experience was ethereal. He knew that it could not last for long.

"Everything which is concealed in hidden places, in towns, armies and the like, can be made visible with reflected light," he wrote as he started a new line.

He had to quote from memory, because he did not have the works of Roger Bacon to hand.

SATURDAY NOON

AT ONE SIDE OF THE ROOM, directly under the windows, stood a metal-plated table which was almost at chest height. There were grooves running across the top of it, and a large pail had been placed underneath to collect the bodily fluids. The table was positioned on a large improvised podium which had been covered in dark cloth, and the overall impact was quite theatrical. It was clearly an attempt to emulate the anatomical theatre in Leiden, and some of the elements of the design were already familiar to Laurentius. Professor Below had been educated in Holland just like him, so his idea of how an anatomical theatre should look had come directly from his alma mater. Next to the podium stood the obligatory skeleton: the anatomy assistant was expected to indicate the part of the body which was being examined at any given time. The skeleton wasn't in the best state of repair, and some of the bones were clearly broken or missing. Someone had glued the lower ribs together, and the taut wire pushed through the finger joints had buckled, causing them to jut out at unnatural angles. There were a couple of shiny white sheets of paper on the wall of the auditorium where mottos such as *memento mori* had been painted, although in those troubled times such advice seemed worse than useless. With all the odd goings-on and constant unrest the students and teachers were rather too vividly aware of death anyway, and would have preferred not to be reminded about it. Maybe that was why there were not as many people as one might have expected at this first public dissection of a human corpse. Professor Below had apparently been telling the city governor for years that the university needed corpses for study purposes, but they had not managed to procure one before now. Given the circumstances there was probably no shortage of suitable material; the delay was largely due to a lack of enthusiasm on the part of the city officials and questions of a technical nature.

"It became apparent yesterday that not a single one of our current students has previously taken part in a scientific dissection," Professor Below began. "I shall therefore have to take Laurentius Hylas as my assistant. I understand he has been present at a dissection in Leiden at least once before."

Laurentius was not taken off guard by Below's proposal, since the professor had stopped him the previous day and informed him that he would like him to be his assistant. He had told Laurentius that he would not have to do anything which required any special knowledge; the main thing was not to pass out at the sight of blood. People could sometimes turn out to be unexpectedly weak-nerved at their first ana-tomical dissection, even if they had experienced war at first hand. According to Below, those who had witnessed death and mutilation in battle could be particularly sensitive.

"War makes people cowardly," Below explained. "Cowardly and superstitious. If you want my advice, don't ever become a soldier."

"Is it not the sight of death which makes people cowardly?" Laurentius had suggested. "Only people who have not expe-rienced death are brave."

"But doctors witness death all the time," Below said with a dismissive gesture. "Death is nothing in itself. It's not death, but fear of death which is key. Yes, indeed. War is full of all kinds of horrors, including human life departing the physical body, and that makes people cowardly. Death is a state of not being and as such it cannot affect us, or it can do so only indirectly. That which is in our souls, which is active, can have a direct influence on us. Without life, the body is just an empty husk."

When Below asked Laurentius to come up onto the podium he felt a sense of dread, the same feeling which usually makes people cowardly. He had been calm and happy the whole morning, but now he could feel the anxiety growing in his stomach again.

"Don't just stand there being shy; come and help me, why don't you," Below said, spurring Laurentius on as he started to unload his instruments in the middle of the table. "As Professor Sjöbergh and I discussed, we might start by acquainting ourselves with the human head."

Sjöbergh stepped up to the table and nodded to Below. Turning to address the whole auditorium, he posed a question which was clearly intended to be rhetorical: "This might not normally be part of an introductory demonstration, but perhaps we could start with the structure of the cranium and the brain?"

A murmur of approval came from the massed students, and one of them even cried out: "Always best to start from the head." This was followed by slightly uneasy laughter. Although everyone had a certain amount of experience of executions and death, the cold-blooded dissection of a human body aroused some apprehension. Just the sight of Professor Below, dressed in his leather apron, placing saws, knives and tongs onto the table was enough to unsettle some of the students, even before he started using them.

Laurentius took up his position on the podium, and almost immediately the door of the auditorium opened and a corpse wrapped in cloths was brought in.

"Aha," announced Below.

The murmur of voices started to die down, and the curious audience thronged closer.

"Lift it up onto the podium right away. Yes, like that, over here," Below instructed.

He started to unwrap the corpse, a look of expert concentration on his face.

"As we can see, rigor mortis is not present in this case." He lifted one of the corpse's arms and let it flop back down. "This indicates that we are dealing with an individual who died more than two days ago. Although there are of course cases in the literature of people never developing rigor mortis at all, particularly those of more advanced years."

He lifted the corpse slightly by the shoulders, deftly moved the head backwards and forwards, and then muttered something to himself, sounding a little surprised.

By now, Laurentius had turned as white as a sheet. The anatomical subject's hair and beard had been shaved off, but he had recognized the face immediately. He could even remember looking into the old man's watery grey eyes, just before he had run off with his cage. Just as he had first started to smell that stench. He instinctively grabbed hold of his nose, but it seemed that the corpse had not yet started to putrefy. It even looked like it had been washed before being brought there. It was safe to assume that the old man had not had such a thorough scrub for a long time, if ever in his life before.

Estonians were reputed to be stalwart sauna-goers, but it was clear from Laurentius' first meeting with the old man that such an activity had not been a priority of his. Now, however, his old body had been rinsed down and was lying there in front of Laurentius, sallow and sinewy like an anatomical drawing.

"As you can see the subject has a slight injury to his skull, but that shouldn't affect our presentation. Assistant, pass me the knife," said Below, getting underway with the operation.

Laurentius approached the table, his legs wobbling slightly, and handed Below a long knife. Below fixed him with a questioning gaze. With good cause, since Laurentius' face had now turned ashen grey, roughly the same shade as the corpse lying on the table. Catching Below's gaze, Laurentius tried to smile, but the result was not convincing.

"First we shall open up the cranium," Below explained. "To do so we will make a circular incision on the head, and roll back the skin. Then we shall be able to saw the bones."

He picked up the knife and made the first incision, producing a few drops of thick, red blood. As he watched the professor busy at work, Laurentius was thinking constantly about their conversation that morning. It was true that there was no reason to be afraid of death: once life has departed the body, it will never come back. But he still felt uneasy. The last time he had seen the old man he was living and breathing, moving about.

"After cutting through the frontal bone, the *os frontale*, I can start on the cranial bone, the *os parietale*. Take note that the join between the temporal bone and the cranial bone, the *sutura squamosa*, is very tricky to saw, and in subjects of this age it is normally completely ossified. It is therefore advisable to make the first incision just above that join."

As Below described the parts of the skull he was examining, Laurentius pointed to the corresponding places on the anatomical skeleton, and the students watched and nodded with serious expressions on their faces. Then Below turned the old man's head to one side, preparing to make another incision, and paused to take a deep breath. In the course of all the pulling about during the demonstration the old man's eyes had come open, and he fixed his pensive and sorrowful gaze on Laurentius. Laurentius could now look into those eyes calmly, free from any guilt. Were there still any signs of life there? No, none at all. The old man's eyes were unfocused, glazed over, like a fish's eyes after it has been lying in the sun at the market for too long. But back then by the barn they had been full of life, bright blue and piercing. Laurentius had looked into those eyes, and that was why the old man was now lying there on the metal table, dead. That was how it always was. Whenever he looked into anyone's eyes for too long, they fell ill or died. There was nothing he could do about it. It was his melancholy, the curse which he bore in his soul, the evil eye, which would not succumb to his reason.

Below started to make a further cut, from the forehead to the ears. At that point, Laurentius was sure that he noticed the old man's eyes flitter slightly. The disgusting smell which he now lived in such fear of started to tickle his nostrils again, barely perceptibly at first. Then he became aware of a foul, thick tobacco taste in his mouth, and he instinctively tried to spit it out. Since the morning, when Clodia had served him breakfast, he had not had to suffer those revolting, hostile stenches. Perhaps it was the sight of death which had heightened his senses' perception of decay and putrefaction? Perhaps Below had not been right to say that witnessing death meant nothing at all. After all, doctors saw the human body, blood, intestines, bones, but they did not see death itself. The true nature of death did not lie in those things. Laurentius started to experience a sharp throbbing pain in his head and soreness in his eyes. He could feel his own blood and bones, and a tickling like when a hair or feather gets in the eye.

"Feathers?" Laurentius' train of thought came to an abrupt halt, and the pointing stick slipped out of his hand. He staggered, reached out for support, and very nearly sent the skeleton flying. It swayed on the thin rod it was suspended from, and its bony arms, which had been held up by wire, flailed about wildly. The skull tilted to one side, and now seemed to be looking reproachfully at Laurentius.

Professor Below turned towards Laurentius with an annoyed expression on his face, and some of the students looked up in alarm, but before anyone managed to say anything, they heard a voice calling out.

"Aaah!" came the cry from on top of the table.

The noise was coming from the anatomical subject, who by now had sat up, and was gripping his head in both hands. Blood was gushing through his fingers as he desperately tried to hold the gaping wound together. What had started as feeble whimpering had turned into a hoarse, frantic wailing. Blood was dripping down onto the old man's shoulders and stomach, and his recently washed body was now smeared with thick red blood.

The students jostled with each other as they tried to back away from the podium, and someone called out "God help us!" Laurentius felt as if he were drunk, and couldn't properly apprehend what was happening. The entire scene was surreal and grotesque.

Only Professor Below kept his calm, leaning towards the old man and explaining: "Everything will be all right; you're with a doctor. A doctor, you understand?" But he shook his head despondently. "He probably doesn't understand German—will someone please explain to him that I am a doctor? I'll take a look at his head. I shall need to bandage him, but if he continues being hysterical and thrashing about like this then I'm afraid it will be impossible." He paused for a moment before shouting above the din which had broken out in the hall. "And who the devil checked the corpse over? I will make sure that he is held to account!"

"Do you suppose…" Sjöbergh started to say in a faltering voice. "Of course, considering that…"

The old man was still yelling in alarm. Given the general commotion and the audience's state of agitation it was quite possible that he thought he had arrived in hell.

"Who speaks Estonian here?" Below thundered angrily. "Come here right away!"

Then he turned and politely addressed Sjöbergh: "There's no need for any supposing here; it's suspended animation, *vita minima*, a common enough phenomenon. Of course, a decent doctor would have spotted it right away. I thought there was something suspect about this one right from the start. Those dilettantes give us nothing but trouble. They could come and study their subject properly with us, but will they ever! Quacks and charlatans, the lot of them!"

Saturday Afternoon

"It does indeed sound strange," Mellinck said, agreeing with Laurentius.

Laurentius nodded worriedly. The morning's events had left him with an exhausted, hollow feeling, which got worse as he recounted the story to the pastor. Everything had seemed so clear at first, almost as if he had been expecting it. Once he was over the initial shock from what had happened at the anatomical theatre he had experienced the strange feeling of lightness again, as if he had just learnt the solution to a problem which had been troubling him for a long time, as if he had suddenly been cured of his sickness. Everyone else had been thronging about agitatedly, but he had just stood there in their midst, somehow removed, as if he were suspended in mid-air looking down on what was happening. The light in the room had become radiant, clear, golden, but all the colours apart from yellow were somehow muted, and many objects seemed to have no colour at all. Standing there in the golden radiance, he had watched as Below, who had failed to get anyone to help, subdued the old man with *oleum dulce vitrioli* and started to stitch up the wound on his head, discussing something with Sjöbergh as he did so. The students, who looked as small as dwarves in a fairy tale, were arguing among themselves, initially in a state of panic, but growing increasingly jolly. It was clear that something bizarre and unusual had happened, but once they had got over the shock it seemed more funny than horrific. Laurentius himself had felt increasingly overcome by a strange, intoxicating euphoria, until suddenly he reached a state of complete lucidity. All of the previous smells and pains had gone. He knew with complete certainty that all he needed to do now was to go to the mortuary and find the peasant woman and bring her back to life. And after that he might even be able to save all the other people who had died or fallen ill from his gaze.

He had hurriedly left the auditorium, rushed down the street and asked the first people he came across the location of the mortuary. People had noticed his grinning face and smiled back at him, happily giving him directions without questioning what he was so looking forward to seeing there. Despite the continuing drizzle he felt as if it were now summer or spring. Even the acrid reek of grey chimney smoke hanging low over the town and the pungent stench of horse dung were sweet and pleasant aromas to him, like the scent of roses. He had gone straight into the mortuary building with a bold and purposeful air and told the guard that he had come from the university under the instruction of Professor Below. A major oversight had occurred with a dead body which had just been delivered, and he had to investigate the matter urgently.

"It was a most regrettable case involving an old man in suspended animation. There are grounds to believe that there may have been other such cases," Laurentius said, adopting an authoritative tone of voice to try to convince the soldier.

"Very well, but perhaps you wouldn't mind looking for the bodies yourself?" the soldier said, seeming eager to comply. He opened a door into a low-ceilinged underground chamber.

Inside, it was even cooler and damper than outside on the street. Arranged across plank beds were ten or so corpses waiting to be buried, all of them cases in which the city was involved in some way. Most of these deaths had been violent, and according to state ordinance any suspicious cases had to be investigated by a judge. Only then could a family member come to take possession of the corpse and lay it to rest, although in present circumstances it would frequently happen that no one came, and the city had to get rid of the corpses itself. There were fears that if the number of dead continued growing as it had then there would be no choice but to consecrate a piece of land beside a cemetery and bury the unidentified bodies in a mass grave for the poor.

Laurentius moved hurriedly from body to body, occasionally peeking under the sheets which covered them. Then he came to a standstill. He recognized those torn foot straps— they were the same ones he had seen poking out from under the sheet when they had carried the bleeding corpse past him, down near the caves. He hastily pulled the cover to one side and looked at the skinny frame of the woman whom he had seen alive only once, after Peter's theatrical performance. The woman's arms and legs had been laid out straight; her hair was down, and her head cocked backwards. Laurentius noticed that her face was covered in tiny cuts. He leant forward to try to get a better look at her in the dim light of the room, and recoiled. Surely she had not been lying out long enough for the crows and magpies to peck out her eyes! All he could see there were two black holes. Laurentius stood staring into the empty voids where her eyes had been. Eventually he placed the sheet back over the body with a dejected look on his face. Now there was nothing he could do.

"It appears that there is in fact no cause for concern; everything's in order here," he explained to the soldier in a dispirited voice. "Good day to you."

He hurriedly left the mortuary, but once outside he immediately came to an irresolute standstill. All he could see in front of him were trees dripping with rainwater; there were no signs of any people around. He looked up at the bare branches, overcome with uncertainty about what he should do next. At that moment a flock of sparrows appeared like a sudden gust of wind and flew past very close, one or two even passing between his legs. The thoughts in his head were also flitting about here and there, whirling around uncontrollably before suddenly disappearing, just like the sparrows. He even felt a little embarrassed about what had happened. Hopefully it hadn't seemed too odd to rush out of the university like that. He was pretty sure that he had seen Professor Below glowering at him disapprovingly. He might even decide to write to Leiden to find out what kind of impression Laurentius had made there. Based on his behaviour just now, it might well be assumed that he wasn't quite right in the head. If they started to investigate his background, it could lead to all sorts of bother. Someone might even bring up the circumstances of his departure from Leiden University. If people kept falling seriously ill or having strange accidents after they came into contact with him, then someone might make the link. Such a conclusion could be dismissed as simple superstition, but someone with a keen intellect such as Below would be able to discern the deeper root causes, especially after what had happened in the auditorium.

"But what actually happened back there?" Laurentius thought to himself.

The old man had come back to life. It could have just been a coincidence, of course. But he still couldn't comprehend how it could have happened. He needed to discuss it with someone, but going to see Professor Below or Sjöbergh would not have been appropriate. The only one left was Mellinck, who had anyway invited him to come and visit. It felt reassuring that he was a pastor, and apparently quite an open-minded one too.

And so he had gone to find Mellinck. At first Laurentius' haggard and distraught appearance had seemed to make the pastor a little uneasy, but once he started recounting the morning's events, the pastor's expression softened. He understood why Laurentius was so upset.

"And so you believe that you somehow caused this old man to come back to life?" Mellinck eventually asked.

Laurentius shook his head apprehensively. He hadn't dared tell the pastor too much.

"There is actually nothing unprecedented about any of this; as Below himself said, cases of suspended animation are pretty common these days," Mellinck mused. "Looking at this from a religious perspective, there is also such a thing as the Lazarus syndrome, of course. It is particularly common during times of strife, and its purpose is to honour God. We know from the writings of St Nicholas, for example, that he managed to bring back to life three boys who had been killed by a butcher. It took place during famine, and the city folk were ready to eat them. They had already been chopped up and hung from meat hooks. But it didn't look like anyone had started eating that old man, did it?"

Laurentius shook his head. "Below had only just managed to make the first incision."

"Of course, there are plenty of cases of anthropophagy here as well," Mellinck said with a nod. "I've heard some really ghastly stories. But that is probably not relevant to this matter. You said that Below had managed to make an incision. Did the cut disappear when the old man came back to life?"

"No, quite the reverse, the blood started gushing out. It was a horrible sight."

"So it didn't disappear, then. What is certain is that a human could never bring someone back to life unaided—God's intervention is required. But in those cases the person is normally fully restored, like those boys whom St Nicholas saved. There are no injuries left on them at all. Of course, some kind of demonic deception is always possible, but in such cases the person doesn't truly come back to life, even if his eyes open. And you say that the whole auditorium witnessed the reanimation?"

"Yes, of course," Laurentius said, sounding slightly put out by the question.

"No cause to take offence," Mellinck said with a smile. "I simply want to weigh up all the possibilities, one by one... But if you want my opinion on the matter, then what we are dealing with here is simply a chance occurrence. Such things have been known to happen, although I do concede that they are worthy of attention, since they provide another demonstration of the extraordinary times we are living in. There have been no comets sighted recently, and they would normally accompany such unusual events. But it may just be that we haven't noticed them. It's recently been overcast all the time, so I haven't been able to conduct my usual astronomical observations."

As Mellinck continued to muse in that vein Laurentius started feeling that he might have allowed himself to get too upset by something which may have been unusual, but was nevertheless readily explainable. Below's suspended-animation theory probably offered the most credible explanation after all.

"By the way, how is that girl whom you took in from the refuge?" Laurentius enquired when it seemed that Mellinck had said everything he wanted to on the topic.

"Ah, her," said the pastor after pausing for thought for a moment. "Not good. Her fever has not yet subsided; I'm afraid that her humours have been put decidedly out of balance. There is nothing we can do other than to keep her in a warm, dry room and try to somehow bring down her cold, damp humour."

"I happen to have some medicinal powders with me which I use for my fever—perhaps you could try them?" Laurentius suggested.

"Really?" asked Mellinck with interest. "What kind?"

"Willow bark, prepared according to a Galen recipe. I normally make a tincture from it, but I haven't had time to recently. The effect is therefore much weaker," Laurentius explained.

Mellinck seemed keen on hearing more about his recipe, so Laurentius had to tell him at length about the results he had achieved with the bark.

"Let's go and try it straight away," Mellinck suggested.

They went downstairs to the ground floor and entered a small room next to the kitchen, where a little figure was lying on a low bedstead, covered in a thin blanket.

"Since her fever is so high we have to allow her to sweat out the cold vapours; they must not be trapped under thick blankets," Mellinck explained. "The ventilation needs to be very good, but the room should not be too cold either. At the moment it's rather difficult to achieve the right conditions. I have had damp cloths put onto her to try to draw out the cold vapours, but without much success so far."

The maid carried in a pot full of hot water, and Mellinck sprinkled the powders into it. "I assume that it doesn't need to be boiled?" he enquired, concerned to administer the medicine correctly.

"I have found that simmering it on a very low heat tends to give the best results," Laurentius replied.

The girl took the pot back to the kitchen, accompanied by Mellinck, leaving Laurentius alone with the sick girl in the tiny room. He could hear her hurried, uneven breathing, and the whistle of air as it passed between her dry lips. He slowly approached the edge of the bed and reached out to feel the child's forehead. It was very hot. The girl opened her eyes and looked straight at him in alarm.

Laurentius wanted to turn his gaze away, but the child gripped his hand and he found himself looking into those sunken grey eyes once again. She smiled feebly at him.

"I know," said Laurentius softly. "*Kuningas.*"

He tried to pronounce the Estonian word clearly, so that it would sound the same as he remembered the girl and the pastor saying it. "I am not a king." He shook his head. "Not any more."

The girl was staring straight at Laurentius, and he noticed that her tired eyes were ringed with dark-purple shadows. There was a weary lifelessness in her gaze, just as he had seen with the old man. By now Laurentius had started to smell death again—his eyes were itching; it felt almost as if someone were pushing their thumbs down onto his eyelids. He crouched down to the ground, afraid that his eyeballs might drop out at any moment, feeling nauseous. At that moment he remembered that Pliny had written that it was impossible to take out a man's eye without making him vomit. On this basis Pliny had concluded that sight and digestion were linked in some way.

Saturday Evening

Through the blue-grey clouds and the damp haze of the atmosphere, the moon looked like the reflection of a lantern, floating on the surface of a muddy pond. Nudged along by the wind, white clumps formed from compressed droplets of water rolled across the poets' celestial body, distending into fibrous strands, creating shadowy blotches and fantastical shapes. It was as if the god of the north winds were driving his subjects relentlessly onwards, demanding ever more from them. Their celestial dance grew wilder and wilder, and the shreds of cloud turned crazy somersaults as they raced across the pale patches of light. The ecstatic dance gradually took on clearer outlines, until suddenly the moon appeared in all its cool radiance. Light gleamed through the cobwebs of darkness, and behind the ragged talons of cloud danger loomed. Thin white strands spun around the heavenly body as it slowly rotated.

Laurentius had already sensed that the light in his room had changed before becoming consciously aware of it. The candle on the table in front of him was guttering in the whispering draught coming through the chink in the window. The sloped ceiling was reflecting the low flames from the smouldering hearth, the flickering red coal light creating incomprehensible contours across the wall. Alsted's encyclopaedia was

267

lying open in front of him. He had been turning the thick tome's pages backwards and forwards for some time, but his gaze was fixed on some point on the other side of the wall, behind the flames, in the emptiness beyond, and he looked completely detached from reality, deranged even. He could feel a sharp scratching pain in his eyes, as if sand or earth had got under his eyelids and he couldn't close them. Maybe it was because he had been reading for too long, striving in vain to comprehend the text before him. The candle had been flickering, distracting him.

He stood up, and started pacing angrily around the room.

At that moment he would have liked to consult the works of Robert Boyle, which Dimberg had recommended to him, but he would have to content himself with what he had. He was sure that someone must have already written about what he was experiencing. Instead of falling ill from his gaze, people had now started to become healthy again. Previously his gaze had been like the look of remorse which Orpheus had cast in Eurydice's direction—loving, longing, but deadly. He had stood in the light, and everyone he had looked at had fled into the shadows.

"But what now?" he asked himself.

Now he was certain that the girl at Pastor Mellinck's would recover. As he had looked into her tired eyes he had suddenly seen the same golden glow which had appeared in the old man's eyes. The air had started shimmering; the walls had become translucent, and he felt as if he were flying high above. Maybe the girl's fever had fallen by now and she was already sitting up in bed, asking after her mother. The maid would bring her something to eat and explain that her mother had suffered a misfortune. The girl would listen as she ate her soup, but the meaning of the words would not fully dawn on her. It might be many years before she would be told the true circumstances of her mother's death. Taking everything into account, this was what was meant to happen. But why?

He glanced impatiently out of the window. Clodia. Clodia was the reason. His parakeet had been with him when he arrived in this country. He had been sick, and only her chirping and her warm temperament had kept his humours balanced. But then someone had fed her something, and she died.

Laurentius opened the window and looked out at the moon.

"Blessed are those who hunger and thirst, for they shall be filled," he whispered.

In the dusky light outside he could see a thin drizzle of rain, falling with a gentle murmur. It looked almost like a white mist which was making everything damp and clammy as it descended. A hazy glow came from it as it spread, flowing like a liquid, lapping up against tree branches, sloshing about in the yard and trickling from the roofs of the houses, washing things which had been long concealed out into the open, just as Roger Bacon had described.

"It is not yet time," he said to himself.

What hour had it usually been when he met Clodia here? Had it happened at night? Laurentius looked at his watch and saw that it was just past eight o'clock.

He leapt up with a determined look on his face and rushed out through the door and downstairs to the kitchen.

"Who is Clodia?" he demanded of Madlin, who was standing there.

She looked straight at him with a thoughtful expression, but she said nothing.

"Who is Clodia?" Laurentius repeated the question.

"Easy now," she said, trying to calm him down.

"Who?" Laurentius asked. He felt his eyes itching.

Madlin came up to Laurentius, put her arms around him, and broke into tears. Laurentius wanted to leap away, but he managed to stop himself in mid-movement and put his arms around Madlin. He patted her gently on the back, unable to think of anything sensible to say.

"Don't cry," was all he could eventually manage.

Madlin felt sturdy but soft and warm in his arms. He could feel her full bosom pressed against his body, and the rhythm of her breathing, in and out in time with the sound of her sobbing. There were kitchen smells coming from her clothes. But she still did not quite reach him; it was as if he were hovering somewhere overhead, watching the two of them standing together. As if he were standing atop a church tower, recklessly craning out of the open hatch of the bell chamber, the wind whistling in his ears, looking down at the tiny people below, their bare heads, their caps and their hats. Just as Descartes had looked out of the window and seen the overcoat and hat. Laurentius stood there, leaning forward awkwardly so that he could hold Madlin as she sobbed fitfully. Behind them was the stove with a flame burning on it, and the knives and forks laid out on the table.

Laurentius started feeling uneasy.

"Very well, I won't ask any more questions. There, there," he said, trying to comfort Madlin.

For some reason he could not understand he felt tears welling up inside him. He took a clumsy step away from Madlin and glanced around the kitchen with a regretful expression. He felt full of sorrow and yearning. It seemed that he had to bid farewell to Madlin and that place.

"Goodbye, Madlin," he said, turning away from her. He all but ran to get away, clattering noisily through the kitchen and out through the door. Madlin slowly pulled the door shut after him, wiping away her tears with the other hand, and Laurentius heard her draw the bolt shut from the other side.

He came to a halt and leant against the door frame, breathing heavily and looking out into the yard. The rain was still drizzling, the cold, thin vapour seeping downwards, illuminated by the cool moonlight. Since the very first day he had arrived in Estonia he had been swathed ever tighter and tighter in that damp breath, until one day he had stopped being aware of it altogether—it had become a part of him. His sickness had been steadily getting worse and worse, and he had been growing more and more afraid, right up until the moment in the auditorium when the old man had come back to life. Then he had felt well again. Healthy, but somehow removed, as if he were no longer inhabiting the same dimension as others. As if he had forgone some part of himself.

"Are you coming?" a voice asked.

Laurentius looked around but he could see no one.

"I'm coming," he answered reflexively, as if repeating the question to himself.

Something soft and familiar brushed momentarily, barely perceptibly against his face, and then Clodia appeared, running up the steps. Laurentius saw her dark, flowing hair and started to follow the glow which was emanating from it. The stair rail felt cold and wet from the autumn night.

"Wait," he called out after her.

The girl laughed and ran ahead.

When he got upstairs to his room the table was laid with bread, a wooden tray full of cheese, and a glittering glass full of clear white wine. Clodia was sitting there next to the table.

"There, help yourself," she said.

As Laurentius approached the table he realized how hungry he was. He broke off a piece of bread and poured himself a glass of wine. He dared not ask any questions or say anything at all. The whole situation seemed too fragile, too improbable, and his eyes were still hurting.

"Clodia," he started in a faltering voice.

She came and stood before him, looking straight at him. Her eyes were like liquid gold, like dark honey, and her breathing sounded like a gentle humming.

NIGHT

I CAN HEAR BIRDS SINGING, leaves rustling, someone's footsteps, and the barely audible sound of a musical instrument being played somewhere in the distance. I push myself upright, resting my hands on the marble which has been warmed in the sunlight, and I turn to look in the direction of the sea.

Where am I?

The clay-brown water seems to become blue on the horizon, and growing out of the dark haze I can see a shimmering shore and the contours of mountains, tinged red in the sunlight. I can smell the sweet scent of bright roses, mixed with the powerful woody aroma of thyme, and I can hear bees humming. There are countless numbers of bees, all around.

I feel as if I have just woken from a dream, and I strive to hold on to that fragile feeling, and the fleeting fragments of memories. I take in the view of the sea, the trees, the garden. There is an *apiarium* down there, a row of beehives standing in a straight row alongside a low wall. The wall winds round the edge of a small plateau, and appears to have been built with almost no grouting. The house where I am has been standing here for a long time—someone came to this mountainside many years ago and built the first walls on the cliff edge; then they made a garden in the fertile earth which had been washed into the plateau. That was how it had to be. I turn around, and I can still hear the distant murmur of conversation coming from the other rooms of the house. As I move towards those voices I come to an atrium containing a pool, and I see a single slanting ray of sunlight shining into it. I notice a parakeet with brightly coloured feathers sitting on top of a tree which is growing in a large ceramic pot. The bird is whistling gently to itself, nodding its head, hopping impatiently from foot to foot, demanding attention. I approach it and it jumps onto my outstretched finger. I instinctively rummage in my belt pocket, looking for some sunflower seeds. But there are none there.

"Where am I?" I ask the parakeet.

"Squawk!" the bird replies, and gives me a painful nip with its beak.

"I'm sorry, but it looks like I have nothing for you to eat," I apologize to the bird.

"Squawk!" it says again. At that moment someone pokes their head round the door of the adjacent room.

"Did you mention food? Come through, we happen to have just started eating."

I look in the direction of the person who addressed me, but they have already disappeared. I can hear the murmur of conversation coming through the doorway, and I assume that must be the way to a courtyard which serves as the dining area in the summer. I carefully lower my hand to let the parakeet jump back onto the branch and I walk down the colonnade which borders the courtyard. A little way off I can see people sitting at a table on long benches—not reclining on couches, Roman-style. I know these people; their faces are familiar. As

they turn to look in my direction I see their dark complexions
and golden eyes, and I hear the membranous wings on their
backs rustle. It is a square table laden with loaves of bread,
jugs of water, wine and fruit. And there are pomegranates,
grapes and honeycomb.

AUTHOR'S NOTE

Melancholy has come to be seen as the ailment of the seventeenth century, but the concept had existed in one form or another since at least the fourth, when Evagrius Ponticus first referred to it in his practical guidance for monks. There, he described the "noonday demon", which caused weariness in the limbs and a troubled mood, or more simply languor and compulsive laziness. During the Antique period and the Middle Ages the condition was yet to have acquired any romanticized connotation, and was described simply as lethargy and sloth (one of the seven deadly sins). It most often affected those engaged in intellectual work, such as monks and philosophers. During the time of the Humanists (and especially in the works of Petrarch), the *acedia* of the Middle Ages came to be increasingly poeticized, and sloth was replaced with the term "spleen", denoting ill humour. It was still seen in negative terms, but the emphasis shifted from lethargy and sloth to heavy-heartedness, despondence and apathy. It was in this form that the concept became widespread during the early modern period—poets and kings suffered from it, and artists depicted it (Albrecht Dürer, among others). The key work on the subject was *The Anatomy of Melancholy* by Robert Burton (written under the pseudonym Democritus Junior). Over the course of nearly 500 pages it provided a thorough analysis of the phenomenon:

When I lie waking all alone,
Recounting what I have ill done,
My thoughts on me then tyrannize,
Fear and sorrow me surprise,
Whether I tarry still or go,
Methinks the time moves very slow.
All my griefs to this are jolly,
Naught so mad as melancholy.

The vice known by the term *acedia*, which had originated in the traditions of Latin-speaking monasticism, therefore acquired a medical diagnosis derived from ancient Greek—melancholy. The condition was similar to our modern-day understanding of depression, although the interpretation of it given in humoral medicine means that there are some important differences.

Humoral medicine was based on Antique conceptions of the world as being formed from elements which were traditionally defined as fire, water, earth and air—although people tended to speak more of heat, coldness, dryness and moistness. These were the properties which gave a substance its essence, and a given material could be described in terms of the specific balance between them. According to Galen, a medical philosopher who was active in the second century and subsequently became very influential, the equivalents of these elements could be found in the human body and were known as the four humours: yellow bile, phlegm, black bile and blood. A person's health, or the type of ailment which afflicted him, would depend on the balance of his humours. Just as it became conceivable to manipulate these four elements within a given substance in order to change it (transmutation), so the purpose of medicine was to manipulate the balance within the human body. If the purpose of alchemy was to achieve the perfect balance, and thereby to produce the perfect metal—gold— then the aim of medical science was to achieve a balance of the humours, in the form of good health. Due to this common theoretical basis, medicine and alchemy remained very closely related for centuries, and the majority of physicians were to some degree also alchemists.

The first stage of the alchemical process was known as *nigredo* or decomposition, which broke down the bonds within a given substance. The symbolic representations of this process were destruction, death, decay and disease. All of these were antithetical to life, but they were necessary in order to rebuild the substance in a new, improved form. The final stage of this process of reconstruction was *rubedo*, which was represented by gold, honey, the sun, (eternal) life and good health, among other things. Gold therefore became a symbol of perfection and good health due to what it represented in alchemy, not purely because of its material value.

Although there were many changes in scientific thinking in the early modern period, alchemy did not fade away; in fact it gained new adherents among the most progressive scientists (including, for example, Isaac Newton and Robert Boyle). Although they declared the theory of the four elements to be false, other theories came to replace it (such as Robert Boyle's corpuscular theory), some of which offered even greater scope for conjecture of various kinds. In medicine, humoral theory survived for many years, and in the seventeenth century it gained renewed importance as a means of explaining witchery.

Modern-day researchers find it difficult to comprehend how people who were otherwise thoroughly rational, and capable of making important discoveries in the natural sciences, could stubbornly continue to believe in witchcraft and witches. However, witchcraft was seen as a scientific problem. According to one sixteenth-century theory, witchcraft was linked to a surfeit of black bile within the body, which caused the witch to experience illusions. This was the view advanced by Johann Weyer in his book *De praestigiis daemonum* (On the illusions of demons). Although the author did not deny the existence of demons or Satan, he generally believed that witches were sick people who were mentally deficient in some way, and saw visions. Evidence that this view was also held in Estonia and Livonia comes from the so-called Thies Werewolf Case of 1692, in which an old man's claim to be a werewolf was ridiculed by the judges, who passed a verdict of "devilish deception". It was not rare for so-called witches to believe that they flew to witches' sabbaths and transformed themselves into various creatures, and they would sometimes even try to prove it to sceptics. In the early modern context witchery was therefore a far more multifaceted and complex phenomenon than our modern-day conceptions of witchcraft. It was an integral part of the world view of the period, which was linked to all conceivable kinds of social ills, from the rejection of established local customs to heretical theology, as well as sickness and madness. This was the context for the widespread belief that it was the old and sick who were most likely to be witches—it was their sickness which was seen as a threat to society, and therefore led to accusations of witchery. Just as outbreaks of infectious disease cause mass hysteria to this day (the saga of "swine flu"; HIV), in the early modern period social tensions, infectious diseases, famine, and so on were often categorized with the non-scientific term "witchery".

The witch's ugly appearance confirmed the presence of sickness—according to Aristotle a human's essence was expressed by his form, the soul. If his soul was sick or damaged in some way, then that would be reflected in his outward appearance. This belief was represented in paintings of the time, in which the traitor Judas was depicted as ugly, for example. Thus a person whose soul was ugly was also seen as physically ugly. This was how the philosopher Thomas Aquinas described it in his commentary on Aristotle's *De anima* (On the soul):

> As he says, there is no more reason to ask whether soul and body together make one thing than to ask the same about wax and the impression sealed on it, or about any other matter and its form. For, as is shown in the *Metaphysics*, Book VIII, form is directly related to matter as the actuality of matter; once matter actually *is*, it is *informed*.

Since the eyes provided the most direct link to the soul ("the window on the soul"), the acts of seeing and watching were effectively seen as an extension of the soul. Just as a seal leaves an impression on wax, so, according to Aristotle's theory of perception, external experiences leave a trace (an impression) on our soul, causing it to resemble our experiences. If those experiences were sufficiently traumatic, then this could negatively affect the soul, leading to (physical) degradation and sickness. Sometimes this degradation of the soul would manifest itself as the "evil eye".

The phenomenon of the evil eye had been recognized since Antiquity, and descriptions of it can be found in the works of authors of the period, who generally linked it to jealousy. In Greek the phenomenon came to be described with the technical term *baskaino*, which in the Latin-speaking world turned into *fascino*. In the third of Virgil's *Eclogues*, for example, it is described as follows:

> These truly—nor is even love the cause—
> Scarce have the flesh to keep their bones together
> Some evil eye my lambkins hath bewitched.

During Antiquity belief in the evil eye was widespread, and laws were even passed to punish people who used it to cause damage of various kinds (an example can be found in *Leges decemvirales*, the codex of Roman law dating from 449 BC). A similar popular belief in the harmful effects of the evil eye persisted into the Middle Ages. There were cases of people believing that the evil eye could be used to blunt a sword or cause harm to unborn or newborn babies. Such a case was described by St Gregory of Tours, who wrote that the Frankish king Chilperic was afraid to show his son in public lest some kind of misfortune befall him. It was similarly considered dangerous for pregnant women to look out of the window for fear that they might catch sight of a crippled or degenerate person, which might affect their unborn child in some way. Children and sick people were seen as particularly vulnerable to bad experiences, since their souls were weak and certain kinds of impressions could distress them. Various theoretical explanations were also developed for the evil eye, based on Antique philosophical ideas and biblical traditions. The thirteenth-century French philosopher Peter of Limoges described the workings of the evil eye or fascination as follows:

> A rabid dog has poison in its brain. A bite from such a dog, irrespective to which part of the body, will later infect the brain or a similar part of the body. It is therefore likely that the lustful vapours which rise from a woman's heart into her eyes also infect her gaze—if we observe the emissions of the gaze which infect a man's eyes and later his heart, we find that they are the same as those which left the woman's heart.

This provides very clear evidence that the evil eye was believed to function like an infectious disease. Illness, manifested by some form of degeneration or demonic behaviour, was considered socially detrimental and had to be rooted out. Efforts to combat witchery were therefore intended to keep society healthy, and could be seen as serving a sanitary or prophylactic purpose. While good health was associated with moderation, balanced elements and gold, for example, sickness was linked to everything dark, to black bile and to demons. A person's entire mortal existence was even seen as a form of sickness, with death being welcomed as a release. This is one interpretation given to the final words of Socrates' dialogue *Phaedo*, in which Socrates mentions that he owes Asclepius a cockerel; with his death he will finally be cured of the sickness known as life. Life itself was often seen as sick, degraded, horrific, demonic.

The horrors of everyday existence were demonstrated particularly vividly during the famines which struck at the end of the seventeenth century. During the summers of 1695–97 there was constant rainfall across northern Europe (including in Estonia), destroying the crops and causing the price of hay to rise exorbitantly. The city of Tartu (known at the time as Dorpat), where the Swedish army's grain stores were situated, established a refuge for penurious women and children. However, the initiative came to an end when it became clear that there were too many people in need of assistance. During the early spring of 1697, at the height of the famine, the misery and wretchedness of the peasantry was said to be so severe that no one could bring themselves to describe it. The situation was said to be even worse than the starvation which was witnessed during the siege of Jerusalem (cf. Lamentations 4: 4–5). There were cases of parents eating their own children, and the children who fled home or were thrown out could themselves end up eating corpses they found lying by the roadside. Faced with a choice between starvation and cannibalism, many people chose suicide, and their bodies could be found hanging from the forest trees, or drowned in the rivers.

In the same period in which Estonia suffered a series of major crop failures which took the lives of around 70,000 people, professor of mathematics Sven Dimberg was working at the Gustavo Carolina Academy in Dorpat. He was one of the first people in the Nordic region to teach Newtonian mathematics, and he was familiar with Robert Boyle's theories on chemistry. Professor of philosophy Gabriel Sjöbergh was also well informed on the theories of Descartes, and professor of medicine Jakob Friedrich Below, who had been educated in Holland, organized anatomical dissections of animals and humans for instructional purposes and to "satisfy public curiosity". Pietist pastors had established schools for the peasantry, and only a dozen or so years had passed since Bengt Gottfried Forselius' initiative in that area. Throughout the course of the seventeenth century a total of fifty-three people were sentenced to death for witchcraft in Estonia, half of them men.* The complainants were normally other peasants who claimed that the suspected witch had caused them, their family or their property some kind of damage. Around fifty years had passed since the Võhandu uprising, which resulted in the burning down of the local mill. According to folk memory this had angered the river spirit, thereby causing crop failure.

* Between 1400 and 1750 around 40,000 people accused of witchcraft were put to death across Europe.

TRANSLATOR'S NOTE

The extract from Dante's *Paradiso* in the chapter 'Thursday Evening' is from *The Divine Comedy*, trans. Charles S. Singleton (Princeton, NJ: Princeton University Press, 1975).

The extract from Thomas Aquinas' commentary on Aristotle's *De anima* (On the soul) in the 'Author's Note' is from *Aristotle's De anima, in the Version of William of Moerbeke, and the Commentary of St Thomas Aquinas*, trans. Kenelm Foster and Silvester Humphries (Eugene, OR: Wipf & Stock, 2007).

The extract from the third of Virgil's *Eclogues* in the 'Author's Note' is from *Eclogues and Georgics*, trans. James Rhoades (New York: Dover, 2005). The quotation from Aristotle on p. 246 is from *The Works of Aristotle: De Anima*. Translated by J. A. Smith, M.A., LL.D. (Oxford: Clarendon Press. 1931).

PUSHKIN PRESS

Pushkin Press was founded in 1997, and publishes novels, essays, memoirs, children's books—everything from timeless classics to the urgent and contemporary.

Our books represent exciting, high-quality writing from around the world: we publish some of the twentieth century's most widely acclaimed, brilliant authors such as Stefan Zweig, Marcel Aymé, Teffi, Antal Szerb, Gaito Gazdanov and Yasushi Inoue, as well as compelling and award-winning contemporary writers, including Andrés Neuman, Edith Pearlman, Eka Kurniawan and Ayelet Gundar-Goshen.

Pushkin Press publishes the world's best stories, to be read and read again. Here are just some of the titles from our long and varied list. To discover more, visit www.pushkinpress.com.

===

THE SPECTRE OF ALEXANDER WOLF
GAITO GAZDANOV
'A mesmerising work of literature' Antony Beevor

SUMMER BEFORE THE DARK
VOLKER WEIDERMANN
'For such a slim book to convey with such poignancy the extinction of a generation of "Great Europeans" is a triumph' *Sunday Telegraph*

MESSAGES FROM A LOST WORLD
STEFAN ZWEIG
'At a time of monetary crisis and political disorder... Zweig's celebration of the brotherhood of peoples reminds us that there is another way' *The Nation*

BINOCULAR VISION
EDITH PEARLMAN
'A genius of the short story' Mark Lawson, *Guardian*

IN THE BEGINNING WAS THE SEA

TOMÁS GONZÁLEZ

'Smoothly intriguing narrative, with its touches of sinister, Patricia Highsmith-like menace' *Irish Times*

BEWARE OF PITY

STEFAN ZWEIG

'Zweig's fictional masterpiece' *Guardian*

THE ENCOUNTER

PETRU POPESCU

'A book that suggests new ways of looking at the world and our place within it' *Sunday Telegraph*

WAKE UP, SIR!

JONATHAN AMES

'The novel is extremely funny but it is also sad and poignant, and almost incredibly clever' *Guardian*

THE WORLD OF YESTERDAY

STEFAN ZWEIG

'*The World of Yesterday* is one of the greatest memoirs of the twentieth century, as perfect in its evocation of the world Zweig loved, as it is in its portrayal of how that world was destroyed' David Hare

WAKING LIONS

AYELET GUNDAR-GOSHEN

'A literary thriller that is used as a vehicle to explore big moral issues. I loved everything about it' *Daily Mail*

BONITA AVENUE

PETER BUWALDA

'One wild ride: a swirling helix of a family saga... a new writer as toe-curling as early Roth, as roomy as Franzen and as caustic as Houellebecq' *Sunday Telegraph*

JOURNEY BY MOONLIGHT

ANTAL SZERB

'Just divine... makes you imagine the author has had private access to your own soul' Nicholas Lezard, *Guardian*